Sunshine Spirit

Sunshine Spirit

Barbara Willis

Published 2014 by Creativia

Book design by Creativia (www.creativia.org)

Cover art by http://www.thecovercollection.com/

For Elisabeth, Meredith and Adam
For Steve
For George

Acknowledgments

There are so many people who've encouraged and supported me in my dream to write; I'm nervous of adding names to these people for fear of forgetting someone. However...

I have fabulous friends who help me; old, new and in between. These friends have encouraged, cajoled, bolstered, listened, shared and read. I send a huge alphabetical thank you to Clare, Dawn, Edward, Lisa, Lynn and Sharon.

I must mention the indefatigable Miika at Creativia and the authors who shelter there and provide support, camaraderie and hilariously random (and sometimes frankly worrying) conversation. Paljon kiitoksia!

The most important acknowledgment is of my most important people, my wonderful family.

Elisabeth, Meredith and Adam provide me with limitless joy, inspiration and pride. Steve gives me huge amounts of time and encouragement. They accept that I spend a lot of my time in a fantasy world with my imaginary friends, but they know that the door rightly closes on that world when we're together.

For Sunshine Spirit I called upon the amazing mechanical and motoring knowledge of my rather brilliant dad, Alan Partridge; the guru for old motorcycles and an unbelievable amount of other things.

The combined Partridge and Willis families offer love, support and laughter; always a part of every day whether near or far, in person or in memory.

Thank you.

Contents

Fate

So now she knew for sure that when you slide into unconsciousness, or die, the last thing you lose is the power to hear. It is also true that the first things you know are sounds and your first awareness noise. This is why a baby recognises and responds to the sound of its mother's voice before it's even born, and why sounds conjure for us a multitude of memories.

Certainly the first thing Jane became aware of now was not a sight but a sound, then lots of sounds. There were thumps, pops and sirens, people shouting. Then odour met the sounds, first one then more; acrid smoke, metallic gas, burning timber and a strange chemical scent - maybe it was more a taste, the way it seemed to linger on the tongue. The noise and smell were partners these days. Sometimes one was sensed before the other, but not for long; they always joined forces quickly. It took Jane a few moments to drag her thoughts together and make sense of where she was and what had happened, slowly waking her senses as though she'd had a deep sleep. She realised that what her senses thought was slumber had actually been unconsciousness. Although the smells and sounds were unpleasantly familiar, experienced almost daily, this time they seemed distant, smothered somehow, shut away.

It had at first been a wail, a high pitched whistling scream that poured into her ears like sand. The scream changed its tone menacingly as it dropped from the sky. The sound turned from firework to bomb. And then, for the tiniest of moments, there had been silence.

It was a sad thing to recognise how much experience everyone now had, how each person knew the sounds, the smells, what to expect.

Jane knew that all those within its grasp had looked heavenwards; whether they were indoors or out, alone or looking into the corresponding eyes of a companion, knowing that there was no time to change an outcome that was already written. The silence meant it was imminent, a moment away. If it was above them, there was little chance; just a few seconds to wish, despair, accept, or pray - not even enough time to cry. If it wasn't directly above them, if it wasn't too near, there may be hope.

When silence reigned there always followed the briefest of moments, seconds only and sometimes not even that, to wait for fate to show itself; the instinctive flash of hoping for one's own salvation, but knowing that meant wishing for another's demise in your place.

For some, after that briefest of silences, there would be the loudest of noises and maybe the shaking of all around them, the floating down of whispers of plaster dust, but nothing more; they would look around themselves in disbelief at their survival, so sure were they that death had been upon them.

For others that instant was indeed the last, followed immediately by oblivion.

Jane's fleeting questioning of what fate had planned for her was answered by a deafening noise; her silent question met by a bellow, an angry roar. In that spilt second she knew it had hit the house or, at the very furthest, next door. But in that burst of knowing, there was also almost a kindness; a gentleness of being aware of everything and nothing before the world switched off and all was still and black.

An ebony cloak shrouded her, kindly removing her from the moments to follow so no fear could be felt as she was immediately entombed by tons of falling brick and plaster, broken walls and furniture. Years of memories lay on top of her.

Sirens called, people shouted and dust settled. The sharp dark silhouettes that peppered the sky and dropped destruction from their bellies as they flew over the city moved on, spent.

Eventually noises seeped through the blind void, creeping through each crack of consciousness, drawing Jane back to the world. The sounds whispered their way into her ears, nudging her mind, cajoling her senses.

She didn't feel fear in those first moments of recognition, but a strange calm. It was over. There was no pain, just acceptance and relief. It took several seconds for Jane to dust the confusion from her thoughts and realise that she wasn't peacefully accepting death. She was alive.

As her mind struggled to recall what, when, how, all Jane could remember was being in the hallway. Luck must have been holding her hand in that moment when she'd been standing right next to the under stairs cupboard. Instinctively, she'd wrenched open the door and thrown herself in - before she could even pull the door to seal the opening behind her, the whole world seemed to move. She'd put her arms over her head and curled over, squeezing her eyes so tight that they watered. Or maybe that was just caused now by the smoke and dust that her eyes absorbed and her lungs inhaled; she couldn't be sure.

As she nervously opened her eyes and rubbed the drying tears away, Jane was disoriented. It was dark and warm and close. She couldn't see it but she knew the small space had changed since she dived into it; it was smaller and sharper and she was now squashed awkwardly into the tiny area that remained. All the household paraphernalia that made its home under the stairs was packed tightly around her, although she couldn't discern the individual identities of any of it now.

She didn't know how much of the house lay on top of her tiny sanctuary as she struggled to move. Coughing in a bid to clear the dust from her mouth and throat, she carefully wiggled her toes, then flexed her arms a little and turned her head slowly from side to side. Then she offered a prayer to heaven, thankful that she was alive and relieved that no-one else had been home.

She'd called out as she returned home, moments before she and the house shook hands with fate; she and fate had parted uneasy friends, but clearly the house and fate had not. At the very least, Jane could be sure that the stairs were damaged due to the smaller space she now occupied.

Her landlady and the other lodgers, Florence, Aggie and Dorothy, hadn't been home. She hoped they were safe somewhere, maybe sheltering in one of the nearby underground stations - she knew her landlady and Dorothy favoured Charing Cross, but that Florence and Aggie usually tried to get to Piccadilly in the hope that an actor or two may also be sheltering there. Ridiculously, despite the desperate situation, Jane smiled inside. She winced as her foot scraped against something sharp in the darkness and she reached her hand past her ankle to check for damage. Her fingers touched her ankle to find something warm and sticky, but there was no protruding bone or flap of hanging flesh and Jane sighed the relief from her body. She wasn't going to bleed to death in this dark little space; she was alive, a few cuts and bruises she could deal with. Her death wouldn't come today, alone in a hole at twenty three years old. It would come another day; maybe tomorrow, maybe next week, maybe in fifty, sixty, seventy years, but not today.

Tapping her hands tentatively around in the darkness she could find neither her handbag nor gas mask. Maybe she'd dropped them in the hall as she'd thrown herself into her sanctuary. Come to think of it she couldn't feel the door either, just rough edges of wood or plaster or maybe brick. She felt above her head and found the underside of a stair, the strength of which had given her safety. There was no heat on any of her prison's walls as her palms padded around in the dark. There must be no fire, she reasoned, just collapse. She thanked heaven again for each mercy shown.

Jane didn't know how long ago the blast had been. She must have been rendered unconscious almost immediately but couldn't be sure exactly when that was or how much time had since passed. Was it twelve thirty when she'd arrived home, or one o'clock? She could feel her watch on her wrist, but there was no way to see it clearly.

When her eyes had adjusted in the gritty little hole that had saved her life she could make out a tiny chink of light, but even holding her wrist up to that didn't afford enough illumination to see the watch's small ivory face. Coughing more brick dust from her throat, she raised her hands to scratch at the little glimpse of freedom. When she tried to call out, to make her location known to anyone who may be close enough, her voice was just a scratchy echo. She coughed again and took a moment to summon up enough saliva to swallow a couple of times. She tried again, this time with more success. After each call she stopped to listen.

As the minutes passed, she quelled the tiny rising fear by reasoning with herself. You're alive, you have air, you're not crushed or bleeding to death. They will find you. Digging away at the little gap brought nothing but sore fingertips and she was mindful that she could dislodge something and make her situation worse. She tried to leave the same space of time between each call for help, playing little counting games to draw her mind from her growing discomfort. Her position was awkward with unknown objects prodding and poking at her, blunt or sharp, and, despite the cold of October, the little hole in which Jane sheltered was oppressive and becoming more so. It was too warm in her lonely lair, but Jane quelled her concern through frequent checks of the walls around her - she told herself that the cause was body heat mixed with limited space and peppered with a slowly growing dose of panic.

She didn't know whether she was still inside a structure that resembled a house, one which might possibly have stood firm if not directly hit, or whether her shelter was now just a burrow beneath an unrecognisable pile of fallen memories. She wondered at the chances of her coming home on the one day, at the one time, that one of Hitler's bombs did. Of all the days for the now nightly bombs to drop into lunchtime, it would be the day that Jane's lunch had been sitting in the kitchen instead of in her bag.

With physical inactivity, Jane's brain took over. Its supremacy over her body, needing no space in which to exercise, was confirmed. Jane drifted to each part of her life and with each visit she felt optimism fade. She thought of her mum and how she would weep in devastation at her daughter's demise. She worried for her and then worried for her friends, her landlady, her colleagues at the hotel where she worked. She silently wept at the loss of her photographs of her parents, tucked in her bedside cabinet. She contemplated the things she wouldn't do if her optimism was unfounded and death came today; the books she wouldn't read, films she couldn't watch, plays she'd never enjoy, fun she'd relinquish. She quietly surrendered the history she wouldn't be a part of; an unknown husband who wouldn't be married and a child who'd not be born, a future Jane wouldn't see.

In silence she sat; squashed and lonely. Then, not knowing how or why, her resolve returned. Her strength was renewed and hope reborn. After foundering temporarily, her faith lurched and staggered until it stood upright again.

'I will not die here.'

She started to sing; anything to lift her spirits and pass the time until her rescue came, as she kept telling herself it would.

Lily of Laguna, By the Light of the Silvery Moon, Roll out the Barrel, Deep in the Heart of Texas, Hands Knees and Bumps a Daisy, You are my Sunshine...

'Jane?' A distant but distinct name was called. 'Jane, can you hear us? Sshhh, everybody, stop a minute.' The sounds that she only now registered, of people moving stone, rubble and wood, stopped.

They were waiting for her response.

'Yes. Yes I'm here!'

'Alright love, we'll have you out in a jiffy. Are you hurt?'

'No, no I'm alright. I'm under the stairs.' The responding voice gave a little laugh.

'Ok love, give us a few minutes - we'll just need to find the stairs.' Jane breathed the deepest, biggest sigh she ever had and lay her head back against the coolest wall of her cell, relieved that her incarceration would indeed be temporary; only now did she realise that she'd again started to think she might die in the little hole.

If it was as bad as it sounded, the noise of footsteps climbing on rubble, of moving wood and stone and the man's semi-humorous difficulty in finding where the staircase might be, Jane was indeed one of the luckiest people in London that afternoon.

The time passed in a daze of noise and movement and calls from her rescuers to each other. Jane heard instructions to lift, pass, listen, be careful. She waited patiently as the activity and noises grew louder and closer, listening to each scrape and muffled shout and knowing that these noises would eventually bring her freedom. The friendly voice called to her now and then to check where she was and to provide a positive progress report and lift her spirits. When the little chink of light suddenly grew into a football sized hole, Jane blinked as she turned her head up to it; she could at last make some sense of what was where. The small opening hadn't been where the cupboard door was, as she'd naturally assumed, and she wasn't facing the direction she had thought. Everything appeared to have been shaken up and thrown back to earth. A grubby face smiled at her though the hole, then a hand reached through and she grasped it like it was the hand of deliverance.

'Alright sweetheart, nearly there,' the voice reassured, and the owner's hand softly squeezed hers before withdrawing to turn itself from a gentle sign of hope to a tool of rescue. And after another age of manoeuvring and lifting, the hole was just about large enough for escape. The smiling face looked in at her once more and reached to her again, taking both her hands in his this time and easing her gently up into daylight and freedom.

Daylight.

Daylight where the house should have been and sky where the hall ceiling should have been.

A cheer went up among the men who had dug her out with their bare hands.

Jane's rescuers guided her carefully, blinking and unsteady, over the rubble and debris towards a little patch of the street that was free from the remains of the house. Her eyes adjusted to find Mrs Cavendish, her landlady, waiting in the street and dabbing at her eyes. Jane looked down to watch her steps towards safety as the last rescuing pair of hands took hers and helped her over the shards of glass and lumps of wood and brick. 'Hello Sunshine. Welcome back,' said the hands' owner. He smiled as Jane, looking up and smiling back, stepped down.

'Thank you. Thank you.' Jane rubbed her hand across her face and through her hair, which felt bitty and dusty. She was a little wobbly and her limbs were stiff; her muscles seemed fused into the curled position she'd been forced to remain in for what her body said was days but her head said were hours. A lady from the Red Cross was soon beside her, as was Mrs Cavendish, and Jane turned back to see the gaping void where two homes had once stood. As Jane turned she caught a glimpse of the man who'd called her sunshine and helped to guide her footsteps down to the pavement. As he walked away into the distance Jane thought that he reminded her of someone, but she couldn't quite see who.

All Clear

When the long howl of the all clear sounded, Mrs Cavendish had emerged from Charing Cross station. She headed home amid shouts and calls, people hurrying; smoke and confusion. She'd found an empty space where her home should have been. Only half a jagged wall remained; her house and that of her next door neighbour had been reduced to one teetering tower of shared masonry. Mrs Cavendish's side sported a cream paper with a tiny floral print; on Betty Millbank's wall at number 22 the paper was blue. A crooked picture hung on Betty's side and a ribbon of net curtain clung to the corner of its frame, the only remaining piece of the nets lovingly bleached and billowing on the washing line like delicate clouds only last week.

Mrs Cavendish was certain Jane was in the house or what was left of it; and she was sure she was alive. She immediately raised the alarm with the rescuers, assuring them Jane was trapped beneath the almost unrecognisable remains of her home.

Now Jane and her landlady held each other tightly as they cried in relief and despair and Jane thanked heaven again for Mrs Cavendish's intuition and the brave men who rushed to the aid of anyone who needed it.

The two ladies were ushered towards the mobile WVS canteen. There, spirited ladies poured welcome cups of tea for the rescued and rescuers alike; people converged from the surrounding streets like animals emerging from hibernation, bewildered and blinking, some dusty and dazed. Old and young surveyed their neighbourhoods and the work ahead. Some cried with loss and disbelief, others with gratitude and relief; a number of people gathered their scattered belongings as they moved, shocked, amongst the rubble.

Jane and her companion were told to head to the rest centre in the local school just a few streets away, where the 'bombed out' and the lost were uniting for information, first aid and help. It was there that they hoped to locate their housemates and their neighbours, fear clutching at their hearts with icy fingers as they hurried along.

The rest of the day passed in a blur. Their home was gone, but they were all safe. The other girls had found refuge at Charing Cross, Piccadilly and, strangely, an Anderson shelter in the grounds of the Savoy Hotel. Knowing where bombs had fallen they'd all made their way home, only to find it missing, and they too had been directed towards the school. There, after frantic searching, they'd eventually found Jane and Mrs Cavendish and each other. Florence, Aggie and Dorothy were all beside themselves with delight and relief at finding their co-residents of number 20 safe and well. They were pleased to report to Jane and Mrs Cavendish that they'd hugged a very much alive Betty Millbank, finding her a little disoriented but otherwise well. All were thankful that she hadn't been at home that lunchtime and neither had her heavily pregnant daughter-in-law; both were now making plans to leave the city for Wales. The daughter-in-law's parents' hospitality would house them for the duration of the war.

The quintet from number 20 parted company in the school hall to locate food, clothing, beds and other friends. Jane found herself being offered food and clean clothes; she forced herself to eat a little despite having left her appetite in the under stairs cupboard, but gladly accepted the clothes. She made her way, with her donated dress and cardigan, a flannel, a tiny nub of soap and a comb, to the pupils' cloakroom where she saw herself for the first time since leaving home for work that morning.

Work. She'd forgotten her lunch and rushed home at lunchtime to get it. Mrs Cavendish had spotted Jane's sandwiches in the kitchen that morning and thankfully so, as these had poked her intuition into action. She said she 'just knew' Jane would have returned for them. The siren, unusually now, had sounded during the day.

The hall.

The screaming whistle of the bomb.

The cupboard.

Work. She'd have to get word to the Grandchester, to tell them what had happened. Although since the minor bomb damage to the hotel just a matter of days before, and indeed the launch of the city bombings at the start of September, upheaval, disruption and change were accepted facets of daily life in London.

Her fingers moved to her cheeks as she surveyed the streaks of dust, blackened and caked into ribbons by her tears. Her eyes roamed to her hair; lord, what a mess. It was now grey, not chestnut brown, being completely covered in dust; a few splinters had been thrown in for good measure and were sticking out of her hair like wooden hairpins. The real pins, holding her hair neatly at the nape of her neck this morning, dripped from her hair like pine needles and long knotty fronds of hair hung down while others still clung desperately in place despite their ordeal.

She held out her hands, turning them over to scrutinize; dirty broken fingernails from her initial scraping at her prison's exit and grimy grey skin. Her clothes next - a ripped sleeve and skirt; the shredded nylons had already gone, removed out of necessity whilst the Red Cross lady cleaned and dressed the nasty cut on her ankle. She'd been barefoot since emerging from the rubble that had once been a home. Well, in truth, she'd had one shoe on but had discarded it knowing that one wasn't much use without the other. It now stood neatly by the front door to number 20 Alderney Street; the front door which now served as a ramp to the rubble. Jane pictured the house that had lain on top of her and was thankful for the selfless men who worked so tirelessly and usually at night searching, helping, finding, and who still had their own day's work ahead of them when every morning came.

Jane washed as well as was possible in the circumstances, changed clothes and combed the worst of the sooty dust from her hair - it still had an immovable film of grey powder which clung to her fingers every time she touched it, but it would stay until she could have a bath and wash her hair properly. She looked at herself in the mirror again. That'll do. I'm still here. That'll do. And she pinched her cheeks to force a little colour to them and returned to the hall.

Mrs Cavendish, the gentle soul, was deep in conversation with a woman behind a desk who had been doing her best to bring order and reassurance to a queue of people, newly homeless and needing the answers to many questions. There was no anger or pushing, no discord or argument. The crowds in the hall, although sometimes animated and emotional, were accepting, positive and pleased to be alive. In their temporary roost they wanted news of loved ones, milk for a baby, clothes for children, blankets, somewhere to stay, the first aid station, some food, fresh water, medicine. The lady answered each question and request with sympathy and a gentle smile; she pointed out which of her colleagues in the hall they should seek assistance from, which queue to join and sometimes jotted down a note for them. She had now turned her attention to Mrs Cavendish.

Jane sat on the floor by the door to the school yard, lay her head back against the wall and closed her tired eyes. She still held her old clothes and donated wash kit in her lap.

The 'phoney war' of just a few months back was over, replaced now by a very real one. The weeks of preparation and propaganda, leaflets and lists, were done. Anderson shelters built in back gardens as instructed, with the recommended earth covering of 15 to 30 inches of course, were no longer used by boys and girls as a setting for their innocent games of war; they were now employed on an almost nightly basis as a true arena for fear and wide-eyed alert. The cold shelters, sometimes flooded and always damp were cheered by their inhabitants with makeshift beds, blankets and lamps. The eerie shadows cast by a flickering candle or lamplight against the corrugated walls either brought alarm or excitement for children, and the noises outside invariably visited trepidation on the adults with the now routine question of what sights would greet them when they emerged blinking the next morning, God willing. God willing. The phrase was tagged on to many a farewell or wish.

'Hello Sunshine. It is you, isn't it?' It took Jane a few moments before she realised the voice spoke to her, then recognition came like the opening of a book and she quickly opened her gritty, resting eyes in response. A man crouched opposite her smiling. 'Nearly didn't recognise you.'

'Oh, sorry, hello,' Jane replied. 'You were helping at Alderney Street earlier?' He'd said Hello Sunshine to her once already today, as she'd emerged from her temporary tomb and he'd taken her hands to help her take those final steps down to the street.

'That's right.' The stranger smiled. 'Heard you singing.' Jane blushed. Of course, that's where the sunshine bit came from - the last tune she'd been singing before being pulled free from her dusty vault. Jane turned briefly to look for Mrs Cavendish but she couldn't see her. 'How are you?'

Jane's attention returned to the man in front of her. 'I'm alright, thank you. A little grubby but that's about it, surprisingly.'

'Jolly pleased to hear it.' He smiled again then nodded towards her ankle.

'Oh, just a scratch.'

He smiled, looking more familiar than he should, and the feeling annoyed Jane. It was the same feeling as trying to recall the name of something you should know but which eludes you; when the answer's almost close enough to taste, but still too far to call to your mind or tongue.

'Thank you for helping.' He shrugged at her thanks, looking a little self-conscious. Dressed in everyday clothes, grubbied by his helping at the bomb site of her home and possibly elsewhere, he clearly wasn't working in any official capacity earlier that day. Jane wondered if he'd been caught off duty and waded in. 'Are you with the auxiliary fire service?' she asked. He shook his head. 'ARP?'

'No, just doing my bit. I was in the wrong place at the right time, or something like that. I don't know. I was heading off to look for some friends, to check they were alright. But then your house needed me first, so that's as far as I got.'

'Well thank you again anyway.'

'I just lifted a few bricks that's all, when they said someone was inside. It must have been horrific, underneath all that.' Now it was Jane's turn to shrug.

'Well, now it's over it doesn't seem that bad. But before I heard the men calling to me I had some awful thoughts.'

'I bet.'

'Did you find the friends you were searching for?'

'Not yet. I was directed here to look for them, or news of them, so fingers crossed.'

'I hope you find them.'

'Me too.' He looked bashful then reached out a hand. 'William Batten, call me Will. Only get called William as my stage name. Or when I'm in trouble.' He winked and Jane took his hand for the second time that day.

'Ah, right.' Too bad Florence and Aggie weren't here to meet the actor. 'Jane Fraser; Sunshine. But I only get called Sunshine when I've just been trapped under a building.' It was Jane's turn to offer a smile.

'Pleased to meet you. Properly.' He hesitated for a moment. 'Look, a bit cheeky I know, but I'm working at the Majesty in The Smile Patrol. If you feel up to it some time, would you like to come along?' With no response from a surprised Jane, he continued. 'I'll speak to Frank at the stage door; go round to see him and he'll let you in and find you a good spot. We're matinees only for a bit, just Tuesday to Thursday until these raids stop. We came off altogether on the 9th last month, after it all royally kicked off, but we were up and running again the next week. Got to keep the spirits up and carry on. By all accounts, the theatre still stands, so it'll carry on for a bit longer too I should think.' He paused to look around as his face turned sad. 'An awful lot of people made homeless today; again. I guess a theatre's the least of anyone's worries.' He seemed embarrassed to be talking of light entertainment amidst the aftermath of yet another air attack.

'Yes, I suppose it is,' Jane said, and then added quickly, 'but we all need something to cheer us and make things feel more normal.' Jane also glanced at the displaced souls around them. She looked upon them as a separate group; all sheltering under the title of homeless although that really meant everything-less. Homes weren't the only thing lost; they'd lost their clothes, papers, family heirlooms, sentimental gifts, photographs. Somehow people smiled through, knowing that life was more important.

Jane didn't recognise that she was now one of the everything-less group, part of the crowd, until Will very gently spoke again.

'Do you have anywhere to go?'

'Uh, no, not yet.' The realisation of her similarity to these people slapped her in the face. Will nodded to the desks along the walls, manned by efficient and organised women.

'Don't worry, I'm sure they'll soon sort you out. I would think there are lots of empty places, now that so many people have left for the countryside and whatnot. Where do you work, is that alright do you know?' He seemed genuine and kind, talking quietly.

'Work's alright; for now anyway. I work on reception at the Grandchester. I hear it's also still standing.' Jane smiled affectionately at the thought of the imposing hotel.

Will raised his eyebrows and smiled. As he did so, a little light of recognition switched on for Jane. She knew why he looked so familiar. He looked like someone she'd seen at work almost every week for two years.

'You could always stay there eh?' Jane laughed at his suggestion, despite the real subject actually being her homelessness.

'That would be rather nice,' she admitted, delighting at the ridiculous thought of taking a room at the prestigious and expensive hotel.

Will stood up but reached back down to shake Jane's hand again, this time in farewell.

A voice cut through the busy mumble of activity calling *Hugh. Hey Hugh!* Will and Jane turned benignly towards the voice that begged attention, then back to each other as Will smiled down at Jane.

'Afraid I've got to make tracks Jane. I need to find the fellas, check all's well. It was nice to see you again - and to see you a bloody sight cleaner too!' Jane blushed and his joking ceased, replaced by an earnest and kind smile. 'Please come along to the show. It would be really nice to see you again.' Then, the moment complete, he winked and called over his shoulder 'The show must go on, Sunshine,' as he walked away.

Onwards

A short while later Mrs Cavendish reappeared, a welcome bustling of maternal activity in Jane's vision, helping to draw her thoughts from those still trapped, injured or worse among the fallen shops, offices and homes. She stirred Jane from the floor and led her to the desk of the lady she'd watched for some time as the lady helped the homeless and the frightened. Jane looked around but could see no sign of Will Batten, who'd clearly been sent somewhere else in his search for his friends.

The kind lady advised Jane on the process for obtaining new ration books; items safely guarded since they were issued at the beginning of the year but now lost forever under tons of masonry. She told Jane where she could get a few more 'bits and pieces' to tide her over – additional wash things, donated clothes and shoes. And where she should go to find somewhere to live.

'We'll get you sorted love, and the other girls; don't worry.' Mrs Cavendish was reassuring and buoyant, despite her great loss.

'Mrs Cavendish, I'm so sorry. Everything's gone.' Jane tucked her arm into her landlady's who patted it and managed not to look sad.

'Well, every cloud love. At least that awful vase of my aunt's is gone. I've been trying to accidentally knock it off the mantel shelf for years.' Mrs Cavendish giggled like a little girl and Jane joined in, both women delighting in the ridiculous amidst the destruction.

Together Mrs Cavendish and Jane went to get Jane's new ration book. Jane signed the declaration confirming its loss and Mrs Cavendish paid the replacement fee, waving aside any suggestion of repayment from Jane. Mrs Cavendish, thankfully, had her own book safely stowed in her handbag along with her meagrely stocked purse, a handkerchief, pen, shopping list, nail file, lucky silver horseshoe from last year's Christmas pudding and the front door key to number 20 Alderney Street, a door that no longer existed.

The two ladies spent the night in the school hall, sandwiched between other displaced individuals and families, all trying to find cheer amongst the sadness and devastation. The next day, after a cup of tea and some toast, they set themselves the task of arranging new lodgings. Mrs Cavendish was keen to see all the girls rehomed in 'nice places' but Jane was the only one who had yet to find an alternative to the flattened house, so the ex-landlady turned her attention to her.

Mrs Cavendish, thankfully, had a small circle of friends who also rented rooms. Without too much difficulty, they were able to find a room for Jane not too far from Alderney Street. When Mrs Cavendish's friend turned to her with an offer of a second room, the former landlady quietly revealed that she would actually be leaving the city and heading for Somerset as soon as she could; although she was loathe to leave the place of her birth and her fellow Londoners, the time had come to retreat to her daughter's house in the countryside.

Mrs Cavendish's daughter had been pleading her mother to come for some months, citing help with the children in the absence of their enlisted father as the main reason. It was, however, just an extra string with which to draw her mother to safety. Mrs Cavendish would now oblige with a large paper bag in one hand (encasing a spare dress, cardigan and underwear) and her handbag in the other, still bearing the front door key to number 20.

After a further night in the school hall, Jane escorted Mrs Cavendish through the bustling crowds of people at Paddington station, some waving from train windows and some holding uniform clad loved ones close on the platform for as long as possible before releasing them. Mrs Cavendish's train was heading west to safety and the two ladies silently waited on platform three for its arrival.

As the train pulled into the station and waiting passengers were stirred into action towards its doors, Jane and Mrs Cavendish hugged.

'Look after yourself Jane love. And keep an eye on the others, especially Florence and Aggie, won't you? Keep my address safe and let me know how you all are from time to time if you get the chance. I've given my address to the other girls, and Betty, and Mary Foster, but I doubt that Florence will write although she'll intend to.' She smiled affectionately at the thought of the whirlwind that was Florence. 'Make sure you keep that ration book with you and…' Jane interrupted to reassure with a hand on Mrs Cavendish's arm.

'Don't worry, we'll all be fine. I'll write, I promise.'

'Thank you. Take care of yourself won't you, and the girls.' Mrs Cavendish squeezed Jane's arm.

'Thank you for everything. We'll see each other when it's all over.'

'We will, love, we most certainly will.' The young woman and the former landlady hugged again and the older woman stepped onto the train. She turned, squeezed Jane's hand, and moved along into carriage B where she found a seat and settled into it for the journey, gently slipping her hand into her bag to check for the front door key to number 20; her fingers wrapped around the cold metal and she closed her eyes and wept silently as the train pulled away.

Beginnings and Decisions

The kind lady showed Jane to her room. She was gentle and softly spoken, but she wasn't Mrs Cavendish. No-one could live up to Mrs Cavendish. Mrs Foster explained the running of the house and left Jane to settle in. Jane thanked her new landlady then sat on the bed as she left and closed the door behind her.

Jane looked around again at the room she'd seen the day before. It was a nice room; basic, but clean and light. Bed, wardrobe, chest of drawers, dressing table, chair. She hung her three donated outfits in the wardrobe and placed her underclothes and nightdress in the top drawer of the chest. She had no need of the other two drawers at present, her own clothes being in a drawer underneath 20 Alderney Street. Slipping off her shoes she lay back on the bed. Monday tomorrow. So much for Sunday being a day of rest. There had been lots to organise, in addition to saying a sad farewell to Mrs Cavendish at the station. Dear Mrs C, and Florence, Aggie and Dorothy; Jane's cherished ex-housemates were now scattered. At the school hall rushed plans had been made to meet on the Sunday, the girls all keen to see each other soon to find out where each would be living.

Jane was still relieved to see her friends again, even though she knew they were all safe. The meeting place had been decided as Hampney Park. Jane arrived to find Dorothy and they were soon joined by Aggie. Florence, flustered, windswept and arms waving at them dramatically had appeared a good twenty minutes after the agreed time. She wafted into their midst like multi coloured silk ribbons in the wind; in beautifully compelling disarray. Even windswept she turned heads. The four young women hugged and kissed with each new arrival. Once all were assembled arms were linked and they marched to Hampney

Teas, a small restaurant at night and tea shop by day that sat just outside the park gates.

Nestled at a table, the girls' news tumbled out; there was much to talk about and update each other on. Their first topic naturally fell into the rubble of Alderney Street, somewhere that for the moment they still called home. The excited chatter of reunited friends that had fallen from their lips moments before was replaced with the subdued acceptance of fate. Words slowed and emotions stirred. Hesitance and sadness replaced the jumble of girly chatter. Dorothy, pretty, delicate and intellectual, dabbed unashamedly at her eyes as they reminisced about the happy times they'd spent under the protective and matronly wing of Mrs Cavendish. Thanks was once more voiced that Jane was safe and the mood lifted with recognition that life was the most precious possession one could have; all of them had escaped with this priceless commodity despite the collapse of their home. They all voiced promises to write to Mrs Cavendish very soon.

The girls' new addresses were shared and notebooks updated. Telephone numbers, where available, were jotted down.

Dorothy, a secretary at a firm of solicitors, had found sanctuary with a work colleague. Another secretary at the practice had come to her aid and offered a spare room for as long as she should need.

'I'll be alright there, but it won't be the same. I'm going to miss you all so much.' Dorothy smiled sadly and all three of her friends leaned towards her at the same time to pat her hand, touch her arm or rub her shoulder.

Florence, pale and blue eyed and with ribbons of glorious red hair, had thrown herself on the mercy of a distant relative who had come up trumps and opened her home to her. Florence worked 'front of house' in two different theatres. Now that shows were no longer daily and her working hours reduced, she had pieced together two jobs to make one, working mainly in the ticket office and cloakroom but filling in with whatever else was required.

Aggie, unable to find anywhere within a reasonable distance of her own workplace, had called upon Florence in anguish. Florence's great aunt twice removed, or so Florence had detailed, accepted Aggie in the same spirit that she'd opened her arms to her young relative. Her home was surprisingly Bohemian and Aggie had been left in no doubt as to where Florence's genes had lain before descending to her.

Aggie decided to lift the mood with a description of her new home. 'Well, I've been accepted into a home that frightens and excites me all at once. Honestly. It's…it's floaty and…inventive? Like living in a technicolor tent that's faded.' She smiled conspiratorially at Florence, who decided to join in.

'Ah, but the parties we shall experience Aggie; just wait and see. And the stories my aunt can tell of the lovers she's had. She was the paramour of some famous painter once, apparently. She still moves in arty circles; wait 'til she introduces us girls to everyone. It's another world. We'll not have time to miss each other, we'll just be too busy recovering from night long parties and dances and raucous revelry.'

'Oh good Lord, Florence, your aunt's a concubine!' Jane gasped.

Florence pretended to be affronted and replied haughtily, 'I prefer the term avant-garde.'

All four girls laughed at the pictures that had been drawn and which had dried and warmed their damp spirits.

When afternoon threatened to turn its attention towards evening, the friends knew it was time to part company and make their way towards their new homes. They all gave more hugs and kisses as parting gifts before they left.

In the blacked out room that night, Jane found it hard to sleep. Every noise startled or unsettled her. Several times she thought she heard the screaming whistle, but an explosion didn't follow. The bumps, pops and bangs were further away. The two nights in the school hall, despite their discomfort, noise and activity, had been strangely more restful and somehow felt safer. The people there seemed competent, in charge and protecting. Now Jane was exposed and alone, away from the people who helped and organised and saved. She supposed mental peace would come when the freshness of her situation dulled, the edges smoothed; they'd still be there but less harsh, less likely to bruise her confidence with fear.

The morning came and Jane rose for work. Normality, at least in its current form, was restored. Jane had lain in the bath the night before, at last washing the dust and the remnants of Alderney Street from her body.

She rose, washed and dressed, delighting in the simple pleasures of brushing clean hair and putting on clean, if strange, clothes.

At work, she'd forget about home for a while as another world took her. Her colleagues would fuss about her for a while, as word of her temporary burial would have spread round the hotel like ink on wet blotting paper. The hotel was a pleasant place to work with a comfortable camaraderie and despite the strict codes of conduct to be followed, as long as everyone did their job as they should, the hotel was a friendly place. Those who worked there generally considered themselves fortunate to be in the employ of such a prestigious hotel and took pride in what they did; the worst employee transgressions were the occasional sloping off ten minutes early by one or two of the chambermaids, once their work was done, or the lightening of the day with a spot of harmless gossip.

An early start for Jane used to mean that she walked the streets when they were quiet and most of the city just waking. For weeks now, it also meant that she walked the streets not knowing what to expect at each corner. A turn of the pavement could offer the relative quiet of a street just stirring, shops awakening, front doors opening, a man whistling, a working day beckoning inhabitants and businesses. Now a bend in the journey could bring a closed road, a lost street, dust or recovery.

Jane's early shift on the front reception desk began at seven and she was, as always, at her post and ready for the day by quarter to. As she foretold, there was much bustling about her and asking after her welfare and her experience. A few of the girls gave her clothes and other necessities which Jane accepted with grace and thanks, moved by their kindness. Not one for the limelight, she played down her ordeal. She was the only one who knew that it would never leave her; that she heard the sounds in her head many times a day; that she jumped at sudden noises and checked the location of her gas mask repeatedly throughout each day; that her handbag had new additions and left her side as rarely as was possible, now harbouring ration book, matches, bandage, whistle...

Jane saw all the usual faces. A few of the guests who had heard about her recent encounter with Hitler had asked after her; Mrs Cartlyn, Mrs Henderson, Mr Callaghan, the Franklins, Dr Bishop. With each enquiry, she smiled and said she was as fit as a fiddle. She made no mention of the loss of her home or the nervous fear, the involuntary jumpiness, which was left behind in the bomb's exploding wake.

Mrs Cartlyn was the first to ask after Jane, in an indirect way; not one for small talk with the staff, she had seen Jane and called out to her across the foyer as she made her way grandly to her car.

'Jane. I'm delighted to see that you are at your desk.' She waved her hand through the air with a flourish and a flick of dismissal. 'One must not let this ghastly business get in the way of life.' And with that she was gone. Clearly Jane wasn't either invisible or faceless to Mrs Cartlyn, something the rest of the staff felt they were. Mrs Cartlyn had given Jane a warm feeling of affection as she, and all who heard, knew that the words the old lady had tossed across the foyer were as close to kindness and friendship as anyone in the hotel had ever received from the formidable old woman.

Mrs Henderson had gently touched Jane's hand and said she'd heard the awful news, Mr Callaghan had tipped his hat and enquired after her health and home, Dr Bishop was kind, the Franklins showed concern. Jane was touched that so many people had asked her how she was, but was also glad when the enquiries from colleagues and guests ceased and she could continue with her day anonymously, as if nothing had happened last week that was different to any other.

The only hesitation on Jane's part that day was as Mr Hugh Callaghan walked away after his enquiry. She'd paused to watch him. It was now his turn to remind her of someone; he reminded her of the man who'd called her sunshine, rather than the other way around.

The hours hurried by; lunch came and went and soon the end of her shift pulled Jane from the front desk and towards the staff locker room. For a few moments she forgot that Alderney Street didn't wait for her return. It was only as she looked in the mirror to push a hatpin through her donated hat that recollection came. She stared at her reflection for a while. Sighing, she picked up her handbag and made a mental note not to forget that it was a different route to walk or a different bus that would take her home, a word which didn't yet summon up images of her new abode.

As Jane walked away from the hotel, her mind tiptoed back to the school hall and the well meaning invite that she'd received there from William Batten. Without realising it her brisk steps slowed a little with her wandering thoughts and, without a doubt or second thought, she realised that she was going to go to his matinee the next day.

Jane found that the thought lifted her spirits into optimism and her lips into a smile.

A trip to the theatre would be fun.

Life was short.

Warmth

Jane's Tuesday shift passed as it always did, in waves of activity and gentle lulls. There were all the usual tasks to undertake; guests to look after, post to sort, bookings to make or change and telephone calls to answer with a smile in her voice. Through all this, though, somewhere Jane felt anticipation. It hovered discreetly, there all day from the moment she rose. It tried to hide in the shadow of the day's activity but was still luminous, a glow-worm wrapped in cotton.

No-one knew of Jane's tentative plan for the afternoon. It hadn't yet been spoken and given life. It was still caged within Jane's mind, which meant that it could be changed or cancelled with no query or reproach from anyone but her. Not that anyone would be interested, thought Jane, except obviously the girls. Jane gave in to a little smile; Florence and Aggie would be excited and smothering, asking and waiting and wanting to know all, Dorothy would suggest sense and caution. Jane would feel a mixture of all of these things.

At the end of her shift, Jane smiled her goodbyes to her colleagues and found her feet taking her quickly to her locker. She was keen not to linger in conversation or on extended duties, as she so often did. As she checked her reflection, tidied her hair and added her hat she paused to question herself and could hear a Dorothy caution. Before she had time to deal with her own probing questions, one of the restaurant girls came in.

'Hello Jane, all done for the day then?'

'Yes, just about.'

'Off home? Getting cold out there isn't it? Still, at least it's not raining.'

'Too true,' said Jane, keen to leave and not to encourage a long conversation. 'See you tomorrow Sally.'

'Yes, see you Jane.'

Jane picked up her handbag and gas mask and left. She stepped out onto the street to head not for home, but to the Majesty. She wasn't really sure what had prompted her decision to act on the invitation offered in the school hall. She'd initially had no plans to go to the theatre, as flattering as the invitation had been from the handsome young actor. But, for some reason, as Monday drew to a close, her thoughts crept towards the apparent suitor. Something had brought him to mind earlier during the day, and he'd hovered in her head patiently until she was in her room that evening. Then he'd managed to entice her thoughts back to him and force a change of heart. What harm could it do? Jane loved the theatre, a very rare treat despite the proximity of all the sparkling theatres of the West End.

Her footsteps fell a little more briskly than usual and she was at the theatre by half past three. Pausing for a moment to look at the posters that called its patrons to enter, Jane was taken in by the romance of the lights and the brass and the treats within. A woman bumped Jane's arm, saying sorry as she continued into the foyer of the grand venue. This disturbed Jane's daydream and she continued past the building to the alleyway at the side. Glancing along the alley before her feet took her there, she saw the sign which announced Stage Door and walked towards it bravely.

Just as Will had said, Frank was there and greeted Jane warmly even before she explained that Will had invited her. Once she'd introduced herself, he said he'd been told she might be coming and guided her though the backstage maze to a spot next to some important looking ropes and pulleys to the right of the stage. There was an excited hush backstage as the show had already begun. Frank quietly explained that she'd be fine standing there and just to stand back out of the way when any actors or stage gang needed to pass. Jane nodded solemnly, but with an undeniable surge of excitement in her chest.

She watched spellbound and without moving for the next hour as the show progressed and people dashed to and fro. The thrill of standing so close to the stage as the show unfolded was something Jane had not expected to feel. And her first glimpse of Will on the stage also brought a feeling that Jane hadn't anticipated. She gasped a little involuntary breath and looked around to see if anyone had noticed. It was so small an action that they couldn't possibly have seen, but Jane felt that the entire backstage fraternity must have seen her eyes widen and her cheeks flush.

At the interval Jane stepped back to let the bustle continue around her. The curtain fell and people dashed onto the stage to adjust the scenes and prepare for the continuation of the show. A hand took Jane's arm and she turned quickly, surprised, scared for an instant that she'd accidentally touched a lever or leaned against a rope.

'I'm so glad you came.' Will smiled down at her. 'Are you enjoying the show?'

'Yes, very much. It's exciting to see everything going on.'

'It's a different world isn't it?' The question needed no answer and Will continued. 'I've got to go but when it's over wait right here, in this spot.' He pointed to the floor unnecessarily. 'I'll come and get you.' With that he was gone, disappearing amongst the organised tangle of scenery, curtains, props and people.

At the end of the performance, the curtain dropped and there was another surge of activity. This time, however, it wasn't the frenetic buzz of change and preparation but a happy throng of back slaps, handshakes and people rushing to change and leave. It was still a hot and busy place, but now it moved a little slower.

A few minutes after the final curtain call Will was back at her side.

'All done,' he said. 'Let's get outside and away from this madness.' It was a madness he clearly loved. He smiled as he led her through the puzzle of backstage paraphernalia, saying goodbye to numerous people on the way through and hearing calls of *see you tomorrow* and *good show Will.*

Leap of Faith

'Did you enjoy the show?' Will asked, as he smiled and held the door open for her. Jane returned his smile as they stepped out into the cold early evening. After the heat and activity of backstage, the quiet of the street outside the stage door and the fresh air on Jane's face was a surprising but pleasant contrast.

'Absolutely. I can't believe the activity that goes on backstage. I knew it'd be busy, but the show that people actually see really is just the tip of the iceberg. It was fascinating to watch the performance from behind the curtain. Thank you for inviting me.'

'You're welcome. I'm glad you enjoyed it. And I'm glad you came. Would you like to go for a drink or maybe a stroll? Something to eat?' He looked at her for her choice, but added just in case, 'Or should I take you home?' He suddenly looked horrified. 'I'm so sorry. I can't believe I haven't asked you about your home.' He shook his head, disappointed with himself. 'How insensitive am I? God, Jane, I'm sorry.' He touched Jane's arm gently in apology, though she felt more touched by his shame than his hand.

'Don't be sorry.'

'Well, I am. Where are you staying now, is everything sorted out?'

Jane smiled. 'Yes, all sorted. I'm staying with a friend of my landlady's. My landlady's gone to stay at her daughter's in Somerset somewhere. There were four of us girls and Mrs Cavendish at Alderney Street.' Will looked worried again.

'Is everyone safe? I mean, I just assumed you were in the house alone.'

Jane smiled, quick to reassure. 'Yes everyone's absolutely fine, thank you. I was the only one home. The girls have all found their own places to stay with friends and relatives; thankfully we're not too far apart. Dorothy, Aggie and Florence are my dearest friends in the world.'

'Glad to hear everyone's alright. What about your things? Do you have all you need, clothes and other stuff?'

'Yes, thank you. I'm fine, honestly. I've got all I need.'

'Alright, but if not I could always ask some of the girls.' He nodded back towards the stage door a few steps behind them.

'That's very kind but I really am fine.'

'Ok. But please ask if there's anything I can do.'

'I will. Now I must apologise for not asking after your friends. You were searching for them at the school hall. Are they safe?'

Will chuckled. 'All over the place, but all safe. Shelter found in most cases, but the chap I share a flat with was asleep in his bed, would you believe. I thought they were all still at the theatre with me but apparently not.'

'I'm glad everyone was safe.'

'Me too. Now, how about that stroll?' He looked behind him and counted imaginary markers on the pavement. 'Ten yards does not a stroll make.'

'Actually, I'd better get home. I've still got a few things to organise after, well, after Friday.'

'You don't sound too sure.' Will raised his eyebrows in hopeful question as they walked a few steps more.

'I just, well, I have things to do.' Jane hesitated. 'I really do need to do some things.' The excuse sounded feeble under Will's scrutiny, so Jane added another. 'And I don't normally accept random invitations from strange men.'

'Are you calling me strange, young lady?'

Jane laughed. 'No.'

'Well, that's a start.' Will turned serious. 'Maybe another time?' Jane nodded self-consciously and smiled. 'Great stuff. Can I at least take you home then?'

'Yes, that would be nice. Thank you.'

'If you don't mind we can take my motorcycle.'

'Oh,' Jane hesitated at the suggestion but Will didn't seem to notice.

'It's just down here.' Will motioned with his arm down the narrow street that ran from the stage door away from the theatre. They walked a little further and turned a corner into another quiet, narrow street. 'Here she is.' Will smiled again as he stopped next to the machine and turned to speak to Jane as he bent down to retrieve something from between the front wheel and a shiny chrome pipe.

The motorbike was black with Sunbeam swirled in gold on the tank. It stood proud and clean, albeit a little worn looking. With shiny chrome exhaust and delicate gold lettering spelling out its name, it whispered 'loved and faithful' to Jane in the growing darkness.

'Here, you must put this on.' He offered Jane the dull round crash helmet that he'd plucked from behind the front wheel. Jane hesitated and Will shook the helmet in front of her. 'No helmet, no ride,' he chided and moved to put the helmet on her. Jane instinctively dodged her head back as he tried to place it on her head. 'Come on, young lady.' She let him put it on and he fastened the strap under her chin. Jane turned to look at her reflection in the window of the adjacent building and grimaced as she turned back to Will.

'Well, that's attractive.' Jane raised her eyebrows and Will stifled a smile as he stepped back to regard her.

'It looks marvellous. All the young ladies are wearing them you know,' he said in mock authority. 'Very haute couture.' Jane moved to undo the strap, but Will shook his head. 'No you don't.' He took hold of her hands. 'As I said; no helmet, no ride.'

'What about you then, you appear to only have one crash helmet.'

'Well, I have a hard head.' He dismissed Jane's concern as he took the handlebars and rocked the bike forward to release it from the rear stand which held it firm. He gestured with his hand as though inviting Jane to board a carriage and, hesitantly, she did as he instructed and he took her left hand to steady her. He hopped on the bike in front and she gripped the seat either side of her. He stood up then and kicked down onto the pedal to start the engine. He had to do this three times before the machine roared to life. Their transport settled into a comfortable grumble as Will sat back down and then reached back to take Jane's hands from the fearful grasping of the seat, and pulled them gently but firmly around his waist. He turned his head to the side to speak to her. 'Now, first I need to know where I'm going young lady. Then, just relax and stay with me. When I lean, you lean. Simple.' Jane nodded even though Will couldn't see her and held tightly to him. 'Don't worry; I won't let you fall off.'

Destination confirmed and no going back, Jane took a deep breath. She found that she liked the sensation of being firmly bound to William Batten and leaned forward into his back. Her pleasure turned to nerves as the motorbike pulled away and she tightened her grip around his reassuringly steady body. She didn't see Will smile to himself as the machine moved off and he felt her body tense, and he didn't see her close her eyes tightly for the first couple of hundred yards.

As the streets passed by, Jane relaxed a little and began to enjoy the new sensations she was given; the freedom of independent motor travel, the lean of the motorcycle as they turned corners, even the wind in her face, but most of all Jane enjoyed Will's firm strength as she leaned against his back and kept her arms firmly wrapped around his waist. It had taken a little while for Jane to feel safe enough to turn her head to look around and not to feel as though she clung to a cliff edge.

London passed by Jane's eyes in a different way than it ever had before. When walking, she realised now, she either kept her head down or looked just at what was immediately around her.

When taking the bus, she only saw the pedestrians that walked the streets and the other vehicles that shared the road.

Now, she took in the buildings as they passed.

There were tall impressive buildings, most still standing proud despite the almost nightly onslaught of fire and explosion; they still held their authority even though prepared with sandbags and windows taped with the now familiar white crosses to protect the inhabitants from broken glass should an explosion be near enough to implode the windows.

Other structures hadn't been so lucky; homes, shops, hotels and offices brought to their rubble reduced knees. Along one broken street a tram lay on its side like an abandoned toy. Some buildings they passed were razed completely to the ground, others still tried bravely to stand firm despite losing two or maybe three of their supporting walls. One house looked to Jane like a dolls' house with the front wall removed. It was as though there had never been a front wall or the door and windows it contained. The rooms stood revealed to the world, exposed but almost unharmed, showing the lives that had once been lived inside; sadly not those of dolls, but of people. These broken and sad, previously solid, constructions reminded everyone not of war but possibilities; the destruction that stared into the faces of all the city's inhabitants every single day, the chance that this devastation could arrive holding hands with death, the possibility that you may well survive despite all the odds that screamed your chances at you.

Above this destruction and bleakness, the bent metal and shattered lives, there was defiance in the air and on the faces of those who remained in the city. Life continued; schools taught, hospitals treated, shops traded, restaurants fed and theatres entertained. Jane's fellow London dwellers kept going; they worked, they slept, they celebrated birthdays, marriages and births and they cleaned up and carried on when destruction came. Strangers became friends in many places; they reached out to each other and most shared what they had, however little. Life was bad and life was good. The important things had become important again.

Jane's mind drifted to those she'd met who seemed almost oblivious to the reality of all of this. Mrs Cartlyn, who had a suite of rooms on the seventh floor of the Grandchester, emitted an air of disgust about 'the whole ghastly affair' and termed the difficulties this brought as 'troublesome'; her delicately powdered nose would turn up at the 'goings on' in the streets seven floors below. She rarely left her rooms but when she did so, was taken by her driver who always ushered her deferently to the waiting Rolls Royce. Mrs Cartlyn waved away any mention of war, as though she were dismissing talk of the latest young persons' craze, something that would not dare affect her and which left an unpleasant taste on one's palette. Jane smiled with an indulgent affection. Mrs Cartlyn seemed to like her, a gift not bestowed on many in the hotel. No, that was unkind. She didn't *dislike* others, she just seemed indifferent to most of them, whereas she would sometimes say more than the minimum required when speaking with Jane. Jane liked Mrs Cartlyn; she spoke her mind and could wither even the most confident person with a glance should she choose to. People either loved or hated her, mostly the latter, especially those who'd been unfortunate enough to feel the whip of her lash-like tongue.

It was with relief and disappointment that Jane loosened her grip as the journey slowed and Will steered the Sunbeam to the curb just a few steps down the road from Jane's new home. Just for a moment, Jane wished that she lived further away. Will switched off the engine and hopped off to help Jane undo and remove the crash helmet.

He took the crash helmet from Jane as she ran her fingers through her flattened hair and then he took her hand to help her disembark.

'Thank you. That was fun. More fun than I expected actually.'

'Wouldn't like to travel any other way,' he agreed. 'I told you I wouldn't let you fall off.' Then he laughed to himself.

'What? What are you laughing at?'

'Sunshine on a Sunbeam.'

'Very funny,' Jane admonished, although she couldn't help but release a giggle too. 'You're quite mad.'

'Best way to be, young lady, best way to be.' Will smiled as he bent to slide the helmet once more behind the front wheel. He stood up then pointed back at the helmet. 'Always there when I come back, don't worry.'

There was a moment of silence before Jane spoke.

'I really had a lovely time at the theatre, thank you.'

'You are *most* welcome.' He stressed the most then looked at his watch. 'I suppose it's a tad unusual to be invited to the theatre only to watch the show alone. I'm sorry it was unorthodox.' He looked embarrassed, despite his confident manner. After a little boy hesitation, he continued. 'Rather than going in now, would you like to go out for dinner?'

With an indulgent smile Jane declined. 'You are persistent. I'd like to, but I have to be at work for seven o'clock tomorrow. And as I said...'

'I know, I know. You have things to do and I'm a strange man.' Will looked crestfallen for the slightest of moments, before smiling and taking Jane's hand. 'Life's very short young lady. There are *hours* until you start work tomorrow. Don't waste time over-preparing with sleep when the city awaits. It's the best time to be out. The lights of London, the sounds and the smells, the magic of a night in the city.'

Jane frowned.

'Bombs you mean, not magic.'

'No, I definitely mean magic. Like I said; the lights, the smells, the sounds.'

'Don't you know there's a war on? There are no lights anymore. It's a blackout William.'

'Ah, but that's where you're wrong Sunshine. When the lights of London go out, that's when the city really lights up. And it's Will, please.' Jane raised her eyebrows at Will and he winked at her mysteriously. 'Jane, life speeds up now. People all around us are making the most of every moment. Things happen quickly. Life has to move faster in case there's limited time to fit it all into. We all need to reach out and grab things; opportunities, life itself. And people.'

As Will spoke his eyes bore right through Jane's, burning into her mind and down though her chest to her core. Hesitance cracked open to become spontaneity, life became exciting.

She gave in. 'Alright. Yes, ok.' Even as she said it, Jane was surprised to hear her words.

'I'll come back for you in a couple of hours.' He bent down slightly to look directly into her eyes at the same level. 'Alright?' Jane nodded and Will turned back to his motorcycle retrieving the crash helmet, unceremoniously plonking it on his head then kick starting the machine into action before he rode off with helmet unfastened and hand waving goodbye. Jane sighed with a suddenly affectionate exasperation and smiled as she turned towards the front door.

'What am I doing?' she quietly asked.

Mrs Foster knocked on Jane's door just before eight that evening to advise that there was a young man waiting in the hall for her. Jane, refreshed and tidy, thanked her landlady, picked up her bag, gas mask, coat and hat and trotted down the two flights of stairs to find Will standing nervously inside the front door turning the brim of his trilby round and round in his fingers. As he looked up and saw Jane he smiled.

'No Sunbeam?'

'Nope. Thought we'd walk. A first ride on her in the daylight is one thing, but putting you on her in total blackout is another.'

Knowing no crash helmet beckoned, Jane carefully put her hat on in the hall mirror as she saw Will plonk his own on behind her. He held open the front door for her and they stepped into the darkened street.

Jane was surprised to feel Will's hand seek hers out and they walked away from Mrs Foster's and along the unlit pavement, both pleased with the contact. They strolled in silence for some time until they came to the river. Will stopped by a bench looking out over the water; he motioned for Jane to sit down and then sat next to her. He lifted his hand to Jane's cheek and with gentle fingers turned her head to face down the river. He waited as Jane caught her breath. The sight she saw was as beautiful as any sparkling lights.

The moon was full and high. In the blackened city it looked brighter than ever before. With no contest from street lights, cars or windows it was free to throw its light out to the world uncontested. The gentle ripples on the river sucked the light to them and blinked brightly back at the sky as they went on their way.

'It's really beautiful.' Jane said.

'It certainly is. I told you London's best when the lights go out.' He looked down to rummage in his deep overcoat pocket and drew out a paper bag and a small hip flask. Jane frowned without realising and Will laughed as he saw her expression. 'I invited you out for dinner and dinner we shall have.' He slid back along the bench away from Jane, leaving a space between them, and lay out carefully on the seat what looked like a starched white handkerchief. On to that he emptied the contents of the paper bag. Two sandwiches, a pork pie and two hard-boiled eggs. He stood the small hip flask against the back of the bench and gestured to the feast with a theatrical wave of his hand. 'Voila! Dinner is served. Better than the Ritz.' He looked to

39

Jane for reaction and she laughed, at which he feigned offence. 'What? You laugh? I'll have you know this restaurant has the best view in London!' Then he added in a stage whisper as he coughed. 'Well, that, and I'm on actor's wages.'

They laughed together and then tucked into a romantic dinner for two of corned beef sandwiches, pork pie and hard-boiled egg.

The Grandchester

As Jane walked along the waking streets of London the next morning, she smiled at her memory of the previous evening.

After their dinner on the bench, Jane and Will chatted for a long time, then strolled alongside the river. Will tried to encourage Jane to dance with him as he sang 'By the Light of the Silvery Moon' but Jane was reluctant. She'd shivered as the night air crept inside her insubstantial coat; Will had again offered her the flask that she'd already declined during their meal. 'Go on,' he'd urged, 'one sip won't hurt, it'll just warm the cockles.' Jane took the flask and tipped it to her lips. The warm but sharp liquid seemed to touch every part of her tongue before it slipped down her throat, leaving a burning warmth in its wake. Jane coughed slightly as she handed the flask back to Will. Returning it to his roomy pocket, Will then rubbed Jane's arms before hesitantly enfolding her into his to warm her almost as though he waited for her to say no. However, Jane liked the feeling and the charm of his nervous delay. 'Come on, let's get you home in the warm. Your landlady will be thinking I've kidnapped you, or dragged you away to join the circus or something.' Then he took off his coat and wrapped it around Jane's shoulders before they walked along the quiet and slumbering streets back to Jane's new home, just as the siren sounded.

The streets Jane now passed in the morning light were surging into life rather than going to sleep. People were heading off to work and Jane hurried along as a few drops of rain began to fall. She reached the welcoming face of the hotel and said hello to the doorman as she passed him. She entered not by the main door in the impressive street frontage but via a side door reserved for staff. Off of the narrow corridor that followed there were five rooms, one was a small storage area, another an office where staffing, rotas and stock ordering were dealt with, the third was a small staff canteen and the last two were cloakrooms. Jane headed to her locker to hang her coat, hat and bag. She gave herself a quick check over in the mirror, smoothed down her dress, straightened her collar and made her way to the front desk, greeting colleagues on her way as night shift swapped for day.

Jane enjoyed her job and loved people. The hotel welcomed new guests daily and, despite the times, was always busy. There were a few guests who had taken up almost a permanent residence in the hotel, such as the irrepressible Mrs Cartlyn, a few who used it as a base where they regularly stayed for days or weeks at a time and those more traditional guests who stayed for one or two nights and then left for good.

Before half past eight, sometimes nine, the hotel usually only bustled with staff as breakfasts were delivered to rooms or tables prepared in the grand dining room. After this, most guests descended from their rooms, deliveries were received, post was sorted and pigeon-holed, telephone calls were answered and a hundred other things happened in the lobby and beyond.

Mr Hugh Callaghan was one of the first guests Jane saw that morning; bizarrely he was returning *to* his room rather than leaving it, having strolled in nonchalantly through the impressive front doors, extinguishing a cigarette just outside before he entered. He raised his hat a fraction and nodded when he passed the front desk 'Good morning Jane,' he called as he climbed the stairs. Jane called a Good Morning Mr Callaghan in return and appraised him as she looked at the back of his retreating form, sprinkled with drops of rain which darkened on the pale fawn of his coat.

He was forever the gentleman, but with a sparkle of cad in his eyes. Always impeccably dressed in a suit and hat, often to be seen drawing on a cigarette as he leaned outside the hotel waiting for a car to pick him up. He stayed at the hotel for weeks at a time but was then often gone for weeks with no prior hint, sometimes appearing to leave in a rush, before he would return calm and natural weeks later. Occasional messages arrived that appeared to put him in two places at once and these only served as dry tinder to the already smouldering rumours. Whisperers at the Grandchester pinned him as a spy; the hotel girls had painted him as a mysterious yet heroic man, destined to win the war single-handedly, and swooning a little under his gaze; the gents drenched him in admiration, a man about town, yet claiming him to be one of them (or maybe, fancifully, them as one of him), always happy to hand out a cigarette, shake a hand, offer a tip in thanks. But most definitely and without a doubt, a spy; for the ladies it meant romance and thrill, for the men adventure and derring-do.

Jane liked him and tried not to get involved in gossip but wondered whether, on some level, the rumours might be true.

Jane's reverie was disturbed by the appearance of Piers Henderson and his beautiful, graceful wife Maria. Maria looked like a finely painted china faced doll, almost transparent in her delicacy. Piers' hand rested in the small of his wife's back as he guided her to breakfast in the dining hall. They were a quiet and pleasant couple. He worked somewhere in the city and would leave after breakfast, always parting from his wife in the lobby, kissing her farewell and leaving for the day. Maria Henderson would either return to their room or wait in the lobby for one of her numerous girlfriends. If it was the latter, they would be gone for most of the day, returning with purchases or overheard giggled tales between them of the delights they had discussed or planned over lunch. Not many could afford such a life and, once more, there was speculation. The Henderson stories weren't as colourful as the folklore that had been written amongst the hotel staff for Hugh Callaghan. The Hendersons were 'weekers', as the hotel staff called those guests who resided with them from Monday to Friday and then left for home; although, if the amount of time spent somewhere dictated where home was then the hotel was more home than the sanctuaries the weekers left London for. In the case of the Hendersons, home was a large 18th century pile in Sussex, the farmland around which currently provided an ample income to add to Mr Henderson's probably substantial city wage.

Jane was stirred by the ringing of the telephone and answered it immediately. As she did so her eye was caught by Mariana Jack. Ms Jack, something in the art world that no-one could quite pin down, floated down the stairs in a filmy Bohemian blouse which swept past her hips to her knees. Her legs were stockinged and her spiky little heels tapped on the marble tiles as she waved melodramatically towards the front desk. In her hand she carried a cigarette which dripped a little ash as she passed in a cloud of expensive perfume and cigarette smoke. Jane wondered if she might be a friend of Florence's unconventional aunt.

Life was not dull at The Grandchester.

'Hello? Is that Jane?' asked the voice on the other end.

'Yes, yes Sir, this is Jane.'

'Jane, it's Hugh Callaghan. I need you to do something for me.' He sounded hurried and the line wasn't terribly clear, as though he wasn't in the hotel but somewhere else.

'Of course Mr Callaghan. How may I help?'

The conversation that followed intrigued Jane only a little and she didn't hesitate to do as Mr Callaghan asked, jotting a few notes down on the pad of paper in front of her as the instructions were given; fresh linen, laundering of all clothes, provision of evening meal in his room for the next week. Jane had become accustomed to Mr Callaghan's hotel requests and his occasional instructions to field calls or take delivery or ensure the safe collection of something.

Unexpectedly, Will turned up at The Grandchester a short while before Jane was due to finish. He was at the desk before Jane noticed him and felt a proud pleasure when she turned to find him there, absentmindedly putting her hand up to check her hair as he greeted her.

'Are you free to come on an outing with me?' he asked without preamble.

'Uh, yes, I suppose so.' Jane spoke quickly for fear of being seen chatting. 'What sort of outing and when?' She visualised another picnic. Will tapped the side of his nose theatrically. 'Wait and see.' Before she could prise more information from him, Hugh Callaghan had also appeared at the desk and Jane immediately turned her attention to the guest. She knew he wasn't the kind to complain about her chatting but he was still a hotel guest and therefore had to receive her full attention first.

Again, ahead of Jane being able to greet him with an offer of assistance Mr Callaghan beat her to it.

'Hello Jane,' he smiled, then turned to Will and offered his hand in greeting. 'And you are...'

'William Batten.' They shook hands.

'Hugh Callaghan; pleased to meet you.'

It couldn't have gone unnoticed now the two men were just inches apart that they bore a striking resemblance to each other. Each man's build, colouring and facial features were hugely reminiscent of the other although Mr Callaghan's slightly greater count of years gave him an air of importance that he seemed unaware of himself.

'And you sir,' was Will's genial reply.

'And you're a friend of Jane's?'

'That's right.'

'Splendid. And where do you hail from?'

'Sir?' asked Will, clearly unsure of the response to give.

'Do you work here?'

'Oh, no. No, I don't. I'm an actor. Currently at the Majesty. Well, until I'm called that is.'

'Ah, yes of course. Well, they're working through the list. You might see the year out before the brown envelope lands on your mat.' He patted Will on the shoulder jovially. 'Anyway, good show young man. Keep the nation's spirits up until then eh?' And with that Mr Callaghan left the hotel with no mention of his earlier telephone call.

'Good to meet you,' Will called after him, before turning back to Jane and raising his eyebrows. 'Something a bit strange about him, but nice enough.' He shrugged and the foyer fell silent for a moment. Will leaned against the counter and turned the rim of his hat round between his fingers. 'So, when do you finish?'

'Give me an hour and I'll meet you out the front if you like.'

'Yes, I like.' Will smiled and left, looking a little like the delayed shadow of the previous person to exit the hotel.

Jane's surprise trip was a ride on Sunbeam for over an hour, after which they pulled up in the yard of a farm. Jane was intrigued by their location and was soon introduced to Mr and Mrs Hall and their children Sylvie, Jacob and Daniel. Their oldest son Harry, serving somewhere undisclosed in Africa, was the point of connection between Will and these friendly and welcoming people.

After a filling meal of sausage cottage pie and ample vegetables, Jane and Will were sent off for a walk.

'What lovely people.'

'They certainly are. It's a shame you can't meet Harry, but next time he's home I'll make sure you do.'

'I'd like that.'

Will explained that he and Harry had been friends since childhood. When Will's family moved to Scotland at the behest of work, Will (then fifteen) had stayed behind and lived with the Halls. Now Will was frequently found at the farm, helping out in

Harry's place. Sylvie and Jacob being ten and twelve were still at school but Daniel, at sixteen, helped his dad on the farm. Mrs Hall, Maggie, was the epitome of warmth and motherhood and on arrival had immediately ushered the two visitors into the large warm kitchen where she hugged Will warmly and then did the same to Jane.

As they walked away from the farmhouse after their meal, Mr Hall called out 'Will, need any TVO top up while I'm in the shed?' at which Mrs Hall was heard to say 'Jack, leave them alone.'

'No, I'm alright for now, thanks Jack,' Will shouted back, smiling.

'TVO?' asked Jane.

Will laughed. 'Tractor Vaporising Oil. Mix it a pint to a gallon with good old petrol and it means I get more mileage now petrol's in short supply. It's a different story on a farm as you probably know; no issues with fuel. I could run the old girl purely on TVO, but that gets a bit more complicated and mechanical. Mixing it is good enough for now; my petrol goes further and that's enough. I generally get sent away with food, socks or TVO; or all three.' Will smiled affectionately on talking of his second family's generosity.

As the evening drew in, from their vantage point on a small hill miles away from the city, Jane and Will watched the lights of London go out.

'Bloody war eh?' Will mused in the darkness.

'Yes, bloody war.' Jane said.

Will was a little startled at Jane's concurrence with a matching cuss word and he laughed.

'So where are your family Jane? Are they in London?'

'No, mum's in Somerset.'

'How come you're here then?'

'Mum and Dad moved here when I was small because Dad worked for one of the banks. Dad died five years ago.' Will gently offered an I'm sorry as Jane carried on. 'Mum and I moved back to Somerset to be near family. I missed the city though; it's my home. So I moved back three years ago, much to Mum's disappointment. I lived with an old friend of my Mum's, Mrs Cavendish, so that eased the parting a bit. Mum knew I was in safe hands with her to keep an eye on me.'

'Will she want you to move down with her, now the house is gone?'

'Yes, absolutely. I've spoken with her several times and promised to visit and everything. I've reassured her over and over. It's not so much the issue of not having Mrs Cavendish watching over me anymore, but the air raids. Mum's had enough of me being here amongst it. It frightens her.'

'She's your mum Jane, it's bound to frighten her.' Will could see both views; a mum's protection versus a daughter's independence. Will also found a third view that he hadn't noticed until now. It was his. He felt his own contradiction of the two women's opinions. He wanted to keep Jane safe, but he also wanted her to stay near to him. 'You haven't thought of moving back with your mum, even temporarily? Maybe you should think about it. London will be here when you come back.'

'Yes, I've thought about it. Actually, no I haven't; not really. Well, I have *thought* about it, but not seriously. Even when I'm scared I don't really ever imagine I'll leave. But I've told mum that I will if things get too bad here and I tell her it's not as dangerous as it seems. She pretends she believes me and I pretend I don't know she's pretending.'

As they spoke a flash lit up the sky and, even though the sound it made was distant, Jane jumped. Will put his arm around her.

'You're brave Jane. Not many would have been buried under a house and not have run away.' Jane shrugged and leaned towards Will's warm body. 'Come on; let's go back into the warm.'

They stood and turned back to the farmhouse leaving London in the distance.

As the evening wore on, Jane was enveloped by the Halls and drawn into their kindness. The younger members of the family were delightful, providing fun and laughter as Mr and Mrs Hall soaked up news of Will's latest job and passed on a letter received from Harry. They were interested but not intrusive when it came to learning about Jane and all were genuinely sad when the time came for Jane and Will to leave.

'We've room for you to stay over,' Mrs Hall invited. 'You don't want to go back tonight in the dark and the cold, with the blackout and the bombs and everything. And with those silly things on your headlamps when you ride your motorcycle, Will, it's a wonder you can even find London.'

'Bless you Maggie, but we need to get back. Work beckons. It's been great as always.' Will kissed Maggie on the cheek and shook Jack's hand. 'Don't worry Maggie, I'm used to riding the Sunbeam with her eyes half closed. We'll be fine.'

'Thank you so much for a lovely evening.' Jane echoed Will, sorry to go.

'You're most welcome Jane, anytime at all.' She looked at Will. 'Bring Jane again soon Will.'

'Yes ma'am,' Will saluted.

'Oh get away with you,' Mrs Hall shooed him with her apron and they left the farmhouse.

Will carefully fastened the helmet under Jane's chin, apologising all the time. 'I'm sorry, I didn't think we'd stay into the dark. I said I wouldn't take you on her in the dark.'

'It's fine, honestly. I'll be fine, don't worry.' Jane found that, for a moment, she too was surprisingly good at acting.

The Halls stood waving from the kitchen door with the light and warmth of the house glowing behind them and children calling and waving from the yard. Will and Jane waved back as they sat aboard the purring Sunbeam before gently moving off into the darkness.

During daylight Jane's nervousness on the motorbike had been easily replaced with confidence by Will's sure and steady lead. But now in the darkness of the countryside at night and with only the very much obscured headlamps to offer guidance Jane held more firmly to Will as he navigated the lanes he'd ridden through a hundred times, closing her eyes as much as she dared.

Dawn

The warmth that had spread through Jane's body during the three weeks since she'd first met Will now coursed up to her lips and culminated in a smile that was clear for all, or so Jane thought. This suspicion was further fuelled by Mrs Cartlyn, who had stopped at the front desk to enquire about her post as she had received nothing for several days. Jane answered the abrupt query with her usual efficient and friendly approach, before Mrs Cartlyn continued.

'I see. Well, it's still most strange. Like a lot of things around here at the moment. Comings and goings at all hours and sneaking about. It's distasteful to say the least.' Jane agreed without agreeing. Mrs Cartlyn started towards the lift, then stopped and turned back to Jane. Jane might have imagined it, but there seemed the slightest softening of Mrs Cartlyn's ice solid eyes. 'In these times, more than ever Jane, any new found joie de vivre that you may have should be tempered with caution.'

Mrs Cartlyn, for all her brusque abrasiveness, suddenly seemed intuitive and concerned. Jane had always known that Mrs Cartlyn had a kind heart and she saw more depth in her than the other staff gave the old lady credit for. She had indeed noticed the young receptionist's glow but Jane felt a little sad to think that, just possibly, a long past broken love affair had caused the old lady to recommend caution. Or maybe she hadn't registered any difference in Jane at all. After all, she'd also mentioned strange comings and goings and sneaking about, but Jane had heard nothing of this from anyone else in the hotel.

Mr Callaghan was now before her and crossed the foyer without turning as Jane put her hand out to answer the telephone.

He carried a small bag and a briefcase and, thinking he must be off on another of his trips, Jane picked up the receiver.

Moments later, as Jane glanced towards the hotel door she saw a motorbike pass along the street and her mind moved back to an outing with Will a few days before. She told herself off for daydreaming and turned to the pile of post on the desk as she balanced the telephone between shoulder and ear. This man was occupying more of her thoughts than was healthy, surely. She'd even, for a split second, thought she'd seen him that morning in the hotel. Perhaps Mrs Cartlyn wasn't the only one imagining things.

The same had happened two days ago. Jane had glanced up from her work to see the back of a man briskly turn the corner at the top of the stairs. For the briefest of moments she'd had the strangest sensation of butterflies inside her chest; until she realised that the figure must have been Mr Callaghan, such was the similarity in the two men's build and gait. From a distance, they could indeed each be mistaken for the other. And in describing them, you could be forgiven for using the same words; tall and straight, broad shoulders, decisive gait, strong features, dark hair, grey eyes, handsome, kind, exciting… Where did a straightforward impartial physical description end and turn to something else? Jane mentally reprimanded herself and carried on with her work.

A familiar voice greeted Jane the next time she picked up the telephone that day.

'Fancy an evening under the stars Sunshine?'

Jane smiled and looked around her in case anyone was to notice her indulging in a personal call which was strictly against the rules. She tilted the receiver a little closer to her lips.

'Sounds lovely.'

'Great, I'll pick you up at seven.'

Just as the smiling girl was about to respond, there was a commotion at the other end of the line. Muffled voices and movement could be heard but not discerned.

'Will? Will?' The line went dead and Jane spent the rest of her day wondering what had happened, innocently cursing the effects the war was having on even the most simple of things such as the telephone lines.

As Jane sat in her room at Mrs Foster's that evening waiting for the voice that would tell her Will had arrived, she worried. She wasn't sure what she thought might have happened but felt more unsettled the longer she mused over the abrupt end to the telephone call. She'd mentioned this to Dorothy when she'd met her for tea just an hour or so earlier. Dorothy was quick to reassure her and confirm her first theory; the telephone lines weren't what they used to be. Dorothy had also smiled knowingly and acknowledged Jane's very obvious concern for the gentleman of which they spoke.

'Sounds like this new friend means a lot to you Jane.'

'Do you know something Dotty? I've only just realised how much. He means an awful lot.' Dorothy's hand reached across the table to squeeze Jane's as she winked and smiled.

A gentle knock at the door startled Jane, so deep in thought was she. 'Your young man's here Jane,' came the voice.

'Thank you Mrs Foster, I'll be right there.' Jane stood up to get her coat and bag.

'Jane, may I come in a moment?' Jane was surprised to hear the landlady's request.

'Yes, of course.'

Mrs Foster entered and looked gravely at Jane as she closed the door quietly behind her.

'Is everything alright Mrs Foster?' Jane stood completely still with coat half on as she watched her landlady.

'Jane, I just wanted to say a few things. I'm not old fashioned and I don't mind at all having your young man calling and sharing the occasional meal and so forth. And I'm a modern woman and I like having you here. But if there's trouble with your young man, or if he's *in* trouble, I can't have him bringing it here. You do understand don't you?' Jane didn't understand, but nodded as she finished putting on her coat.

'Mrs Foster...' The words wouldn't come to voice the confused questions that suddenly rolled around in Jane's head.

Mrs Foster put her hand on Jane's arm and smiled. 'Go on and see him Jane; I've delayed you, don't keep him waiting any longer.' Jane smiled and nodded and the two ladies left the room together. Mrs Foster hovered on the landing as Jane started downstairs. 'Jane?' Jane turned to look back up. 'Be careful dear.'

Will was waiting in hall as he had previously and turned towards her as he heard Jane's footsteps descending the stairs.

As he did so and Jane saw his face, she stopped. The mute questions sparked by Mrs Foster now found words in her head. Will winced and lowered his eyes.

'Sorry,' he said as Jane rushed down the last few stairs and touched his battered face.

'What happened? Why are you sorry?'

'I'm sorry to turn up looking like this.' He gently moved her hand away from his face.

'Oh goodness Will, don't be sorry. Just tell me what happened.'

'I came off the Sunbeam; into a ditch.' Will tried to smile and then winced again. His eyes moved away from Jane's as quickly as they met. 'Anyway, there's no real harm done. Just a few cuts and bruises and a scratch or two on the petrol tank.' Jane was still horrified, looking at the fresh bruises on his face and the raw crimson of the grazes along his jawline. 'Really Jane, I'm fine.' Now he looked at her in reassurance. 'It looks worse than it is I promise. Come on,' he glanced back up the stairs 'let's go.'

Taking Jane's arm he led her out into the dark evening. 'There's a dance at the Medway a couple of streets away. Would you like to go?'

Jane looked down at her tidy but pre-loved dress. 'I'm not really dressed for it I'm afraid.'

'Nonsense, you look a picture. Come on.'

The evening skipped along in a flurry of music, as Jane and Will danced gently and chatted. Will brushed into insignificance all mention of his accident and resulting injuries, but Jane noticed his sometimes restrained movements and the occasional grimace as an unseen pain caught him. No-one else seemed to take much notice of Will's battered face so Jane tried her best to follow suit, at least in front of Will. When he wasn't looking it was a different story as Jane took in every mark on his face and every pained movement that he thought she didn't see.

When the air raid siren sounded Will was quick to usher Jane from the Medway and down into the nearest underground shelter swapping the fresh cold air of the street for the close, almost smoky, smell of the station. The rush and tumble of weeks before was largely replaced with a more calm approach. Although people were mostly quick to find shelter when the familiar siren called, there was a more composed and less frantic approach. Despite the sound being one that everyone sadly knew well, the sudden starting of the wail always brought dread even if its well-known calling was no longer answered by so many with an urgent rush. As Jane and Will descended the stairs towards the corridors and station platform, they saw many for whom this was like a second home. People came armed with flasks and gas masks, blankets and food, and carrying small children who in turn clutched teddy bears and dolls. They were accustomed now to the nightly outing.

'Come on, this way,' Will urged as he led Jane though the people as best he could. They stopped by a wall where there was room to sit. Will took off his jacket and wrapped it round Jane's shoulders then lay his scarf on the floor for her to sit on. 'Here. It'll be cold on the floor.' He looked around. 'I'll see if there's a chance of a cuppa anywhere.' He put his hands on her shoulders. 'Don't go away.' Jane didn't get chance for response before Will was gone, disappearing amongst the milling crowds.

Jane watched the hordes of people around her who sought sanctuary as she did each time the siren sounded and she thought of her friends, wondering where they were now and searching faces just in case.

It was likely that, wherever she was, Florence would flutter her long lashes and find men eager to assist her in finding a place to sit or a cup of tea to warm her. If Aggie was with her, Florence would ensure that her friend's safety and comfort came hand in hand with her own. Dorothy was always organised and efficient; she probably had her air raid bag with her - it was now always close to hand and containing items she felt essential for a stint in a shelter; small blanket, flask of water (refreshed daily), biscuits, book, modest supply of first aid essentials, torch, whistle. She'd put together the bag after they'd lost Alderney Street; if Jane had had a whistle and a torch her rescue would no doubt have come sooner was Dorothy's comment. She gave a sage forewarning to be prepared for the worst, meant for all the girls to heed. They'd all readily agreed but Dorothy and Jane were the only ones to act so diligently upon the words.

Jane felt a chill run through her as she leaned back against the tiles of the station but couldn't be sure whether it was the memories or the cold that made her shiver in the subterranean shelter. She pulled Will's coat more tightly around her and slid her hands into the pockets. Her fingers touched something cold and she pulled out the contents of the right pocket. Some loose change and a key. She put the coins back but turned the key over in her hand. It looked like a hotel room key but with a plain rectangular metal tag attached, instead of one carrying a number as you would expect. It looked very much like the keys at the Grandchester, but Jane reasoned that all hotel keys probably looked similar. Maybe the Grandchester wasn't the only hotel who had the curled top of each room key coloured silver; Jane had previously assumed that this was an eccentric quirk of the hotel, but clearly it wasn't so rare. Anyway, the Grandchester had an oval tag attached to their keys with the hotel name emblazoned on it along with the room number. She put the items back in the pocket but, without thinking, felt around inside the left pocket too. She knew that she was looking for the Grandchester tag. It wasn't there.

She touched the breast pocket to hear paper. As she wrestled with the temptation of delving further into Will's coat, guilt overwhelmed her and she withdrew her hands from its warmth. It wasn't long before Will, smiling, appeared weaving through the crowds to proudly offer her a steaming mug of tea.

'What would we do without the WVS and the Red Cross?' he smiled. 'They do a sterling job; never far away in a crisis.'

'Absolutely.' Jane sipped the tea carefully, her fingertips itching to turn the key over again as if touching it might explain it.

Will put his cup on the floor then slid down the wall to sit next to Jane. He nodded towards the crowds. 'It's filling up but there's nothing much doing outside at the moment. Let's hope it stays that way.'

Somewhere inside the station a baby cried, children laughed and a small group of people were singing. Two children dashed past, chasing each other through an imaginary game.

'Will, I meant to ask earlier...' Jane wanted to ask about the key but didn't; it was just a key. 'When you telephoned me, was it after the accident?'

Will seemed to hesitate 'Uh, no. No, it was before. I telephoned before.'

'There seemed some commotion at your end when we spoke. What happened?'

'I don't know, I think we got cut off,' was all he said. Jane didn't respond as her mind found suspicion and her fingertips once again found the edges of the key.

When the crowds tumbled out once more into the world above, they looked round with trepidation wondering what they might find. As people dispersed, homeward bound, to see what damage was done and which buildings stood firm, Jane and Will stepped onto the street. Activity surrounded them, but the previous night's bombardment seemed to have been centred on a different part of the city and they walked along streets that remained unchanged from when they'd last seen them.

They'd slept fitfully underground, Jane with her troubled head against Will's shoulder and Will leaning back against the wall. The morning brought optimism with its light, despite the tired eyes that greeted it. Jane looked at her watch, which Will noticed.

'Not much time before you start work is it?' he asked.

'Sadly not. I could quite happily crawl into bed for an hour or two.'

'Did my shoulder not pass muster young lady?' Will feigned distress as he grasped his chest. 'I'm hurt. I'm offended to the core.' He staggered against the wall and Jane looked around to see who might be watching the faux drama.

'Will, stop it. People will think you're really hurt, especially with your face like it is.' Will stopped his act and stood straight.

'Sorry. Bad taste I suppose.' They continued to walk towards Jane's new home, commenting on the thankful lack of fresh damage around them but knowing that other areas had experienced the wrath of war instead. They reached Mrs Foster's front door and Jane handed Will his jacket.

'Thank you for that.'

'You're welcome.' He slipped the jacket back on as Jane located her front door key and turned it in the lock. 'I'm in rehearsal most of today and then I'm working tonight.'

'Can you work then, looking like that?'

'I told you, it's nothing much; it's more visual than debilitating. But a dab or two and this'll soon be covered up.' He touched his own jaw, but Jane could see that he did so carefully. 'They're trying out an evening performance to see how the box office does. Fingers crossed the Germans don't decide to come too. Can you come along? Show starts at seven thirty.'

'I'll do my best.'

Will took her reply as a yes. 'Great. See you tonight.' He leaned forward and, taking Jane completely by surprise, he kissed her. When she was released from his arms he hopped down the two steps to the pavement, waved and was gone; he looked once again like someone else as he walked up the road. He turned at the end of the street and called back, cupping his hands round his mouth to aid the travelling words 'I have a surprise for you later! Don't be late.'

Frank, subdued, greeted the now familiar person at the stage door and let her in. Jane had become a regular guest backstage during the weeks since her first nervous visit and comfortably weaved through the activity and bustle to find a spot in the wings, where she waited. She didn't see Will as she waited for the performance to begin, but that wasn't unusual; most of the time he didn't appear by her side until the interval or, occasionally, after the final curtain call. However, one of the chorus girls did appear at Jane's shoulder. She whispered quickly into Jane's ear then took her hand and guided her through areas of the theatre she didn't know, until they came to a dressing room. Inside there were numerous dressing tables and mirrors, with wigs, make-up, hats and other small items littering the tables and hanging from mirrors. Costumes hung around the room and there was the scent of make-up, perfume and powder in the air.

As Jane entered, she saw Will sitting at one of the dressing tables staring at his reflection in the mirror, his eyes vacant to the real world and seeing something in his mind that Jane couldn't. The dancer retreated and discreetly closed the door behind her. As Jane approached, Will turned his head so slowly it was almost sinister. She held her breath for a moment before speaking.

'Will. What is it?' Jane stopped behind him and he turned away to look at her through the distance of the mirror. They looked at each other in the glass. Jane searched for new wounds but only saw the traces of his previous injuries underneath the strong stage make up, invisible to an audience but detectable here.

'Harry was coming tonight; he was coming to meet you.' Jane was engulfed by a chill. 'He was home on leave, or supposed to be.' Jane feared the words to follow. 'But Jack telephoned. They had a telegram today. It came today.' There was nothing more to be said and Jane let her arms and her tears speak for her. She hadn't known Harry, but she knew his family after all the visits to the farm and she knew the friend he'd been to Will and the son and brother he'd been. She'd heard anecdotes of their past antics and couldn't help but share the excitement that emanated from Will when he'd talked of seeing his dearest friend again the next time he was home.

The surprise that Will had happily planned, the meeting of two people of great importance to him, would never happen.

A soft rapping on the door a short time later told them that Will had five minutes before he was due on stage. The large man who gently opened the door a crack asked if Will was 'alright to go on' and Will cleared his throat and answered yes to the man's obvious relief. Will quickly wiped his eyes, kissed Jane's hands and stood up.

As Will left the stage at the end of the show, his fellow actors and the backstage crew turned their usual post show back slaps and congratulations to handshakes, shoulder pats and condolences. Will changed quickly, unable to make eye contact with anyone as he acknowledged their kind words with a mute nod and all the while searching instead for Jane with his pained eyes. Once she was by his side again he took her hand and they left the theatre, walking into the night without a word to crack the air between them.

Jane waited for Will to speak first.

'Missing in Action,' came the words as they eventually stopped by the river. Jane squeezed Will's hand.

'Then there's hope, Will.'

'No. He's gone Jane. We all know he's gone.'

'How are Maggie, Jack and the children?'

'As you'd expect; broken but brave. I need to go and see them.' Will sighed, wrecked and tired by his grief. When he next spoke it was as if the words were real to him for the first time, like he only now absorbed their meaning. 'He won't be back Jane. He won't ever come home.' Jane was quiet. 'What will Maggie and Jack do?'

'We'll look after them. We'll look after them all for him.'

The pair strolled on in silence, with Jane praying the siren wouldn't sound yet and disturb Will's contemplation. Finally, it was Will and not an air raid that intruded on the quiet.

'I'll look after them Jane, don't worry. I've been thinking about this all afternoon since Jack called. I can't be there to work the farm full time, but some money would help them. When the war's over, they'll need to take people on. You know about Harry and there was another chap, Jim, but both left to join up. Jim was sent home minus his legs.' Jane gasped and Will squeezed her hand. 'And now Harry's gone too. It's really hard for Jack and Daniel; there's so much to do and they only just manage. But knowing it was short term, that there would at least be three of them again one day, made it seem easier. They really need to take on help now, maybe get one of the girls from the WLA.' They stopped to sit on a wall. 'I need to take over where Harry left off, even if I'm helping in a different way. They'll turn down financial help of course, but I'll get round that somehow. I can see my call up looming so I need to do what I can now, before I'm sent off somewhere; even if they just sit on the money until they need it most. A girl from the land army would be a great help to them, but that's relatively short term. Cash can do so many things for them.' Jane nodded when he looked to her, not sure whether he was seeking sanction or just understanding. 'I know that nothing, no-one, will ever fill the Harry shaped hole they have in their souls. If I can't be about to offer practical help now and then, I'll at least help some other way. It's not much but it's something.'

'You do more than you think Will. You're part of their family, that's very clear.'

'But now the family's broken Jane and a piece will always be missing.'

Jane didn't know what to say in response, knowing it was true, so again she said nothing hoping that her company was as important as her words.

Will walked Jane home, kissed her goodnight then said he was off to collect the Sunbeam and ride to the farm. Although Jane felt it was too late to be riding over there that night, she again stayed silent. Her words would be weightless tonight, like a baby's breath on a dandelion clock.

'I'm sorry to rush off Sunshine. But I have to go.'

'I know.' Jane smiled gently and squeezed Will's hand. 'Tell them all I'm thinking of them.'

'I will.'

'And I'm thinking of you.'

'I know.' Will smiled for the first time that evening.

In Will's absence Jane felt a little lost. There was no under-study for his role with Jane as there was with his role at the Majesty but he did manage to telephone Jane at the Grandch-ester every single day he was away; just a quick exchange to check her safety. Jane knew he saw the fire in the clouds over the city and heard the sounds of death being dropped from the sky. Jane offered the same reassurance to him that she presented to her mother, although she knew that this would not give Will the comfort that she hoped it gave her worried parent. Her mother closed her eyes to news of the devastation and told herself she believed her daughter's comforting words, Will knew what it was like when the bombs came and that no family was immune to the horror; her mother prayed she'd soon welcome her daugh-ter's arrival in Somerset, Will knew that Jane had no intention of running away.

It was during one of Will's brief telephone calls that Jane's eyes came to rest on an empty hook.

All the hotel's room keys had a numbered hook on a large polished wooden board on the wall behind the front desk. If a room was unoccupied its hook held three room keys.

On checking in, a guest would be given their key. Should they request it, for example in the event of a couple occupying a room, they could have two keys. The third key, a spare, was kept on the hook. The 'hook key' was only used by staff in the event of an emergency and was immediately returned to the hook. The staff wondered whether their private phrase of 'they're off the hook' when letting a locked-out guest back into their room had been leaked and was indeed the origin of the expression. Cleaning and maintenance was done by utilising a separate set of master keys, carefully looked after by the housekeeper, her staff of chambermaids and the hotel handyman, so the absence of any hook key was a very temporary situation. A hook key was only ever missing for as long as it took an employee to reach the room in question, unlock the door and return the key to the front desk.

The empty hook that caught Jane's eye belonged to room 37; Hugh Callaghan's.

After her brief conversation with Will, Jane carried on with her daily tasks but found herself glancing at the vacant hook frequently. Throughout the rest of the day, the key remained absent. Hook keys were never missing for more than an hour but no-one came to return the key to its home. No-one mentioned needing the key, and everyone who had access to use it had passed the desk more than once without returning it.

Before Jane left for home she also checked the pigeon hole for room 37. There was no post or note to explain the key's absence and Jane couldn't shake the feeling that she knew exactly where the key could be found.

As Jane collected her things, one of the chambermaids who was having a break looked up.

'Lucky you, off home?'

'Yes. That's me done. I'm shattered for some reason.'

'It'll be the sleepless nights with the raids I bet,' the maid smiled.

'Probably.'

'I don't know about you but I'm so tired I think I'm ruddy seeing things.' Jane chuckled and nodded as if to confirm a similar state of fatigue, but the girl continued. 'No, seriously. I saw Mr Callaghan disappear round the first landing the other day, heading up towards his room as I came down. Then a few minutes later I was in the foyer and I saw him go up again I swear.' She shook her head. 'I don't know; it's either lack of sleep or I'm losing my bloody marbles.' She laughed as she stood up to get back to work. 'Anyway, back to it. See you tomorrow Jane; fingers crossed for some decent sleep tonight eh?'

The girl crossed her fingers and waved them behind her as she left the room. Jane replied 'Yes, fingers crossed' but the girl had already gone by the time Jane forced her lips to reply.

Jane sat down.

She sat statue still for some time before leaving.

With trepidation, Jane waited in the hallway at Mrs Foster's for the knock on the door that would say Will was back.

Whilst hovering in the staff room, Jane had eventually forced the questions from her troubled mind. Her mood changed to nervous and excited as she then hurried home. She hastily took a bath before changing into the best clothes she had and checking her reflection a hundred times. There would be a sensible explanation, she told herself as she fiddled with her hair in the mirror yet again.

As she sat by the telephone table in the hall, Jane tried not to feel so eager to see the man who had now given flight to a flock of questions. Despite all her concerns, the feelings she had for him outweighed her doubts by far. She knew there would be rational and acceptable answers but didn't want to seem suspicious or unfeeling by asking for these.

When chatting to her three girlfriends the previous day at Hampney Teas she'd carefully probed for their opinions, trying to be vague. They weren't fooled by her hypothetical question, voiced as though hinting for their view on a work colleague. Jane refused to have the true story drawn from her, but had already gleaned three different approaches to the same situation; have it out, be tactful yet firm and delicately prise the answers free through cunning.

Jane felt a surge of anticipation when she heard the Sunbeam pull up outside. There was a slight delay and she pictured Will pushing the motorcycle onto its stand, removing his crash helmet and sliding it behind the front wheel before jumping up the two steps to the front door.

Knock, knock.

She took a deep breath and walked to the door.

The moment she opened it Will scooped her up to kiss her. When he let her go she was pleased to see that in the few days he'd been gone, his bruises had faded and the grazes weren't as angry or raw. This time when she touched his face he didn't pull away.

'You look a picture Jane. I've missed you.' He hugged her again. 'What would you like to do tonight?'

'I don't mind. I'd like to hear about your visit.'

'How about we stay here for a while? Will Mrs Foster mind?'

'I'm sure she wouldn't. She's visiting family this evening anyway.'

Will theatrically nudged her and winked. In his best villainous cad voice he smarmed, 'We're all alone eh?' He raised his eyebrows in exaggerated suggestion.

'If you hadn't already been beaten up, I'd do it myself.' The moment Jane said it the smile dropped from her own and Will's faces, both somehow falling into their own thoughts on his injuries. Will's smile returned quickly and he laughed.

'The Sunbeam beat me up alright. She's more jealous than any woman.'

Jane smiled, but was sure it didn't look genuine and they walked to the kitchen where she put the kettle on to boil.

'Are you hungry?'

'No, just a cuppa will hit the spot thank you.'

While the tea was made and a few biscuits searched out, Will told Jane about his visit to the farm. As was expected, Harry's parents were being strong for their remaining children. Daniel was a very mature sixteen and was trying to absorb and soften the pain for his younger siblings in any way he could. Jacob and Sylvie were grieving outwardly, in contrast to their parents' and brother's inner pain. All were trying to be brave. Will explained how each of them had a different grief; he said he'd never realised how many types there were.

'They have some good friends and people have been very kind.'

'How are you?' Will shrugged in response, as Jane paused in loading the tea tray.

'I don't know. I feel numb sometimes. Sometimes I forget. Sometimes I'm angry.' Will waited for the teapot then lifted the completed tray and carried it to the living room as Jane followed. They sat together on the settee and Will continued. 'Before Harry went, we had a long talk about this happening.' He felt the need to lighten the mood with a quip. 'Not tea and biscuits, obviously. We talked about death and fear and those we'd leave behind. But the main thing was that we talked about doing the right thing. That's often the hard thing isn't it? Knowing what the right thing is. Harry knew. He knew straight away; the rest of us have caught up now, those of us who didn't understand the urgency, the *they'll call us when they need us* brigade. Even though we talked about dying I suppose it's human nature to somehow believe we'll be alright, that it won't be us. We wouldn't do half the things we do if we were truly aware of our own mortality would we? Being able to say that we did the right thing is what we should all aspire to.' He started to pour the tea. 'I'll be mother. Although my mother would frown because it's not had time to brew.'

'Did you tell Jack and Maggie that you and Harry talked about dying?' Jane accepted the cup and saucer that Will offered and put it down on the table.

'Yes I did. I wondered whether I should and I decided yes. I told them because Harry said that whatever happened, whether he came back whole or broken or didn't return at all, he'd done the right thing. And I wanted them to know that he said that. I knew he hadn't talked about dying with them; he brushed off any talk of it.'

'Did it help them to know how he felt?'

'Yes, it did. It helped me too.' He patted her knee quickly. 'Come on sunshine, what's our plan for the rest of the day?' Will was clearly keen to end the sombre conversation. 'No work for me tonight so the city's our oyster.'

'Oh gosh Will, I don't know. What would you like to do?'

'Well, as I'm topped up to the hilt with TVO and feeling frivolous, let's just get out of the city and go for a ride. We'll see where Sunbeam takes us shall we?'

'That sounds perfect.'

Tea finished and cleared away, Jane descended the stairs wrapped up warm and ready for the outing. Will eyed her up and down. 'Gorgeous, but your legs'll be cold. It's pretty chilly out there.'

Jane shrugged.

'I'll be alright.'

'Hang on.' Will raised a finger and dashed outside. Soon he returned with the small bag he'd taken to the farm. He plonked it on a chair and rummaged around in it for a moment, before pulling out a pair of trousers and offering them to Jane. 'Here you go, whip these on.' Jane crossed her arms.

'Really?'

'Yep. You'll look a treat, honest.'

'Will, they'll fall down.' Will put up a finger to silence her then took off his belt and offered it to her.

'There we are. If it's too big, I'm sure you have something you can use, a scarf or something.'

Jane sighed.

'Wait here then. I won't be a minute.' She trotted upstairs and soon returned wearing Will's trousers and with a blue scarf in her hand.

'Perfect.' Will smiled. 'You look perfect.' He took the scarf from Jane and, as she held up her arms he carefully threaded it through the belt loops on the trousers and tied it up. 'Smashing.

Come on.' He took her hand and they were soon riding through the busy streets on their way to anywhere.

Answers

When Will stopped the Sunbeam and they climbed from their seats, the wind felt colder. It was milder in the city, between the buildings and amongst the activity. They'd stopped in a small town and hovered next to the bike as they glanced around deciding what to do next.

'Shall we just wander?' Will asked, taking Jane's hand.

'Yes, sounds good.' They walked along the empty shopping streets for a while before ending up perched on a wall watching the town's inhabitants in the early evening.

After considering the three options her friends had given, Jane knew which one it would be. Her relationship with Will would be honest; there would be no subterfuge in trying to glean any revelations from him. She had questions for him to answer and would ask him outright, no messing.

'What part are you playing Will?' Will looked down at his feet uncomfortably for a second.

'I don't know what you're getting at Jane. At the Majesty?' He looked innocent.

'What part are you playing with me?' She paused but he didn't respond. 'Ok, let me give you a list then, some ideas. Someone called you Hugh at the school hall the first day we met; I know they called it to you and you know that your resemblance to Mr Callaghan is uncanny. You say you came off your motorcycle but it wasn't damaged, there's not a scratch. I looked. You turned up at Mrs Foster's completely battered, like you'd been attacked. Who comes off their motorcycle and lands so hard on their face as well as their body?' Will didn't take his eyes from her as she spoke. 'That was the same day our telephone call was supposedly cut off, only I know that's not what happened Will. I heard the commotion at your end. And I saw you at the Grandchester, I know I did. You came in, walked across the lobby and went upstairs. And one of the maids saw Mr Callaghan walk up the stairs twice in the space of a few minutes. I know one was you. Why did you do that?' There was no response. 'Why were you there? Don't bother saying it wasn't you.' As Jane watched him, Will bit his bottom lip. 'And I know you have a Grandchester hotel key in your pocket.' Will sighed, puffing out his cheeks, and looked forlornly at Jane. The pause seemed to go on forever as she waited.

'Ok.' Will looked into Jane's eyes with a seriousness he never had before. He turned from the joker, tossing out glee and spontaneity in his wake, to something else. She'd seen many things in his face over the last few weeks. She'd witnessed fun and teasing, softness, sadness and distress, careful concern, gentleness, but never this depth of dark seriousness and confession.

He was a predator caught, a villain unveiled, a trickster revealed; or an innocent accused.

'Your Mr Callaghan. Hugh. He asked me to help him out and offered to pay me. He asked if I'd...well...he asked if I'd *stand in* for him for a day or two.' Jane didn't know what explanation she expected but, of all the wild things that she could imagine but give no name to, it absolutely wasn't this. If it wasn't for the expression on Will's face, she'd have told him to stop messing about. 'The person at the school hall the day we met obviously thought I was Hugh. The job was easy, Hugh said, just go to the hotel, borrow some of his clothes, go out and about, stay at the hotel a night or two and then leave.' He turned his body towards Jane's. 'I could earn some cash by staying two nights at the Grandchester, eating good food and staying in a nice room, all paid for? He asked me some weeks back, saying he'd seen me at the Majesty. I thought it was all a bit odd. Understandably. And I declined. But then I bumped into him again; or he bumped into me, who knows. Anyway, he asked again and I said yes. I had to say yes this time Jane. I need the money now, for Maggie and Jack, before I get called up. But he told me not to tell anyone, especially not you. That was all part of his instruction. It was *ask me no questions and I'll tell you no lies.*' Jane sat wide eyed, stunned silent. 'I wanted to tell you Jane. God knows how I wanted to tell you. I wanted to invite you up to the room, to call room service, to pretend we were part of the Grandchester set, have some fun. I wanted you to be one of those ladies of luxury, to be a guest at the hotel for a little while and not to work there. It wasn't any fun on my own. It sounded exciting, but without you to share it with me it was just a job.' He was apologetic, eyes lowered like a schoolboy caught out, hand deep in the sweetie jar.

Jane tried to ignore the softness of Will's eyes as he painted an attractive picture of the two of them, luxuriating for free at the Grandchester. If she allowed her eyes to see the vision, she might blush, or tingle head to toe, or say 'what the heck, let's do it, let's be somebody else.'

But Jane forced her head to beat her heart down. She had to stop the little tapping of anticipation growing into a mad thumping beat of excitement and daring. Sensible Jane triumphed over the newly impulsive, live for the moment Jane; the latter had been coaxed further to the fore every day by the spontaneous Will and was getting harder to deny.

'Despite his instruction you're telling me now. Why couldn't you have told me then?'

'Because it's all over now. Hugh eluded to there being some peril. I thought that was over the top, even knowing what all your hotel gossips say about him. But I couldn't take the chance of putting you at any risk. I had in mind that maybe he was just wanting to get ahead of some debt chasers or something, wanted to nip off somewhere and do some business while people thought he was still here.'

'And he gave you money to do this?'

'Yes.' Jane frowned at his admission, inviting further explanation. 'He left it in his room for me.'

'What about the motorcycle accident?'

'There wasn't one, you were right. The Sunbeam wasn't being tidied up; Hugh borrowed it. The real accident came when I left the hotel. Two chaps in the street.'

'They attacked you because they thought you were Hugh Callaghan?' Jane was visibly shocked and Will nodded. 'He put you at risk like that? What did they want? Did they want money?'

'I don't know what they wanted. They ran off when two ARP wardens saw us and got involved.'

'I can't believe Mr Callaghan would do that to you?'

'Jane, he didn't know that would happen.'

'You think? You said he told you there could be danger, playing at being him. He asked you to be him knowing that there were men who wanted to do that to him.'

Will took Jane's hand. 'Sunshine. Please. Hugh felt bad when he came back and saw me. He offered me more cash, and somewhere to go. But I didn't take any more money Jane. And I couldn't leave. Jane, you can't let on that you know. You mustn't say anything.' Jane hesitated for as long as she could before she weakened under Will's pleading gaze.

'Alright, I won't. But please don't come near the hotel again. If it was a case of mistaken identity, it can happen again. Is that why he offered you somewhere to go, because it might happen again? What if those men see you another time, somewhere else?'

'It's ok Sunshine.' His eyes wouldn't let her go. 'Honestly, it's done with now.' Jane felt his reassurance wrapping around her hesitation, but feared its glaze of safety wouldn't last. Questions bumped frantically round inside her head, struggling against worry and fear.

After first introducing Jane to the Halls, Will had talked to her of their hardships and his worries for them with their eldest son away. Despite the relative comfort of living on a farm when it came to the availability of vegetables and milk, their life was a hard one in many other ways.

Even before the war had finally hit with its full force, the farm had been seeing a downturn in its profits. Will helped out as much as he could, with labour and small gifts. They had always turned down what little financial help Will could offer, so he'd been creative with the things he gave them. Now that Harry would not return, Will felt his responsibilities even more keenly. He couldn't soothe the pain of loss but hoped to ease some of the other worries that now weighed even heavier with the death of their first born.

Jane knew and understood this, loving Will all the more for his own love and sense of responsibility for the Hall family.

Jane also knew that with limited theatre performances Will's wages were being asked to stretch further than they could; it was enough to ask his wages to cover his own rent and food at times. All these things had made Hugh Callaghan's offer attractive to Will, and Jane feared that any future requests to share an identity would be hard for Will to turn down. His priority was taking care of Harry's family. At any cost it seemed.

Jane wanted to share her concerns with her girlfriends but her silence had been begged by Will; he'd promised Hugh his discretion. Jane's next catch up with Florence, Aggie and Dorothy was hard. The girls were excited to hear of Jane's flourishing romance but could not know of her deeper fears. Added to Jane's assurance of secrecy was her fear that any break in confidence could somehow put Will in further jeopardy. So, with secrets locked away, the friendly chatting and updating continued and the foursome parted company happily with the usual hugs and kisses and instructions to take care. Jane watched her friends go their separate ways and continued to carry her worry around on her own.

The next time Jane saw Hugh Callaghan, she smoothed on a veneer of routine and pleasantry. Underneath, hard scratchy dislike rubbed against it. She'd always liked him but now tasted disappointment and betrayal instead, as keenly as blood from a bitten tongue. And bite her tongue she did, now that he seemed able to put someone else at risk the way he had. That the person concerned was Will made the act even more unpleasant and, even though she wasn't, Jane felt like she was smiling at the man through gritted teeth. Bitterness weaved its way into her and prodded a nasty bony finger at a usually kind and gentle heart.

On a cold Saturday afternoon the Halls greeted Will and Jane with the smiles and hugs she knew they would, enveloping them again within their family. Their farmhouse offered welcome warmth and light on a cold grey day. A month had passed since they'd received the piece of paper that thousands of families dreaded; a few lines of writing with the power to shatter lives, a paper bomb. Yet the mood at the farm wasn't sombre. At the moment, it was almost possible to pretend that slip of paper hadn't come, that it had never existed. Harry wasn't supposed to be there now so he didn't ask to be missed. But when his leave might have come around again, when the war was over, when he should have been out in the fields, sitting at the table, sharing their lives, then the family wouldn't be able to pretend any longer.

As for the telegram itself, Maggie Hall had slipped it into a box then returned the box to a shelf, safe in her wardrobe. She'd read it only once and wouldn't look at the words again for years.

Jane and Will were staying over at the farm this time. Jack had a beam to strengthen in the barn and Will was there to help. While Jack, Will and Daniel worked, Maggie, Sylvie and Jane kept them fed and watered and shared other tasks around the farm and in the kitchen. Jacob was playing with the dogs and generally making a nuisance of himself in the barn, but nobody seemed to mind.

There was an unspoken need for normality amongst everyone since the war had started and, with the loss of a piece of them, every little part of life became more precious to the Halls; even things that would have brought exasperation, remonstration or a cross word were now things to be savoured.

Every day, Maggie wished to be picking up the glass of water Harry routinely left by his bed and forgot to bring down to the kitchen, in the early morning Jack missed Harry's muddy boots always lying on top of his when he got up to start the day, Daniel longed for the good natured but bothersome ribbing Harry insisted on giving him about the sisters who lived on the next farm, Sylvie wanted to hear Harry call her Young Missy in his irritating impression of a school master's voice and Jacob craved the maddening rubbing of his hair every time Harry passed.

When work in the barn was complete for the day, animals cared for and the men washed and changed everyone sat at the scrubbed farmhouse table to eat. The mood was the same as during their previous visit, only different. There was a new and subtle distance to be found occasionally in Maggie's eyes, Jack had a slight greyness about him that wasn't there before, Daniel seemed to have changed into a man overnight and the two youngest family members were not quite as chatty or giggly as previously. But to the outside world, with no knowledge of how life looked before, the family might appear no different to any other. Life carried on. The only break in their conversation and evening meal came when the dogs began to bark outside. Jack went to check, muttering something about foxes, but returned not long after to report that all seemed quiet, smiling and adding 'daft dogs' to his report.

Jane knew there had been occasions since *the news*, when Will had visited the farm alone, when he'd talked to Maggie and Jack about Harry and how they'd cope without him. This visit, however, was not to organise or plan or discuss the gaping loss, but to give some routine back; to laugh, smile, work, share meals, to chat, get to know Jane, make time for each other.

Once Sylvie and Jacob were in bed, the adults chatted and played a game of gin rummy, winning and losing matchsticks. When Daniel was shooed off to bed, Jane and Maggie fell into their own conversation as Jack disappeared outside for a cigarette and Will followed.

When sleep beckoned for the four who were left, Maggie showed Jane to the spare room where she'd already put Jane's small bag.

'We don't use this room very much. Should have really, but the boys always wanted to share. I've put Will in Harry's, in Harry's bed.' The name of her first born seemed to trip over an invisible obstacle on Maggie's tongue and her eyes met Jane's. Jane held Maggie's hand for a moment, knowing that no words would be quite right. Composure unsteadily regained, Maggie smiled, 'If you need anything love, just ask.' With that she retreated quickly to head for her own room where she wept in Jack's arms every night.

Jane's room had white walls that seemed to lean in slightly further the higher they reached. On one was a dark frame containing a biblical print. A small sink stood to the side of a window, where a deep sill reached out to the glass in the old cob wall. There was no curtain adorning the small window frame; it was high and deeply recessed and there were no neighbours to pry or streetlights to protect the slumbering from. Jane sat down on the bed which was very soft and deep, covered by crisp white sheets and a soft pink blanket. On the bedside table was a small jug of water and a glass. She kicked off her shoes and lay down, letting her thoughts walk around freely in her head.

Jane wondered if she might hear the softest of tapping on her door and be able to spend some more time with Will, but no tapping came. She didn't know that he had indeed planned to tiptoe down the landing to visit her and he didn't know that she hoped he would.

But, in the darkness of night, in the room that once housed three brothers, Will had been sitting up with Daniel and Jacob talking quietly about Harry, answering their questions and squashing their fears. When morning came some of the large clouds that had gathered above Daniel and Jacob had been blown away by Will, leaving only the wispiest of hazes. The brother who was their confidante, tormentor, ringleader, supporter, teacher and idol was laid gently to rest.

Chores beckoned early the next morning, then church, more chores and lunch. They all went for a walk after the table was cleared and the Sunday lunch dishes washed. Animals checked and tended, afternoon strolled into evening and soon it was time for Will and Jane to leave.

The farewells were hard, but promises were made to return soon and a little paper wrapped package of cake slipped into Jane's hand, along with a parcel for Will. Gifts and bags stowed, hugs shared and kisses blown, and the pair were once again alone on the Sunbeam in the darkness.

Some time into their journey, as they sped down the lanes homeward bound, Will turned and shouted back to Jane. She thought he said 'The bike's not right' but the wind and the noise of the engine made it hard to tell.

A moment later, she knew she'd heard right as Will tensed.

The front of the Sunbeam seemed to wriggle from his guidance. Then Jane felt the wheel beneath her move in a way she knew it shouldn't, almost snake like, and in an instant the motorbike tipped to its side. Will's foot shot out attempting to right it again, which he seemed to do for just a second before the machine slithered its own course, and crashed onto its side as it slid scraping and crunching towards the hedge. Jane thought she screamed but wasn't sure. All noise was confused, mixed and muffled. The whole incident took seconds and silence followed.

The next moment, as the immediate aftermath brought disorientation and clouded thought, saw a frantic Will scrabbling to his feet then falling to his knees at Jane's side where she lay awkwardly in the darkness a few yards from the stricken cycle.

'Jane, Jane, are you alright?' His hand touched hers then moved quickly to her neck, frantically checking for a pulse. As she stirred, his checking of her became almost frenzied; gentle but hurried hands touching her ankles, legs, back, arms, face; checking for breaks and blood in the darkness. Finally, he slid his arm underneath her to lift her gently away from the cold ground as he nursed her against him. His palm curved round her face and he was so close she could feel his nervous panting breaths.

'I'm alright Will,' Jane was quick to reassure, as gentle but still frantic fingers unfastened the strap of her crash helmet and lifted it from her. He leaned down as she tried to sit up, her disorientation fog lifting.

'Slowly Jane, hang on, let me help you.' As she sat up she was amazed that no part of her seemed more painful than a blossoming bruise. An involuntary wince from a pain in her shoulder and a palm feeling the sting of a graze in the cold seemed the sum of her pain inventory, which was thankfully complete with no loss of limb or blood. 'Are you hurt? Where do you hurt?'

'Nowhere much, my shoulder and hand are a little sore but that's all.' She held out her left hand and Will kissed her palm in the moonlight. 'Are you alright Will, are *you* hurt anywhere?'

'Don't worry about me, I'm fine. I told you before, I have a hard head.' Jane couldn't see much in the dark of the lane. 'I'm so sorry Jane. I said I'd look after you.' All Jane could tell from the dim headlamp and the moon was that Will had now turned towards the prone motorcycle. 'I don't know what happened.'

'Was it mud on the road or something?'

'No, didn't feel like it. It was mechanical. Something didn't feel right with the bike.' He turned back to Jane. 'Are you sure you're alright?'

'Yes.'

'Honestly?'

'Honestly.'

Will wrapped her in an embrace to whisper 'I can't lose you.'

Once he'd tenderly helped Jane up and made her sit on his overcoat on a small bank of grass, Will manoeuvred the lifeless motorcycle into a nearby field and unstrapped their belongings.

'Can you see if there's much damage?'

'Can't see much, but I don't think it's actually too bad bodily. We'll have to walk on and find somewhere to get a bus or something though. I'll telephone Jack tomorrow and ask him to come and take Sunbeam back to the farm. Can't head back there now; we're half way home anyway. Maggie'll be frantic when she finds out. She'll blame it on the lights. She hates me riding in the dark with Sunbeam's eyes half closed.' Jane didn't like the obscured lights on the machine either, but didn't say anything. When the war was over being out at night would feel like daylight, when street lights shone and headlamps were once more fully revealed with their eyes wide open. Will took Jane's hand to help her to her feet again and they walked slowly along the dark lanes. 'I'm so sorry.'

'Stop saying sorry; accidents happen.' When there was no response from a brooding Will, a little light suddenly turned on for Jane and she stopped walking. Will did too. 'It wasn't, was it?'

Will turned in the semi darkness.

'Wasn't what?' he asked the question even though he knew what was coming.

'It wasn't an accident.' Silence. 'The dogs barking. Someone was there and they did something to the bike.' As the flood of thoughts tumbled out in words, Jane's anxiety rose but her voice became a whisper. 'They knew you were there.' Will took both of Jane's hands in his to steady her. 'Did they follow us?' Will pulled Jane into a tight embrace. 'Will, someone thinks you're Hugh and they tried to kill you.'

Will's voice quaked for a moment as he started to speak. 'Jane, I don't know. I'm not sure what's going on. I'll speak with Hugh. As soon as we get back we'll get you on a train. I won't let you out of my sight until you're on your way to Somerset. The further away you are from me the better, just until I know what's going on.' Despite her distress, Jane's response was firm.

'Well, that's not going to happen.'

'What's not?'

'I'm not going to Somerset. If anything, I'm more help here than anyone as I'm at the hotel and near to Hugh. How can he put you in danger like this?'

'Jane, please. For me, just go to your mum's. I'm sure this can all be sorted out and then I'll call you, or I'll come and get you if you like.'

'No, I'm staying. You can't make me go so you can stop talking about it.' Resigned and frustrated, Will didn't argue. He just sighed deeply and held her even closer, almost absorbing her in a bid to offer protection. Then they walked on in silence.

The next day brought an overall ache to Jane's body as she woke and tried to turn over. Her shoulder seemed no worse than any other part of her. Her palm was grazed but otherwise fine. As she dragged herself to sit up she couldn't discern what ached; it felt like every muscle in her body was one entity and had been jarred. It was strange that she felt more discomfort now than when she'd been buried underneath a house. That event now seemed long past and surreal, even if it had left a footprint of jumpiness behind each time Jane heard an unexpected noise.

Mrs Foster had answered the door to Jane and Will in the early hours of the morning. Her face initially showed surprise which quickly slid to disapproval which, just as quickly, turned to concern when she took in the full picture and the expressions on the faces of Jane and her companion. A brief explanation was all that was needed for the landlady to begin bustling about for emergency brandy and cups of tea and warm blankets, despite the returning and bruised travellers assuring her they were fine.

After Will had been brandied, warmed and mothered over he left despite Mrs Foster offering him the settee for the night. Jane watched him go, fearful for his safety but unable to voice the imperative caution to him in Mrs Foster's presence. With Mrs Foster there she couldn't follow him, beg him to stay or take any action other than to benignly say 'stay safe' as he left. His voice told her 'see you tomorrow Sunshine' while his eyes betrayed disquiet. After his departure, Mrs Foster shooed Jane up to her room with a mug of Ovaltine, which Jane wasn't particularly keen on, an extra blanket and a hot water bottle.

As Jane made her way downstairs the next morning, trying to work the stiffness from every joint and muscle, she was met by her landlady in the kitchen.

'Now you're not going to work are you Jane?'

'Yes Mrs Foster. I'm fine, honestly, just a little stiff.'

Her landlady eyed her with suspicion. 'Well, if you say so.' Jane touched the kind lady's arm and smiled.

'I really am absolutely fine.' The landlady smiled back suspiciously and continued her chores as Jane took her hat and coat from the chair and prepared to leave.

'You should eat breakfast.'

'Thank you but I don't really feel like it at the moment.' Then, to appease, she added, 'I'll get something when I get to work.'

Mrs Cartlyn

As Jane answered the telephone, dealt with enquiries, made bookings and smiled happily at guests her thoughts were somewhere else. Today, her thoughts weren't warm romantic ones, filled with pictures of Will, but unpleasant frightened ones bound together with suspicion. The fear of bombs and crashing buildings, her previous visitor, almost felt like an old friend. She knew a bomb was a bomb and a siren a siren. But this new danger was a secret one which hadn't shown its face, so she didn't know what, or who, to be scared of. She didn't know the signs that should set off the alarm. Her stomach turned in apprehension of the moment she'd see Hugh Callaghan and whether her demeanour would reveal to him the new depths of what she knew, or thought she knew. She wasn't an actor like Will; she didn't know how well concealed her angry, suspicious and confused thoughts might be.

With a mixture of relief and deflation, she didn't see Hugh that day or the next. Nothing notable happened at all. The only thing different in life during those three days was the paranoia that Jane and Will tried to hide from each other. Will pretended that he wasn't continuously looking over his shoulder and Jane felt torn each time they parted company, petrified for his safety. As she crossed the lobby at work on the third day Jane saw Mrs Cartlyn walking towards her, clearly with the intention of speaking to her.

'Good morning Jane.'

'Good morning Mrs Cartlyn, can I help you?'

'Yes, Jane, you can. When you have a moment, I'd be pleased to see you in my room.'

'Of course,' was the only reply Jane could give in her utter surprise. Mrs Cartlyn nodded then turned to walk towards the lifts.

Ten minutes or so later, Jane knocked on the door of Mrs Cartlyn's seventh floor room. She heard the old lady call for her to come in so she opened the door and peered inside.

'Mrs Cartlyn?'

'In the sitting area, Jane. Come on in, don't dawdle.' Jane entered the room quickly and closed the door gently behind her. In Jane's role she didn't need to enter any of the hotel guest rooms and was newly surprised whenever she passed an open door and caught a glimpse of the luxury within. In the best rooms the space stretched before your eyes, leading to sitting room then bedroom and bathroom. The windows were tall and swathed in fabric and the furniture and furnishings expensive. Jane scanned the area for her host who was found sitting next to the ornate fireplace, in which stood an impressive floral display.

'Come here girl,' she beckoned. Jane hurried over to her.

'Mrs Cartlyn?'

'Sit down Jane. We need to talk.' Jane couldn't help frowning as she sat down opposite the ageing but formidable woman.

'I'm sorry Mrs Cartlyn, I don't understand. If there's a problem with anything at all, I'm sure the hotel would be only too pleased to...' but before Jane could finish her assurance that the hotel could deal with any problems she may have, Mrs Cartlyn interrupted.

'No Jane, I have no issues with The Grandchester, its service or its staff; although the linen could be crisper on occasion. Let's get straight to the point.' Jane stiffened in her chair, with no idea at all what Mrs Cartlyn was about to say.

'It appears that Mr Callaghan, as dashing and heroic and patriotic as he may be, has put your young man in some peril.' Jane opened her mouth to speak but was silenced by the raising of a hand, old and seemingly frail but clearly with the power to stop fresh words in their tracks. Jane noticed the glint of diamonds as the hand returned to the owner's lap. 'Often life runs its own course regardless of our actions, but there are times when one should intercede. Don't ask me how I know about your William Batten and his arrangement. Just know that I like to keep abreast of things.' Jane was struck dumb. 'My late husband, rest his good soul...' she paused a moment to choose her words, 'was an interested party in matters of security and subterfuge. We met through our shared occupations.' Mrs Cartlyn paused to allow the absorption of her words. 'As I may have mentioned before, there's been a certain amount of unexpected to'ing and fro'ing in the hotel recently; people where they shouldn't be, being who they aren't.'

Jane, stunned, didn't move or speak. When at last she processed the words, she wondered whether she had even breathed during the revelation and the ensuing silence.

Mrs Cartlyn was intimidating and sure. Jane had always known there was more; but she'd suspected softness and warmth beneath the harsh and spiky exterior not secrecy and an almost masculine power. She was lost for words.

'Jane.' Her named was spoken. 'Jane.' She took a few moments to shake off the surprise, the complete bewilderment, which had settled on her before she could respond. 'Jane, would you like a drink? You look a little pale.' Softness? Not sure. But humanity? Yes. Jane shook her head at the offer.

'No, thank you Mrs Cartlyn. I'm just a little, just a little...'

'Stunned? Shocked? Scandalised?' Mrs Cartlyn almost smiled. 'It's a sorry fact but also, conversely, a useful one that when one sees an old woman (or indeed an old man) they don't see their story, suspect their history or acknowledge their past youth. They don't see a strong young woman carrying babies or working like a Trojan, they don't picture a handsome and virile young man fighting for his country or his family. We were all young once Jane. Everyone has a story to tell and some will surprise. Dare I say it, a few might inspire or even revile but we all have a story.'

'Mrs Cartlyn, I don't mean to offend by my surprise.' Jane offered diplomacy, fearing her shock may have caused affront. She had believed without question that only three people knew of the arrangement between Hugh and Will, but just as astonishing were Mrs Cartlyn's own subtle but shattering revelations.

'Jane, I'm not at all offended,' she said smiling. 'Your wonderment is reassuring. The fact is the provision of anonymity from one's past is a blessing.' She straightened in her chair. 'Anyway, explanation over; that's as much as you'll get so don't ask any questions. Do not poke this tree for fruit.'

'I'm sorry, I'm completely lost Mrs Cartlyn.'

'Don't be sorry Jane. Only apologise when you've done something wrong. My disclosure serves only to provide you with some reassurance and add credence to my words. You're not alone, Jane, and you need help; both you and Mr Batten. Hugh has put the pair of you in an untenable position.' Of all the things Mrs Cartlyn had disclosed, exposed and confided, this Jane did understand. 'I can help Jane.'

'I'm sorry but I don't see how Mrs Cartlyn.' The woman clearly knew what was going on, or at least had as much idea as Jane, so there was no point in trying to lead her gently away from it. And despite Will's pleading, now that she had stumbled across someone who seemed aware of Will's folly (and someone, thankfully, who Jane liked and trusted) she felt relief and camaraderie. 'I don't wish to be rude, but fear that's how this will come across; why would you want to help?'

Jane thought maybe Mrs Cartlyn would cite a soft spot, religion, boredom, lack of her own family, altruism, humanity...

'It's a favour to an old friend of mine; Dora Cavendish.'

Jane was glad she was sitting down.

The old woman looked almost pleased with herself to have dropped such a revelation and watched Jane's reaction.

'My Mrs Cavendish?'

'Your Mrs Cavendish.'

Mrs Cartlyn waited.

'How?'

'Jane, I've known Dora Cavendish for many years; longer than I knew my husband. We lost touch a long time ago, but she contacted me before she left London. She asked me to keep an eye out for you in the absence of anyone else to ask. She could never have guessed I would do any more than note your safety and report to her that all was well with you and your former housemates. I think she wanted a spy in the city, to keep tabs on you and her other ex-lodgers. As it turns out, her request couldn't have been more intuitive could it?'

'That does sound like Mrs Cavendish. Can I ask how you know each other?'

'No, you may not.' Mrs Cartlyn saw Jane's face drop, so added 'We were in a similar line of work when we were girls. I owed her a favour or two.' Jane's questions ran into hundreds sprouting from how different the two women seemed and how the paths of their lives, their fortunes, had clearly been so conflicting. 'What's the strongest part of a tree Jane?' Jane was sure that she visibly jumped at the strange question.

'The trunk.'

Mrs Cartlyn shook her head. 'What holds the trunk up?'

'The roots?'

This time Mrs Cartlyn nodded. The analogy wasn't lost on Jane. Mrs Cartlyn knew Jane understood. 'You don't always see what shapes someone Jane, or what bolsters them, or what holds them up, or holds them back. As I said, everyone has a story.' Jane certainly knew that, after the last few minutes. 'Enough idle gossip now. I know what I know and that's that. Now, down to business.' Mrs Cartlyn straightened in her chair. 'Jane, the best thing that you and Mr Batten can do right now is leave the city.' As Mrs Cartlyn was talking she turned to a small walnut side table against the wall and pulled open a small drawer. She withdrew some keys and turned back to Jane, still talking. 'I have property and I have a house that's empty. It's at your disposal. A lady called Mrs Grey keeps an eye on it for me and I've telephoned her to say there may be visitors shortly.' Jane's addled brain struggled to grasp the last few strands of convention, trying to hold on to anything ordinary. Mrs Cartlyn said nothing, appreciating the plight of the poor girl that she was surprised to have a fondness for; Jane, in turn, was one of the few people in many years who had crossed the old lady's path and not found it stony and hard.

Moments passed with Mrs Cartlyn's hand outstretched in offering, holding the keys out to Jane. Eventually Jane's own hand slowly reached forward to take the proffered items. As she did so, Mrs Cartlyn spoke again. 'Mrs Grey will make up the beds and so forth and give the place an airing. She'll stock up the logs and put a few things in the pantry. The place is always fresh and clean, ready for visitors.'

'It's very kind of you Mrs Cartlyn, but I really don't think it's necessary.' Mrs Cartlyn's hand rose to silence the younger woman.

'Oh it is Jane, trust me.'

'But I'm sure it will all be sorted out. It's just a case of mistaken identity. Intentionally mistaken at first, I agree, but I'm sure the continued confusion can all be ironed out.'

'That is exactly the point Jane; mistaken identity, yes, but *guided* mistaken identity.' The woman's voice was firm. 'Mr Batten was supposed to be mistaken for Hugh; one really can't just turn off the fact that certain people think he is someone else. Hugh is an honourable and decent man, whatever doubts you may have had considering his recent arrangement with your beau.' Jane's secret self jumped at the term Mrs Cartlyn used to describe Will. 'However, his country and his duty come above all. Even above daily honour and decency. He's exposed your

Mr Batten to some danger. Until the situation is resolved, one way or another, you both have to be somewhere else. It isn't a case of just telling someone they've made a mistake.'

Jane looked directly into Mrs Cartlyn's eyes to find sincerity, competence and command.

The decision was made.

'That's ridiculous Jane.' Came Will's categorical response that evening. Jane looked around to see if anyone else out for a stroll in the early evening might have heard Will's firm, and rather louder than normal, voice.

'Why is it? Why is it Will?'

'Jane, if I leave I have no job. No job means no money. No money means nothing more to send to Jack and Maggie. Not to mention nothing to live on.' He closed his eyes then, sighing, opened them. 'I trust your judgement Jane, and your faith in the old lady, but I need to stay. I'd like you to go though. As I've said before I'd feel happier if you weren't here while I sort this mess out. If you won't go to your mum's, go to Mrs Cartlyn's place.'

Jane shook her head. 'I'm not going on my own. We go together or not at all.' Will took Jane's hands and kissed her cheek.

'What a bloody mess eh?'

'Will, please. Mrs Cartlyn said you're safe while Hugh's away. That's why I've not seen him and, unbeknown to us, why there's been no danger. They know he's not here, but once *he's* back *they'll* be back. Whoever they are. He's due back tomorrow Will and you have to be gone before then.'

'Look Sunshine, I really think your old lady has blown this out of proportion no matter how good her intentions are. Maybe she does have a mysterious past, or her husband did, or they both did, I don't know. But have you thought that maybe Hugh's just in trouble with someone, gambling or a woman probably.' He smiled cheekily. 'As soon as he pays his debt, monetary or otherwise, things'll be fine.'

Jane withdrew her hands from Will's sharply to emphasise her mood. 'Unless it's *you* who ends up paying his debt.'

'Maybe the beating was the debt paid; angry husband appeased. Maybe your faith in Mrs Cartlyn is misplaced.'

'Will, we're going round in circles. I thought you trusted my judgement. I can't put my finger on it, but I trust her. She knows so much more about Hugh than she'll say. I think you're wrong; I think Hugh is involved with something big and secretive, national security or something. And I don't think he would have risked your life for anything so minor as appeasing a jealous husband.'

The seriousness seemed lost on Will; after his initial fear for Jane immediately following the accident he seemed to have calmed and put everything into his own perspective, but his perspective didn't match Jane's.

Will again grabbed Jane's hand in one of his and wrapped his arm around her waist. Spinning her round he started to hum Waldteufel's Skaters' Waltz.

'Come on Sunshine, lighten up. Dance with me, come on.' Jane couldn't help but let herself be whirled around as the dark mood clouds above her dissolved to make way for blue sky and sunshine. A few people smiled as they walked past the dancing duo, and went on their way in a brighter disposition. When the dancing was finished, Will walked Jane home.

Despite the warmth of the waltzing, their goodbye was different. Will was jovial and sweet, while Jane was quiet and a little curt. As the door closed behind her Jane sighed and closed her eyes for a moment before her feet led her up the stairs. Before she turned at the top there was a knock at the front door. It could only be Will in that short space of time so she turned back, calling to her landlady that she'd answer it.

Jane opened the door to find Will leaning against the doorjamb and smiling apologetically.

'Fancy going to the pictures tomorrow night?' Jane sighed inwardly at his complete lack of absorption of their earlier conversation. She wasn't sure if he'd consciously dismissed it or denied it had even taken place. He seemed intent on carrying on as if the suspicious accident, the beating and Mrs Cartlyn's warning were imaginary. 'Come on, it'll be nice,' he prompted at Jane's silence. He tilted Jane's chin up with his finger and flippantly enticed with a raise of the eyebrows, 'You can ride on the sloper,' he cooed, jesting about the ancient bike. In the absence of the battered Sunbeam, now languishing in a barn, Mr Hall had re-commissioned an almost twenty year old motorcycle. It had waited patiently at the farm, rarely used but kept in acceptable working order 'just in case'. In fact, it was the very vehicle on which Will had learned to ride, nicknamed for the angle at which the petrol tank sloped. 'Please. For me.' Will smiled the most disarming smile in the world, assuring Jane's immediate submission. She nodded despite wanting to reprimand him. 'Good stuff. We'll see The Philadelphia Story.' Then he added in his best James Stewart voice 'I'll pick you up at 6.30.'

The girls harboured concern and anger in equal measure and weren't afraid to say how they felt, although each favoured a different approach to the problem, dilemma, crisis.

All three girls had been delighted to learn of Jane's burgeoning romance. Jane knew they'd like Will but was still relieved when each confirmed the fact. They all warmed to him immediately and maybe even felt the secret presence of a tiny wish that they were Jane. They all knew that Will was very special to Jane and could see, without question, that he felt the same towards her. On the occasions that they met him, there was no feeling of 'odd one out' or of him being an interloper to their tightly formed group; he was an extension of that unit and was welcomed happily by Dorothy, Aggie and Florence.

When Jane said she needed to speak with the girls, Dorothy foretold a rushed union, Aggie predicted new life and Florence prophesied Jane leaving the city.

Instead of all these forecasts, each aptly connected to Will, they were instead told that someone was trying to kill him or at least kill the man they thought he was. The whole idea seemed more than ridiculous, until Jane's face told them otherwise.

'I'd go to the police or the war office, or something. Someone must be able to help. Isn't that their job?'

Florence shook her head at Dorothy's suggestion. 'No Dorothy. That's no good. If it's top secret they'll deny any knowledge. One man's death is a by-product. No, Jane, you need to fight fire with fire. Don't ask me how yet; I'm still working on that one.'

It was Aggie's turn to put forward a proposal. 'Jane, can't you two run away?' The picture of fleeing lovers lit a small fire in Aggie's romantic eyes, although this was quickly extinguished by a good dousing of concern. 'Although I don't know how or where.' She frowned, aware that the holes in her daydream were big enough for the lovers to fall through and land flat on their faces at the feet of reality.

Jane found herself smiling despite the horrors in her head. She should have confided in her friends straight away and now felt guilty that she hadn't. However, their warm unflinching friendship rinsed through her guilt. She should have known the girls better. Despite their dispersal after the demise of Alderney Street, the girls now closed ranks around their friend.

Jane let out a long sigh as she thought of their approaches to her problem and replied to each one.

'There's no-one to turn to Dorothy; not in any official capacity anyway. I already broached that with, well, with someone. What they didn't say gave me the answers they wouldn't say. It's all like something from a spy novel. And Florence we can't fight these people, mentally or otherwise. Believe me, I've run over every scenario a hundred times. If we knew who it was, could we tell them they have the wrong man? No. And even if we knew who or where they are, I can't imagine booking an appointment and there being a friendly chat over a cup of tea with them accepting the explanation and apologising for their error.' Jane turned to Aggie and smiled. 'And we had the chance to run away Aggie. Mrs Cartlyn gave us the keys to a home that she owns but we're still here.'

'Hang on. Hang on. Back pedal please. Mrs Cartlyn from the Grandchester?' Aggie asked as all the girls, surprised, waited for Jane's answer.

'Yes. She's a very wise lady with a well hidden gentle streak.' Florence half huffed, half snorted at the kindness in Jane's words.

'Well I thought she was scary, but you know best,' Aggie added.

'Yes, on this subject I do. I know when I've told you bits about the Grandchester guests before I've probably painted her as a bit of a dragon and, yes, she might seem remote and harsh at times but really she's not. Anyway, regarding her house, Will refused to go.'

'And just why did she offer you her house? How would she know you needed one?' Florence's interest had been poked. Jane looked at each of the girls, all waiting.

'Alright, here goes. Mrs Cartlyn has contacts and pointed out the seriousness of Will's situation. She's being kind to me.' Jane hoped that explanation would invite no more questions, but added. 'And that's all I know so don't ask me anymore. Please.'

The girls were all silent until Dorothy spoke. 'Why is it that wars need to be fought? I mean, I know the politics and all that, but why are so many innocent lives taken, or broken, or changed forever? We tell children not to fight, to sort things out like grown-ups. But that's just what grown-ups do, they fight.'

No one moved until Florence, fiery, theatrical, red head tapped her cigarette on the edge of the ash tray. 'It seems to me girls that the solution to Jane's problem is simple.' The other three all watched her expectantly but Florence's eyes remained on the ashtray. 'Someone needs to kill the real Hugh Callaghan.' And she bent the stub in two as the cigarette snuffed itself out right on cue, adding dramatic emphasis to her joke. Then she raised her eyes to Jane's to show that no glint of mischief or mirth was behind them.

Her joke was unveiled as a suggestion.

After a weighty silence which went on for much too long, all the others spoke at once. That's ridiculous. You're joking. You're mad. That's absurd. Leave the theatrics at the theatre. You're being no help whatsoever. There was head shaking and tutting and other demonstrations of horror, dismay and dismissal. Florence said nothing and the silence returned as all the girls looked at each other, waiting for someone else to speak. In the end it was Dorothy; she spoke calmly and quietly.

'Well, without wishing harm on the man it may well happen anyway. These people have been targeting Will, thinking he's Hugh. I would guess that it's only a matter of time before they get the right man and Hugh gets what they've been trying to give Will. Hugh obviously knows the risks in his...line of work. So maybe, you know, maybe that's his...well, his destiny, or at least a possibility he's accepted. Will just needs to lie low. Once Hugh's gone, Will's free.'

There was another brief silence as all the girls thought about this.

'But what if they murder the wrong man?' Jane's words cut through any thoughts of a positive outcome. And the word murder was used for the first time. 'They've been pretty useless at getting the right man so far.'

Florence had been quiet since throwing her suggestion into the air, and had been calmly thinking it through. 'Or maybe they just don't know the right places to look.'

'Are you suggesting that they should be told where to look?' Aggie's distaste of Florence's ideas left a sour burn on her tongue as she wrapped words around it in disbelief. 'That's as bad as doing the job yourself Florence,' she gasped 'you'd have a man's blood on your hands just the same.' She reached her hand to cover Florence's and almost begged, 'You're not really saying that we should hand him over are you?'

'No, of course she's not.' Jane scoffed. 'Are you?' She too turned to Florence.

'No. That would leave the informant vulnerable, exposed.' Florence waved her newly charged cigarette-bearing hand for emphasis and Aggie's hand retreated in relief.

'See.' Jane turned in triumph and relief to the others and smiled a *see, I told you* smile unaware that Florence had six more words to say.

'I'm saying we kill him ourselves.'

Six Words

Six words can change a life. Just six.

I love you, please marry me.

Britain is at war with Germany.

I'm saying we kill him ourselves.

Just six.

In the last few months a number of events had taken place that changed Jane's view from her vantage point; the loss of a home forcing initially unwelcome independence from her friends, being trapped underneath that home in less than the blink of an eye giving her sight in the ensuing darkness of how fragile life could be, a chance meeting with Will showing her that life and love continued, and indeed thrived, during times of shadow and fear.

All of these events either proved a theory or added a personal experience to things which Jane already knew. She could be strong and independent; no-one was immortal; love didn't stop because the world became aggressive.

But one conversation, indeed one sentence from one friend in one conversation, had so shocked Jane and the two others present that they couldn't speak coherently. After the first flurry of dismissal, when the trio realised that their friend's words held no jest or pun, there was nothing to be said. Nothing had ever shocked Jane so completely. Shock wasn't even a big enough a word to describe how she felt. She didn't know her friend at all. She was a stranger. A stranger who had just suggested murder, as casually as you might suggest a trip to the countryside.

In horror and astonishment the girls soon found reasons to part company. Only Florence seemed unchanged; Jane, Aggie and Dorothy felt tainted as they hurried on their way to different destinations.

As Jane lay in bed that night staring blindly into the darkness unable to close her eyes, she couldn't help but torment herself with thoughts of Florence's words. She couldn't bring herself to use the term *suggestion*, even in her head, as that gave credence to the six shocking words. The disgust she felt at the thought of what Florence had said sloshed around like sticky, dirty mud.

Her mind spoke to her heart.

Doing such a thing would make you no better than those trying to harm Hugh.

The sloshing turned to swishing and the mud diluted as her heart replied.

But the risk is Hugh's chosen course, not Will's.

Muddy waters that had turned clear became cloudy again.

Jane shook her head, but the thoughts remained, arguing with each other. Right and wrong. Good and evil. Life and death. She closed her eyes and placed the cold pads of her fingertips on her eyelids, pressing gently to dispel the polluted images behind them and evict all evil thoughts.

Maybe passion was heightened during war. Actions and decisions that would otherwise not be taken were forced. A sense of urgency, of live for the moment, of what the hell, had taken over. People were more outspoken, stronger. They married quickly, grabbed opportunities, made the most of every day. But did they suggest cold blooded murder?

No. They didn't. There was no excuse.

Florence's words weren't a magnified response of what she might have said a year ago, to be dismissed as a live for the day reaction; they were bomb-dropping change everything shocking.

Jane sat on her bed, almost ready to go. She slipped on her shoes and checked the contents of her bag. Her coat lay on the bed next to her, ready to be shrugged on as soon as she heard the doorbell. Twenty past six. Will was always on time; in fact he was usually at least five minutes early, so she knew she'd hear the door at any moment. But even six thirty brought no bell or knock. A quarter to seven gave no sound, or seven, or ten past. Jane told herself she'd wait for quarter past and didn't take her eyes from her watch. That was enough. The moment the delicate black hand finally moved to the three she stood, picked up her coat and bag and was gone.

At the end of the street she hesitated. She looked up and down, scanning faces. The face she searched for, the one that had the power to trigger a warm shiver in her chest, wasn't among them. She knew something was terribly wrong.

It wasn't lost on Jane that Hugh had been due back that day. His return meant that those looking for him might also be back.

Jane knew Will was riding the sloper to meet her, and she knew which roads he'd choose. It would take her longer than the bus, but walking would ensure she missed nothing and could take an accurate route. At her own pace she could stop where she wanted. Of course, this assumed that Will was already en route. If he hadn't yet left home, she wouldn't be with him very fast. But, she reasoned, if he'd been delayed before leaving the flat he would have telephoned to explain. There was a telephone in the hall just outside; he would surely have called. No, he must be on his way. Although Jane was perfectly aware of the scenarios that haunted the outskirts of her mind she was just about able to keep them at bay, not letting them stay behind her eyes long enough for her brain to register the images.

Jane's feet fell faster than usual, her arms swinging purposefully at her sides. Every turning to every street and alley reneged on their promise to show her Will. Still she strode on, determined. She felt a little cross, like a mother searching for a naughty child who has outstayed a curfew or misbehaved. Jane was getting angry as she walked; Will had been stupid but, unlike a child, he should have known better.

The further Jane walked, the faster her gait until she was almost running. Run, look, run, look. A few people glanced at her as she hurried past but Jane didn't see them. She was almost at Will's flat and still no sign. Her mind swayed between concern and anger as she reached the building where Will lived. It had once been a large Victorian family home, converted into flats some years before as so many beautiful buildings had been. She leapt up the front steps to open the door and step into the porch. She opened an inner door and walked through to the large entrance hall. On the right was the door to the flat that Will shared with a young actor/writer friend. She knocked impatiently at the door, not waiting for a response before trying the handle. Surprised to find the door unlocked, she opened it and peered in.

'Hello? Will?' She could hear movement in the flat, before she heard the voice.

'Jane? Hang on... wait there a minute.' Each word Will uttered seemed forced, like it was hard work. Jane had heard enough to know that something was wrong and stormed forward, looking for Will. She found him struggling to stand, half crouching by the door to the small kitchen. He knew without turning to look at her that Jane was approaching, despite his request. 'I told you to wait.' He was reluctant to turn towards her as she stooped and put her arm around him to help him stand. He pushed her arm away. 'I'm fine, please just go Jane. It's not safe here.'

'Will please, let me help you.' Jane ignored his plea and tried once more to assist. This time Will let her and they shuffled into the bedroom. Will sat on the edge of the bed, still bent over, head down and turned from Jane. She knelt before him, wanting to see but dreading the sight of the face he tried to hide.

Finally Will sighed and turned his face to hers.

'Oh God, Will,' she said, and her hand covered her mouth, drawn to her face with an intake of breath. She touched Will and he flinched as he changed position to ease a pain that Jane couldn't see. Her calm kicked in. 'Right, lie down while I get you tidied up. Then we're getting you to the hospital.' Will's hand grabbed at Jane's as she started to unbutton his blood stained shirt. He looked as though he was about to speak, then said nothing. She gently eased the shirt down his back and pulled the sleeves from his arms as carefully as she could. She took off his shoes and helped him swing his legs onto the bed and lie down.

This done, Jane searched the bathroom and kitchen and returned with a bowl of warm water, towel, face cloth and a bottle of antiseptic. 'Right then, let's sort this mess out.'

Despite her efficient and brisk tone, Jane's nursing was gentle; she winced inside each time she touched the cloth to Will's many bloody marks and bruises. She could only imagine what sort of beating he'd taken; his face and chest bore multiple red marks, some already turning a dark shade of grey. Blood seemed to be everywhere. She'd closed her eyes momentarily as she helped him remove his shirt, as if the marks might be gone when she opened them. His ribcage had clearly been pummelled and there were strong marks round his arms, as though they'd been held tight, restrained from fighting back. Jane tried not to think of it as she worked to soothe the pains with tender strokes of warm water.

Will's mischievous spark wasn't misplaced for long and he smiled. 'The things I have to do to get you to undress me.' Jane gave him a disapproving glare; she didn't need to tell him that it wasn't the innuendo that bothered her but his making light of the beating he'd received.

When Jane stood and picked up the bowl of bloody water, Will took her hand and spoke again; he spoke softly but made his decision clear. 'No hospital,' he said. Jane looked at him for a moment before heading to the kitchen without comment. She returned with a tray bearing a large glass of water, some aspirin and a cup of tea.

'These pills will barely touch it, but it's better than nothing if you're not going to the hospital.' She handed Will the water and tablets which he took half lying down as he leant on one elbow, clearly doing so through some pain. 'I bet you've broken some ribs; heaven only knows what else is damaged inside. And your nose looks broken.'

'It *feels* broken,' he smiled, the expression looking wrong on his beaten face. 'I'll live.'

'Not if they have anything to do with it.' Jane wasn't going to be soft about his stupidity just because he was in pain. She looked at Will expecting further dispute, but he was serious.

'I know.' His lack of denial surprised Jane and she softened.

'So will you tell me what happened?'

Will sat back against the pillow awkwardly and sighed. 'I was getting on the sloper when they came up behind me. No-one was about and they walked me off down some alley. I couldn't do much against three of them; two of them held me down. I really thought that was it Jane. Then I woke up behind some bins with the most God awful headache and every part of my body screaming except my voice. I don't know why they left me. I'm guessing they were disturbed by someone or something and made the mistake of having a bit of fun first, rather than just doing the job. Maybe they were in the mood to give someone a pasting and thought they'd do that first, I don't know. They could have done a lot worse in the time they had.' He shifted his position slowly. 'I know I won't be lucky a third time.' Will took Jane's hand. 'I stumbled and limped back in here and passed out.' Jane tried not to put pictures to Will's tale. 'It just turned real Jane. I can't have you anywhere near me when they come again.'

'Well, I'm not going anywhere on my own.'

The two of them looked at each other as though their thoughts could pass between them wordlessly. 'Alright, we'll leave.'

First Flight

Mrs Cartlyn's house was easy to find; her directions were perfect, as was everything else she'd arranged. She'd procured a car for their use as long as they should want it, saying it was more comfortable for the long journey and more practical for the transportation of baggage. Mrs Cartlyn didn't say that the car was more discreet, that the car was safer. Will had argued against taking it, although he had smiled affectionately when he'd first seen the little Austin 7 Ruby with its smart maroon body and black wings. He'd said they wouldn't be staying away for long and they'd be taking minimal luggage, so thank you but no. Mrs Cartlyn firmly assured them both that the car was wiser as they should take all they needed to ensure there was no call for a return to the city in the near future. The matter was settled. They couldn't argue with her, knowing somehow that any dissent was futile.

When the travellers arrived after two hours of journeying with their thoughts, they were both a little surprised. They didn't need to say anything as the expression they each displayed was a mirror of the other. The address of Richmond Row had unwittingly given the impression of a row of houses, terraced together and an integral part of the town in which its address fell. Instead they had skirted round the edge of habitation, following their host's instructions down road and lane and away from the town itself. Ten minutes after sight of the town disappeared behind them, they slowed down to read a sign announcing Richmond Row, after which they turned left through a gate and continued up a short curved driveway to park in front of the house. Jane thought it looked very much like an old vicarage and wouldn't be out of place as the address of the local reverend or doctor. A large family home but respectable and unpretentious, it seemed a shame that it wasn't inhabited by a big family with lively children dashing round the garden but was instead used as infrequently as Mrs Cartlyn had suggested.

The couple stepped inside the front door. All was quiet. To the left and right were closed doors; the staircase rose in front and the hallway ran away from them towards the back of the house. Jane looked at Will then tentatively opened the door on the right to peer in. A large informal dining room; Will opened the door to the left, 'Sitting room,' he said. They walked together down the hall to find a bright and welcoming kitchen; the larder had been stocked as well as it could and fresh greenery placed in a vase on the table. Jane looked out of the window to the back garden then turned to Will.

'I'll put the kettle on shall I?'

Will nodded, 'I'll take the bags upstairs while you do that.'

'Let me do it Will, you shouldn't be lifting.' Will raised his eyebrows, ignoring her offer, and turned to walk towards the front door and the bags they'd left there. Jane didn't bother to argue and instead hunted down cups and saucers, tea and milk and soon heard Will upstairs; he was back at her side just as the kettle started to boil.

'Nice house,' Will said, looking around him.

'It is.'

They were at a loss as to what to talk about. Will pulled a chair out, wincing Jane noticed, then sat down and immediately stood back up to lift the kettle from the stove and fill the teapot. Rather than sit down again, clearly finding it more comfortable to stand, he walked to the back door and looked out for a moment then he slowly crossed the room again. He located a spoon then lifted the lid of the teapot and stirred the tea round and round.

'So here we are. Safe and sound.' He looked uncomfortable as he replaced the lid, picked up the pot and turned back to the table. 'Shall I pour?'

'Yes please.' Jane still didn't know what to say in conversation. She'd wanted them to come to the safety of this house but now didn't know what to do next. Their situation was a complicated subject to broach, so Jane steered clear. 'You're still in lots of pain aren't you?'

'Nah,' he said, 'Just stiff from the drive, that's all. All healing nicely don't you worry.' He still looked awful, although his cuts and bruises didn't detract from his smile and cheeky boyish face. 'I really need to give Maggie and Jack a call to see how things are. There's a telephone in the hall.' Jane was thankful that the family wouldn't be able to see Will until he looked better.

'Don't tell them where you are.' Will gave Jane a *do you think I'm stupid* look.

'They wouldn't tell anyone.'

'I know, but then you'd have to explain why it was a secret. You don't want them to have any more on their plate.'

'I know, I know, of course I won't say anything.' Will sighed and ran his hand through his hair. 'You know why I was trying to earn more cash, and now I've made everything even worse. Now there's no money at all while I'm not working.' Jane stood and walked over to Will who wrapped his bruised arms around her. 'I've put you in danger, I've stopped working, I've deserted Maggie and Jack and the kids.' Before he could carry on Jane shushed him softly.

'When it's all over and sorted out, we'll put it all right with them don't worry. Maybe we can go and stay for a day or two when we get back home. In the meantime, we've scrabbled to-gether enough cash to survive so don't worry.'

'So you're paying for my mistake in more ways than one.' He looked low for a moment, then the real Will stepped in and he perked up. 'I'm going to ask around the town for some casual work. We shouldn't be here long, so Maggie and Jack might not even notice we've gone, but I'll try and pick up some work while we're here.' Jane smiled back, although she wasn't quite as confident that their stay would be short. 'We'll use this as a little holiday. We can be,' he put on an upper class accent, 'Mr and Mrs William H.C. Batten, resting at their country home after the former's jolly unfortunate accident aboard his yacht.' Will's narration turned to character acting as his voice became Cary Grant's. 'Damn it all, darling, those ropes should never have been left like that!' Jane shook her head, affectionately exasperated, but at least the old Will was back.

Mrs Grey had ensured the house was ready for its two guests, filling the kitchen pantry, stocking up logs next to each fireplace, putting fresh towels in the bathroom and clean sheets on the bed in the best bedroom. Jane hesitated in the doorway of the bedroom when she finally went upstairs to unpack her few things. By the time Will came up to look for her, Jane had located more sheets and blankets, made up a second bedroom and emptied her small case in that room.

Jane could hear Will on the landing, then he appeared at the door to the second bedroom where she was looking at the view of the drive and front garden from the window. She turned on hearing him.

'Ok, two rooms is fine. But you have the bigger one,' he said.

'No, this suits me fine honestly. It's pretty in here; I like it.'

'Ok,' he shrugged 'but I can't promise I won't sneak in and ravage you in the night.'

The next few days passed surprisingly quickly. The town was less than half an hour's walk away and the countryside surrounding them picturesque. They could almost forget the war that still carried on and the reason that they were staying at Richmond Row, playing at all the normal routines of life and pretending there was nothing more.

Will's tender body was quick to heal and he soon moved almost normally again; the pain was gone, he promised, and Jane could almost see his bruises fading. He didn't admit to Jane that the pain, although manageable, was still there and needing concealment. He was pleased that his muscles and bones would now allow him to find local work and he'd already been asking around. With so many young men absent, Will knew there shouldn't be too much difficulty finding someone in need of a strong pair of arms. Indeed, Jane had silently decided that she too would have more success looking for a position that had been vacated by a young man; there was currently no shortage of women in their traditional roles but of young men, or people able to do the work of one, there was.

Mrs Cartlyn had not made any contact; before they left she had said she'd be in touch when it was 'appropriate' for them to return. Jane didn't even want to guess the implications of that word. It was Friday and, after eating, Jane and Will had spent the evening listening to the wireless and talking. Some time just before eleven, Will put the fire guard across the grate and they both left the warm sitting room for the cool hallway, where they climbed the stairs. As usual they kissed goodnight on the landing and retired to their rooms.

Jane was woken some time later by a noise outside. She turned on her light and checked her watch - twenty past two. It was probably an animal, maybe a fox or badger, scouting for an easy meal. It sounded like it was in the front driveway. Jane swung her legs out of bed and padded across to the window. Nothing could be seen in the complete darkness of the countryside. Even the moon couldn't illuminate around corners to throw light into the shadows.

Jane left her room for the landing. She immediately bumped into a tall body also on the landing in the darkness and let out a cry which was muffled by a hand that wasn't hers.

'Sshh,' whispered the owner, 'it's me.' Jane relaxed under Will's hand as it moved to her shoulder, relieved to hear his voice in the dark.

'I heard a noise,' she whispered back.

'Me too, put out your light.' Jane hurried back into her room to do as he asked and realised he'd followed her. She could just about make out his silhouette near the window. 'Someone's out there.' Even the words made Jane shudder. Will turned towards the door. 'Stay here, I'm going down to check it out.'

'Will,' she started, but his response stopped her in its firmness. 'No Jane, stay here.'

He left the room and could be heard heading slowly down the stairs in bare feet. Jane moved to the landing and peered down. It was difficult to see anything in the darkness, even though her eyes had now adjusted. She hesitated so he wouldn't know, then followed Will downstairs despite his instruction; she was surprised that he'd turned away from the front door and gone through the kitchen. Maybe he was hoping to gain an element of surprise by walking round the side of the house rather than straight through the front door to confront whoever or whatever skulked in the driveway. Jane followed suit. The kitchen door handle turned but the door didn't open and it took Jane a moment to realise that Will had locked the door behind him. He clearly knew her better than she knew him and she cursed him under her breath. Not knowing if or where there might be a second key, Jane returned to the front of the house to look for movement. Nothing could be seen from the window. She fumbled around the front door, but couldn't find that key either. More cursing followed. Seconds were ticking by and Jane needed to be outside.

She pushed hard on the window catch and felt it slide across. With a good shove she pushed the dining room sash window up and, without pause, quickly climbed onto the sill. With a slide and a shimmy and a small bang on the head from the frame she dropped out onto a small flower bed. Not registering that she was still barefoot and inappropriately dressed, Jane looked around. Standing completely still now, she listened. She slowly moved forward still listening carefully and looking with eyes wider than ever in an effort to increase their vision in the night.

Then noises hit her ears. Scuffling and skidding sounds, shoes crunching gravel not the scratching of animal feet. Jane hurried towards the sounds, to the side of the house. No discernible words could be heard but there were definitely the noises of human conflict. Heavy shoe-clad footfall could be heard and she knew that Will was barefoot. As Jane ran to the source of the noise, she knew she would find Will doing battle with whoever had been skulking around in the dark.

She was frightened, picturing men with guns and Will being outnumbered and outfought. A cloud shifted in the sky and the moonlight now picked out fighting bodies. Jane could see there were only two people struggling to overpower each other. Anxiously looking around, she was satisfied that no-one else either lay in waiting or was poised to wade in. In a frantic bid to help, Jane's eyes darted round for a weapon. A terracotta flower pot volunteered itself and was soon in Jane's hands. In the flurry of movement and stumbling bodies Jane dodged back and forth several times, knowing even in the semi darkness which body was Will's. The men were clearly tiring and neither one used more than his own strength of fist in his bid to overpower the other. The two men rolled and struggled on the pathway. The unknown man seemed to get the better of Will for a moment with Will struggling beneath him.

As soon as Jane got a clear shot of the second man's head she brought the pot crashing down on top of it.

Even in her anger and very base instinct to protect Will from harm, she cringed as she felt the pot hit the hard but soft surface of the man's skull. It was a vile and foreign sensation. Instantaneously he dropped to the floor. Everything had happened so quickly; from climbing out of the window to murdering a man had taken Jane less than a minute. It seemed to happen all at once; the struggle, the lifting of the pot, and the dropping of the pot at the very moment that Will had shouted 'No!'

Will pulled himself up from the ground and moved to touch the man's neck, checking for a pulse, as the stricken figure lay face down in the dirt and the dark. Jane was frozen in time, her hands still in the position they were in the moment the pot had left them. Stirred from her shock by Will's voice, Jane's eyes still didn't stray from the prone body on the floor.

'He's breathing, but out cold.' At the words, Jane's relief was immediate and overwhelming.

'He's not dead?' Will shook his head. 'Who is he? He's come after you hasn't he?' In the moonlight Jane couldn't make out the expression on Will's face, but she could hear in his voice his surprise at her question.

'Jane, it's Hugh Callaghan.' Jane's questions changed and multiplied alarmingly, but were then halted temporarily as her natural human decency overpowered them. Will was still kneeling next to Hugh, trying to support his battered head as Jane knelt down too. 'Come on, we have to get him inside. It's freezing on the ground and we need to look at his head.' The head Jane had smashed a pot on. Will gently lifted Hugh, staggering a little as he stood up holding a man who was his equal in size. Jane tried to support his head as they walked. 'The keys are in my pocket.' Will tapped his right elbow against his side to indicate the whereabouts of the keys that had tried to imprison Jane. As they reached the front door Will saw the open window as a white net curtain billowed in and out.

Will laid Hugh on a sofa in the living room and rushed to fetch blankets and a pillow from upstairs. When he returned the pair made Hugh comfortable and checked all his vital signs before Will turned his attention to Jane; he'd also collected a pair of his socks and a jumper from his room and he took Jane's hand to move her from where she knelt to tend Hugh. He motioned for her to sit in an armchair where he pulled the socks onto her cold and grubby feet and the jumper down over her head as she slid her arms into sleeves that were too long. 'You must be frozen,' he said, 'dancing around in flowerbeds barefoot and in your nightie. What will the neighbours think?' He kissed the top of her head. 'I'll get the fire going again,' he said as he stood up to take the matches from the mantelpiece.

'Thank you,' Jane said and offered a sad smile. 'While you do that I'll get some water to clean him up.' She looked towards the prone man as she stood and moved to the door. 'The cut looks worse than it is I think because of the blood in his hair, but I don't know what other damage I've done.' She was worried that she'd caused him some irreparable damage that they couldn't see. Turning back from the door she watched Will. 'Are *you* alright Will?'

He didn't turn from his position in front of the fireplace as he lit a match and held it carefully to some fresh kindling.

'Of course I am.'

'But you haven't even recovered from the last beating that was Hugh's fault.' As the new flame breathed life once more into the grate, Will turned to face Jane.

'This was just a scuffle Jane. There weren't really many blows exchanged. Well, except the last one.' He winked. 'Honestly, I'm fine. A little tender in places, that's all.'

'I'm not convinced.'

Finding no sincere way to reassure Jane, Will resorted once again to his cheeky humour. He stood and started to unbutton his shirt as he managed somehow to loosen his belt with the other hand. 'If you want to check me over, you're more than welcome.'

Jane tutted her disapproval loudly and walked to the kitchen. Will couldn't see her smiling all the way.

Jane and Will spent the rest of the night watching over Hugh, listening to him breathe and praying he wouldn't stop. He didn't stir until just after eight the next morning. Will had just returned from the kitchen with cups of tea, as Jane lay curled up asleep in a chair. She woke to find Will hovering next to Hugh who was sitting up slowly, his hand reaching to his head.

'What did you hit me with, a hammer?' Hugh asked, half smiling.

Jane's eyes lowered. 'A plant pot?' She shuddered as she said it.

'How do you feel? Should we call a doctor? Given the circumstances we didn't get you seen last night; maybe we should have?' Will started to doubt the previous night's decision.

'No, no, you did the right thing.' Hugh was being very magnanimous considering he'd been assaulted, Jane thought, but then he was sneaking about in the dead of night so he wasn't completely blameless. 'I've had worse than a bump on the head, believe me.' Jane was relieved that there didn't appear to be any lasting damage, but that relief was quickly turning to anger.

'Why are you here Mr Callaghan? We left London because of you. Now you might have put Will in danger again. Did you know what you were asking him to do? Why would you risk his life?' Before Jane could throw any more questions at Hugh, Will touched her shoulder to stop her.

'Jane, they were my decisions too. Please let the man rest.'

'It's alright Will. Jane has a point. I'm sorry Jane,' he said, 'I know I have apologies to make. I understand how you feel. Let me assure you that I wasn't followed here. And it's Hugh, please.'

'Hugh, how did you know where we were?' Will spoke again.

'Please don't ask me that.'

Will hesitated but then nodded in understanding; Jane wasn't so quick to acquiesce. 'Did Mrs Cartlyn tell you? Is she alright? Did you force her to tell you?'

'Jane she's absolutely fine and, no, she hasn't breathed a word to me. Of all the people in the world, you can trust Esther Cartlyn with your life.'

'If you won't tell us how, you can at least tell us why you're here.' Will was slightly more accepting of Hugh's need to keep certain secrets.

'Yes, of course.' Hugh straightened and leaned forward towards the young couple, touching his head again as his change of position caused more throbbing in his bruised skull. Will was sitting on the arm of Jane's chair and took her hand as Hugh spoke. 'I won't beat around the bush, Will, I need you to do one last job for me.'

Jane washed and dressed as quick as she could, fearful of making it downstairs after Will. She was scared of what they would discuss without her and whether the ever suave and persuasive Hugh could convince Will to do the one thing that she begged him not to.

As soon as Hugh spoke the words she feared, Jane had stood up. She told him that she was sorry he'd had a wasted journey. She'd told him he could stay for lunch but then he should leave. She left the room before either man could see her cry.

As she hurriedly dressed then sat on the bed to put shoes on, she heard a gentle tapping at her door. It was Will, stepping in and pulling the door behind him.

'Jane, please, we need to find out more; I can't just say no. If it wasn't important, he wouldn't be here.' Jane didn't comment. 'Look, everyone has to do their bit; God knows Harry did his. What kind of man would I be if I didn't do my bit too? And I'm going to fight in this war anyway. I may as well do this first.' He stepped forward to take her hands. 'This might be just as important.' Jane's heart sank at the words and she knew then that his consent was inevitable. 'I don't want to overplay my part, but what if doing this really means something?'

'I know you'll be part of the war, Will, but please not this way.' Now Jane almost begged. 'I accept that you'll join up or be called like all the other lads, but this is different. This is an *unknown* enemy, Will; faceless, anonymous. Hugh's inviting you into trouble, asking you to step into the line of fire.' Will pulled her to her feet.

'I hear you and I understand, honestly. But let's just listen to what Hugh has to say, ok?' Jane couldn't answer. 'Sunshine?' He wrapped his arms around her.

'Ok,' came the tiny defeated response.

Nothing more was said on the subject all morning. Hugh had cleaned himself up and Will hovered about Jane as she prepared lunch. There was a limit to what she could do for three on rations for two but she'd learned to be a little creative in the kitchen, as had every other woman in the country, and was pleased that vegetables were still plentiful in the small market town. As the three sat down to Woolton Pie, Hugh spoke.

'I do appreciate this, considering all I've put you both through. Not just this,' he indicated the food in front of him 'as lovely as it is, but letting me stay and hearing me out.' Jane went to speak, but Will touched her hand and she stopped.

'It's the least we can do after assaulting you.' Will smiled and Hugh reciprocated, nodding. He rubbed his head theatrically but on seeing Jane's serious face, he stopped and withdrew his hand quickly.

'I really am perfectly fine Jane. A plant pot is no match for a head made of rock.'

Jane forced out a small smile, still feeling a wild mix of emotions about the previous night's melee in the garden. Always the one to do the conventional, behave and be a peace keeper, Jane had frightened herself.

While Will had been fetching the bedding for Hugh the night before, Jane had watched over him in the living room. She started shaking uncontrollably as the shock finally tapped her on the shoulder. When faced with a threat to Will's safety, some deep survival instinct had taken hold of her; the pot had been on the floor, then in her hand and then brought down to break on Hugh's head within seconds or maybe not even seconds. No thought had been given, no plan made and no consequence considered. By the time Will returned laden with blankets Jane had already sunk her nails into her clenched palms, forced her breaths to come long and slow and found her composure.

Now she looked at Hugh as they sat round the kitchen table, relieved that he was unharmed except for a bruise; in fact his scuffle with Will seemed to have caused little damage. Jane reminded herself that she hadn't known it was Hugh when she'd tried to stop him, or render him unconscious. Or kill him. But she knew deep down that she'd have done the same whether she'd known his identity or not.

'Jane?' Will's voice broke into her thoughts.

'Sorry, I was miles away,' she said to both men lightly.

'Don't worry. I was just saying that I didn't mean to startle you last night.' Hugh sipped his glass of water before he continued. 'It was just the best time to come. I was just about to knock but I heard movement by the house so I headed round the side.' He looked to Will. 'You obviously had the same idea. It took me a while to realise it was you, and then I was…incapacitated.' A charming smile beamed towards Jane and she blushed a little. 'The thing is, as you know, I need to ask you this one last favour.' He looked at Will and Jane with a new expression. Gone was the smiling flirtation, now it was down to business.

'Fire away then,' Will looked back at him with equal seriousness, using words he might later have regretted had he recalled them.

'I need you to be me one last time Will; but more obviously so.' He paused to study the two other faces at the table; one open and listening, the other guarded and suspicious. 'I have to leave the country, but I can't be seen to. When I leave this time I don't believe I'll be back. No-one must know I've gone until I'm far away. You both know that there's more I can't tell you than I can. I wish I could put your minds at rest and say there's nothing to worry about, but I'd be lying and I won't do that. I will understand if you say no. But just let me say this; sometimes the future of many people relies on the actions of one. That person may never see the outcome or realise their importance, as they might be one of many cogs. But if just one cog doesn't turn... well, you know what I'm trying to get across. Analogies are dire, but they serve their purpose.' The room was silent. Jane's lips were pursed tightly in an effort not to speak. She watched Will's eyes move from Hugh, to the table, to the door, to his glass, anywhere but to Jane.

'Hugh, maybe we can go for a walk and talk things over?'

'Of course.' The men both stood at the same time. Jane followed suit but Will took her hands, an action which made her exclusion clear.

'Jane, stay here sweetheart. I'll clear up this lot when I get back.' He indicated the table. 'Please don't worry Sunshine.' Jane's eyes gave him both a warning and a plea. He leaned down, kissed her and turned to the door.

'Thank you Jane,' came Hugh's voice as the men left by the back door. Jane didn't know whether he was thanking her for the meal or for letting him lead the man she loved into greater danger.

The man she loved? Maybe a better description was the man she would kill for.

Jane closed her eyes and lay back in the warm bath. She had cleared away in the kitchen despite Will's promise. Then she'd wandered aimlessly around the house before deciding to have a soak in the bath while she waited for the men to return.

Someone needs to kill the real Hugh Callaghan.

Florence's words shouted out in Jane's head and her eyes opened, startled.

She sat up, shocked that she should find herself reliving that conversation. She wondered if her subconscious mind was trying to communicate how serious this had all become. If she let Will do this thing for Hugh, which she just knew he would attempt to, a life she needed to preserve, one as important as her own, could end. Hugh was a good man, she didn't doubt that, but his duty to his country was what forced his hand. If Will's death was an unfortunate side effect, Hugh would of course feel sadness at the outcome but no regret for the action which caused it. And surely, if the whole purpose was to trick people into thinking Hugh was somewhere he wasn't, then for him to be dead in everyone's eyes would be the ultimate deception and one that would last as long as Hugh did.

Jane practically leapt from the bath.

She wrenched the stopper from the plughole and was in her room dressing quicker than she ever had in her life; her clothes felt uncomfortable against damp skin and pulling on her last good pair of stockings over wet calves was a job in itself, proven impossible when she saw the ladder running up from her fingernails. She cursed as she ripped them off, threw them on the bed and hurried downstairs bare legged and barefoot. She didn't know how long the men would be gone; she hadn't heard them return but quickly checked the downstairs rooms anyway. All was empty and silent. Jane dashed back into the hall and picked up the telephone.

She dialled the number and waited.

'Florence? Florence, I need your help.' Thank heavens it was her. Thank heavens for the matinee show and the lull in the cloakroom after the start of the performance. 'I need someone to tell me what to do. Can you talk for a minute? I'm in such trouble. Will's in such trouble.' The voice on the other end soothed, telling Jane to breathe, to calm down, to speak more slowly. 'I need to see you. Can you meet me?'

Florence always seemed to bring the city with her as she waltzed into any shop, theatre or club. She was exceptionally pretty and supremely confident. But today was an exceptional day; she seemed to know that discretion was more important than entrance and her face betrayed relief when she found Jane sitting in a corner. The two friends hugged tightly.

Jane blessed Florence as she discovered how she'd managed to leave work at short notice, calling in favours from some of her colleagues and arranging for urgent but discreet shift cover and transport. Thankfully, she had more than one would be suitor who was happy to assist in her flight to visit her very poorly great aunt.

'God, we've all been worried Jane. When you said you were going to see your mum, we knew it was wrong. We guessed that it was all to do with this Will and Hugh business. Good job we didn't contact your mum looking for you.' Her voice was low and whispery, conspiratorial.

'I was sure you'd all work it out. I'm sorry I couldn't say anything.' Jane squeezed her friend's hand. 'How was your journey? I'm so sorry to ask you to come all the way out here.'

'It's not a problem; I just pretended I was on the Orient Express with Mr Gable or Mr Flynn, or maybe both of them.' Florence winked.

'I promise I'll repay you the fare,' Jane said, trying not to smile at her friend's cheeky innuendo.

'Jane, I know a chap at Paddington; he gave me a good discount.' Florence winked again. 'Anyway, that's not what I'm here to talk about.' She'd waved away all talk of anything but Jane and looked at her pointedly. Jane took a deep breath in preparation.

'It's all gone horribly wrong Florence.' Then she qualified her statement. 'Well, it wasn't horrible at first. It was actually lovely to be alone with Will. The house, the town, the garden, it was all so… normal. It was like there was no war for a few days, no Hugh Callaghan and no danger. There was no-one but us, together. Then Hugh turned up and now he wants Will again.'

'To do what?'

'I don't know exactly. They went out just after lunch to talk about it and that's when I called you. Will came back after a while to reassure me and to apparently talk it over, then he said he was going to go back out to talk some more to Hugh. But we didn't talk it over, not really. He won't tell me much; just that Hugh wants Will to be him for a few days 'but a little more high profile' this time, whatever that means. Will can't talk to anyone else about it, so all he's got is Hugh asking him to do it and me begging him not to. It's serious Florence. Whatever it is, it's going to put Will in huge danger.'Jane tried not to cry. 'He's going to risk his life for this.'

'That bastard Hugh Callaghan, who does he think he is? What do you need me to do Jane? Just say the word.' Florence was surprised to think that Jane might be considering acting upon the suggestion she'd previously made, but she knew that Jane was completely devoted to Will and Florence would do anything she could to help her friend. For Florence life was clear cut, black and white; no grey. Right was right and wrong was wrong. You did or you didn't. You lived to the full, or you died.

'I need Mrs Cartlyn's advice. She told me not to contact her, so would you do it? Will you go and see her for me please? That's all I ask.'

Florence smiled and covered Jane's hands with her own. 'Of course I will, darling. Of course.' Florence was surprised that the request was so simple.

'Thank you.'

'You don't need to thank me darling; I'll do anything you ask.' Florence's eyes opened wider. 'Anything.'

To have friends who would die for you was one thing, but to have a friend who'd kill for you was quite another.

Jane had left a note for Will who was already back by the time she returned. He hurried into the kitchen as she came in through the back door.

'God I've been worried about you. Where've you been? Don't do that to me again, please.' He wrapped his arms around her.

'Pot and kettle Will,' she commented and he drew back to look at her.

'Touché,' he smiled. 'Where were you?' Jane left his arms and picked up her note from the table, wafting it towards him.

'I told you in my note. I went for a walk to look around the shops in the town. It's a nice afternoon and I couldn't just sit here waiting for you.' She paused. 'You're doing it aren't you?' She glanced around for Hugh.

'He's still out walking.'

'Answer my question Will.' He leaned against the table and looked at Jane, offering no reply, no explanation and no plea. Jane nodded. 'I knew…' Jane couldn't say any more and wept instead, despite trying to contain her tears. 'I knew.' As soon as the first teardrop fell free Will was holding her again.

'Oh Sunshine, I'll be alright, I promise. But I have to do this; I must finish this thing I've started. That'll be it then. As soon as it's over we'll go away, stay with Maggie and Jack or your mum until…' He stopped and started again. 'We'll go away. I promise.' He pulled back to look at her and tilted her wet face up to his with his hand. 'I promise.'

'That's three promises Will. And I don't think you'll keep a single one of them.'

'I will Jane. We'll go to the farm or we'll go to Somerset. I don't care where but we'll go. And it will all be over.' He smiled the smile that Jane couldn't resist. 'I promise.' And Jane counted four.

Will said that Hugh would be staying that night and for two more after that. A further bedroom was made up and quiet plans made between the two men. Will gently explained to Jane that he wanted her to know as little as possible. Jane argued that the less she knew the more panicky she became, but Will would still not tell her exactly what Hugh had asked of him. All he would say was that he would return to London ahead of Hugh. He asked Jane to stay at the house for at least two more weeks. Jane agreed as it was easier to appease him than argue, but knew that she wouldn't stay. She needed to be near Will, no matter what he was up to or what he asked of her.

Jane still hoped that all the planning and subterfuge would come to nothing. She prayed that the danger could be averted and the whole episode closed as soon as Florence had spoken with Mrs Cartlyn. Mrs Cartlyn would have the answers. Mrs Cartlyn would know how to stop Hugh's plan bearing fruit.

The first evening passed uncomfortably. The wireless gave its news and its music and Jane read snatches of one of the many books lining an alcove of the living room; she tried to concentrate but it was hard. Will and Hugh chatted between listening to the radio and reading the newspapers and tried to draw Jane into the chatter, a veneer, but she found it hard to feign a smile as her stomach churned. She thought of Florence and Mrs Cartlyn, her friends in the city among the bombs and the blackout, her job, her mum, the Halls and the men who looked for Hugh.

Hugh rose and Will looked up. 'Just off for a smoke. Care to join me?' Will shook his head.

After Hugh left, Will moved to sit next to Jane. 'Come on Sunshine, smile for me.'

'I can't.' Will took her hand. 'Come on, we've got time for a spot of dancing before he comes back.' He pulled her to her reluctant feet.

'Will, no.'

'Come on, you know you want to. I don't have any corned beef sandwiches or pork pie, but we do have Glenn and the band.' He nodded to the radio then called to it, 'Play on Mr Miller.' And Mr Miller and the band played as Jane swayed half-heartedly and Will tried to encourage her into enthusiasm in his arms.

'You don't have to do it you know,' Jane whispered into Will's neck as they danced.

'Sshh.'

'Say no Will.'

'Sshh.'

They wouldn't discuss it again.

And Hugh turned from his vantage point in the hall and went up to his room before they saw him.

The waiting around was awful, but it did give Jane an excuse to meet up with Florence again the next day by claiming she was going for a walk into town to ease the tedium. Jane's dis-comfort at asking her friend to act as a go-between and make the lone journeys to and fro was eclipsed by the comfort and re-assurance she received from her. Will said he'd join Jane for an outing but she left the house before he had the chance, sneak-ing out way too early to meet Florence but knowing that was the only way to avoid Will's company or his guessing that she was up to something. She hated going without him and missing the opportunity to spend some more time together. Jane walked quickly, giving Will no time to catch up when he realised she'd gone; by the time he did, she be among shops, or by the river, or able to avoid him.

Now finding herself with two hours to fill before meeting her friend, Jane discovered that in a pleasant town on a bright winter's morning it was surprisingly easy. Happy in her own company Jane's pace slowed to take in the houses and shops, the pretty riverside, the morning activity. She bought a newspaper and used some coupons to buy a few things to bolster their evening meal. She nodded and smiled to people as they passed and found a seat tucked away near a bridge where she watched a troubled world go by and read the newspaper as it shouted headlines of 'Call goes out for scrap metal' and 'Hitler says decide.'

Florence wasn't waiting when Jane entered the small park at the edge of the town. She looked around, growing more concerned with each second. As the clouds darkened and tiny drops of water started to fall, she started to question herself; had their arrangement been clear, was Florence alright, did Jane have the right time, was Florence alright, was this the right place, was Florence alright?

A hand touched her arm and Jane spun round. For a second her mind couldn't work out if her eyes were broken. Time paused for a few moments while Jane's brain spun frenzied circles inside her head. Maria Henderson in all her delicate, sophisticated beauty stood before her as it started to rain. She linked her delicate arm though Jane's.

'Come on, let's get out of this rain or we'll be soaked to our scanties,' she said as she led a stunned Jane to a little covered seating area amongst the trees. They sat down, sheltered from the rain, as Maria Henderson gently brushed rain droplets from her coat then looked at Jane who was still struck dumb. Mrs Henderson smiled kindly and took Jane's hand. 'You look numb Jane. I'm sorry if I frightened you.'

Jane's words stuttered from her lips 'I wasn't expecting you Mrs Henderson. What a, what a...' Jane struggled with her next word '…coincidence?' Her companion shook her head. 'I didn't think so.' Jane sighed and closed her eyes, then breathed slowly to calm herself. 'Is anybody in that godforsaken hotel what they seem?' she asked the air without opening her eyes.

Amid the sound of the now heavy rainfall Jane heard an elegant giggle. The delicate gloved hand holding hers squeezed before its owner answered. 'Sometimes.' Jane knew that the lips that spoke were smiling and turned to look at Mrs Henderson. She swallowed, trying to moisten a mouth that was now as dry as sandpaper.

'Mrs Henderson, where's my friend? Is Florence alright?'

'Florence is fine Jane. She delivered your message just as you asked. She wanted to come back to you but we couldn't let her; it was safer for me to come.' Jane retrieved her hand from Mrs Henderson and pressed a hand on the bench each side of her body to steady herself. She took another deep breath.

'How did you stop her coming?'

Mrs Henderson smiled, knowing what Jane was thinking. 'Just by explaining who was better placed to help, Jane, don't worry.'

'Alright, I accept that. And?'

'And I have something for you.' Jane noticed Mrs Henderson's gloved hand absently move to cover the handbag which lay on her lap, as if to protect its contents.

'Is it a message from Mrs Cartlyn? I need her help.'

'And I'm here to give it Jane.'

'I didn't know you and she were friends Mrs Henderson?'

'We don't lunch and so forth, but we have mutual acquaintances and a good amount of faith in each other. If that makes us friends, then we are. And please, Jane, it's Maria.'

'Alright, Maria. But I have to warn you that now I'm getting more confused and more frightened by the minute'

'Jane, I have something for you.' With a graceful manoeuvre Mrs Henderson unclasped the handbag and slipped her hand inside. It withdrew, then took Jane's hand and pressed something small and cold into it. The elegant hand covered Jane's, keeping the identity of the object a secret. 'Life's not simple anymore,' she sighed, 'and I don't think it ever will be again to be honest. I believe innocence has been lost.' Jane tried to pull her hand free but the delicacy of Maria's hand was deceiving and it held tight. 'Jane, I don't need to point out that war is unjust; nothing about it is fair. But it's not just on the battlefield itself that sacrifices are made. Normal people have to do things that,' she hesitated 'that, just a few months before, they couldn't have imagined in their worst nightmares. People take risks, force action and embrace fate.'

'I understand that Mrs Henderson... Maria. I see that you're, uh, not quite what I thought you were. And clearly, neither is Mrs Cartlyn. Nor Mr Callaghan. Well, ok, maybe we all had our doubts about *his* occupation...' Jane offered a rueful little smile and Maria joined her. 'But all this doesn't help Will. Clearly he's caught up in something he hadn't planned to be. I asked for Mrs Cartlyn's help.' Jane had momentarily forgotten about the small object in her own hand that was still a secret to her. 'Do you know what I should do?'

Maria nodded.

'Most people don't know themselves very well at all until faced with adversity. We don't know our own strength until we're threatened, or someone we love is.'

'You mean Will has the strength to deal with this himself? That's not an answer.'

'No Jane, I mean you.' Jane looked down as the elegant lady loosened her grip and she unfolded her hand to see what this refined but paradoxical woman had placed there. 'It's Hugh or Will, Jane.'

A small bottle with a paper seal over the top lay innocently in Jane's hand; a small bottle that, once dispensed, could eliminate the problem in the space of a few hours.

Jane sat on the sheltered little seat for a long time after Maria left. She'd tried to give the bottle back, but Maria wouldn't take it. Jane was no wiser than she'd been earlier with regard to what Will was soon to do for Hugh. All she knew now was that Mrs Cartlyn and Maria Henderson were sanctioning, suggesting, that Jane should administer the toxic contents of this bottle to Hugh Callaghan. The plans Hugh had made, and which Will was to aid by taking his place, would fail; Maria had been clear on that point although she hadn't revealed what the plans were, or what would go wrong, or how she knew.

No matter what happened now, now that this bottle had been given to Jane, her life would never be normal again; even when the war was over, even if Jane ate, slept, lived, worked and behaved as before. Because she had been given this murderous item, this weapon, the decision was now hers.

She was angry and sad at the same time. These two women that she never really knew before, who were just patrons of the hotel, had now revealed themselves; but in doing so they became even less familiar. Knowing more about them she knew them even less. And they'd now put the power of fate in Jane's nervous hands.

Whatever happened now, it would be because Jane did or did not open this bottle.

Jane knew that even disposing of the bottle would equal a decision; because she'd had the choice.

And whatever action she took, she would now always look back and wonder if it had been the right decision.

Jane lost all track of time walking back to Richmond Row in the aftermath of the downpour, until she heard the frantic voice chasing her and getting closer as she neared the house. As it closed in on her location, it shook her from her stupor. The strong arms grabbed her so hard she almost fell over, but the arms that had unsteadied her now caught her in an embrace as she stumbled.

'Jane. Oh my God Jane.' Will was angry, tearful, reproachful and relieved at the same time and berated her as he held her, touched her face, kissed her and stroked her hair. He seemed to do it all at once. She noticed how wet and bedraggled he was and felt a stab of shame, knowing that he must have been desperately searching for her in the pouring rain. 'I told you not to do that again. Jane, I told you not to. I've been looking for you and worried sick. Hugh's looking too. God, we thought, I thought...' Despite the soft lips and the strong arms that revelled in her safe return, Jane felt detached as the tiny bottle weighed heavy in her bag.

Jane heard Will call the Halls that night and listened from the landing. It sounded to her as though he was checking up on them in case he shouldn't be able to again. Unsaid farewells could be heard in his words.

Jane had rocked between conflicting thoughts ever since her meeting with Maria. At first she planned to tell Will everything, but then decided not to. He would be appalled. He should be appalled. But he wasn't faced with losing the one person he couldn't live without and Jane was; wouldn't he be torn if faced with the same impasse? Jane thought she could feel shreds being ripped from deep inside her chest.

No, if she told Will he'd stop her. If she told Will he'd save her from murder. If she told Will, he'd make the decision. And he wouldn't make the decision to save his own life over another's.

Time was ticking loudly in Jane's head, she could almost hear the hand of the clock moving each time it crept a fraction closer to the moment when Will was due to leave. The seconds ticked by as heavily as if Jane was part of the clock itself; a cog like Hugh had spoken of. But no matter what she did, she couldn't stop the movement, the pressing forward of time.

Her cog wasn't the pivotal one Hugh had talked about, stirring all the others to action, but the tiny one that was dwarfed and surrounded and could do nothing but be forced to move when the others did.

Tonight would be Hugh's third and last night with them; a decision must be made. If the choice she made was the one which, until a short time ago, wouldn't even have been in her head then she must act soon. *That* choice had a time limit.

Jane slipped the bottle into her dress pocket before heading downstairs to make lunch. The atmosphere was lighter than previously and Jane wasn't sure whether the buoyant mood the men displayed was for her benefit, or whether it was their subconscious denial of what lay ahead.

Jane watched Hugh as he stood outside the back door lighting a cigarette and strolling casually among the dead or dormant plants, beaten down by winter. She knew she didn't hate him, she didn't even dislike him; he was a good man doing what he thought right for his country, of this she was sure. But she was angry with him and it was anger like she'd never felt before. Unwittingly or not, he had led a good man into a dangerous and dark situation. That good man had chosen to continue with the plan that could mean his own demise. That good man had chosen to walk Hugh's path, fully aware of the risks, as he believed it led the right way.

Jane, of course, was proud of Will's honour and bravery and his promise to finish what he started and to do what he felt was right. She was also incensed at his honour and bravery and desolate at the thought of his desertion; of forsaking their relationship, and possibly his life, for this.

Even though her knowledge of Will's situation caused her immeasurable fear, somewhere inside she knew that Will's choice made him the man he was and the man she loved. This task had started as a means to help his dearest friend's family but it was now a matter of honour and of life or death; the life or death of others. It was a case of doing what was right for an untold number of people he didn't know and would never know. It was a choice that many others had also made and were still making.

Jane felt shame at her own choice of Will over any one person, or indeed any number of people whose futures might depend on his and Hugh's actions.

'Alright?' Familiar arms embraced her from behind and she jumped.

'You scared me. Yes, I'm alright.'

'How about we go for a nice long walk later?'

'That would be lovely.' Jane turned round in Will's arms leaving sight and thought of Hugh behind her, just the glowing tip of a cigarette in the distance.

Had the darkest shadow not been hanging over Jane, it would have been a beautiful day. After lunch, Jane and Will walked. They walked hand in hand for miles and talked and listened. Neither one of them mentioned the following day's plans and neither one of them wanted to. They ate their evening meal in a pub in the town and strolled back through the lanes in the darkness, giggling like children when Will tripped into a pothole and stopping to listen to the silence which still sounded odd to them after the noise of the bombs in London. They knew that if they stood outside during the night they'd be able to hear the unmistakable rumbling of fighter planes above and then in the distance the bellowing thunder of a city under attack.

As the pair reached the kitchen door, they were surprised to see it ajar and looked at each other to convey a hundred words in an instant. Will gently pushed Jane behind him and stepped silently inside. He picked up the bread knife which lay on the draining board and still made no sound as he crossed the room, one hand holding Jane behind him. He turned enough to whisper, 'Stay here, don't move,' through Jane's hair, his voice so low it was almost inaudible, as he quietly padded along the hall.

Jane held her breath, her eyes darting round in the dim light of the hall lamp; she didn't know what she was looking for. Her heart thudded loudly in her chest and she could hear her own breathing, thinking it must sound as loud as thunder.

Jane ignored the instruction to stay put and started to follow Will as he entered the living room; before she'd even taken two steps the house was completely in darkness; whatever light had been on had been extinguished. In that same moment, there was movement, a scuffle, and running feet came towards her; someone grabbed her but her scream was stifled by a large hand and the owner growled 'Under the stairs Jane; take this,' and pushed her up against the staircase. The door at her back was opened and she was roughly pushed down and backwards by a hand on top of her head. 'Don't be afraid to use it,' the voice demanded. Then the door was shut and Jane was alone. She shook as she realised what she held, pressed onto her by her assailant. She dropped the gun to the floor and edged away from it further into the familiar lessening space of an under stairs cupboard.

Jane was shaking with fear, unsure what was going on or where Will was or why the lights had gone out. Despite the low growl of his voice she knew that the man who'd forced her under the stairs as he armed her with a gun was Hugh; the weapon he'd shoved into her hand was surprisingly heavy and was now on the floor somewhere in front of her. She was in a place that scared her more than being exposed in the house. Hugh wouldn't know that the very place he pushed her for safety was the one place she couldn't stay. She felt around carefully and recoiled as she touched the edge of the gun. Surprisingly, she flinched more when her hands instinctively rose above her head and she felt the angular underside of a stair; it was a feature that had once been her salvation but which had since grown within her to mean enclosure, stale warmth, loneliness and burial.

Jane, shaking, reluctantly picked up the weapon and pushed the door gently with her other hand. She knew the door was ajar but no light illuminated the opening. There were noises somewhere in the house, but it was difficult to tell where they were coming from. She pushed the door further and crouched lower as she edged through the gap, stopping just outside, almost on her knees. Although she couldn't see anything her eyes opened wider, pupils large, optimising her vision, absorbing all they could.

The voices were upstairs, threatening low voices; or maybe they were in the dining room, Jane felt disoriented and wasn't sure. She couldn't make out any voices in particular; not Hugh's, not Will's. Trying to decide what to do, she stayed crouching by the stairs. The moment of reckoning for Hugh, and maybe Will, must have been forced; Jane looked down in the dark, not seeing but knowing what was in her hand as her fingers wrapped tighter around the cold metal. It was the second time that day that she held the means to death.

Footsteps came into the hall and Jane's grip on the gun tightened as she slid it under her coat and into a deep pocket. Her heart beat so fast it almost buzzed. The lights came on and Jane blinked as her eyes focused on a man walking towards her. Sombre suit, smart appearance, short dark hair, benign facial expression.

He held out a hand to help her up, which she did not take as she stood. They looked at each other.

'Come with me.' He moved towards Jane, who stepped back as his fingers wrapped tightly around her upper arm and he led her firmly but not roughly into the living room. There she saw Will and Hugh and another man. Will was sitting in an armchair, perched awkwardly on the edge. Hugh also sat, but leaned back in his chair almost casually. His body language said relaxed but his features said guarded, calculating the situation. The third man, very tall and broad, stood with his back to the fire and facing the door. All three looked up as Jane and the other man entered.

On her entry Will immediately stood and rushed to her side. 'Get your hand off of her,' he snarled slowly and the man released his grip. Will pushed his body between them and walked Jane to the chair he'd vacated. All eyes watched. When Jane was sitting, with Will standing guard at her side, the man at the fire spoke.

'We don't have any issues with you Mr Batten, or your friend, although your similarity to Mr Callaghan has caused some confusion.' Jane heard an accent clouding his voice that she couldn't place, although it sounded predominantly English. 'Mr Callaghan here isn't what he seems.' Hugh puffed out a laugh, shaking his head. Jane looked at Will who watched Hugh, then they both turned to look at the man who spoke.

'If we're not the problem, you can let Jane leave.' Jane's eyes shot to Will but before she could speak, the other man replied.

'No need. We have some business to talk over with Mr Callaghan then the three of us will be off. You won't be bothered again.' He glanced down at his large wristwatch.

'Hugh?' Will turned to Hugh who held up a palm in response.

'It's alright Will, you and Jane will stay here. I'll be quite alright with these gentlemen.' Hugh smiled at Will, who wasn't moved to respond with a matching gloss.

Jane's hand sought out Will's and he held it tight in reassurance. The man at the fire spoke again.

'Jim here will keep you company while we go and have a little chat. Then us three'll be off.' Despite his almost breezy words, there was a menacing hostility underpinning everything he said. His insincerity was thinly veiled but he didn't seem to care, as his mouth smiled but his eyes remained dark and hard. He walked towards the door and beckoned Hugh to follow. As Hugh passed, his hand patted and then squeezed Will's shoulder. Will didn't recognise whether this was message, reassurance or farewell. He did know, however, that it was also an acceptance of fate.

Hugh and the unnamed man left the room and closed the door. Jim didn't leave his spot by the door or say anything as they passed. Will still sat on the arm of the chair that Jane occupied and they looked at each other again. Will stood and walked towards babysitter Jim who visibly tensed.

'I would say it was nice to see you again, but I'd be lying.' Will's sarcasm prompted the huff of a laugh from Jim.

'Will?' Jane couldn't piece together the connection for a moment, then Will replied without turning.

'Jim was with some of his friends last time we met, Jane. They left me with a few parting gifts.' Jane wanted to attack the man who stood opposite Will. Had she been close enough she'd have spat in his face.

'So what's the story then Jim?'

'You've been conned,' he said.

Will laughed. 'I don't think so.'

'Really? He's not what you think. You've been had.'

As Will decided what to do or say next, loud voices could be heard. Hugh and the man were having a heated argument. Will turned back towards Jane and walked past her to the fireplace. He bent down in front of it.

'What are you doing?' The man sounded suddenly nervous, possibly unsure whether he should check on his collaborator and Hugh whose voices provided a narration of their escalating confrontation.

'Getting chilly. The fire needs stirring up.' Will took the poker and jabbed at the glowing embers then tossed a log onto the fire, temporarily quelling its power and heat. He didn't replace the iron poker in the stand, but stood very slowly. Jane felt an immediate nervous fear as Will turned and faced the man who fumbled with the door handle behind his back.

Will had risen with intent, intimidating in his demeanour. Then in a fraction of a second he'd launched across the room and the two men slammed into each other.

Jane could do nothing; she stood as soon as Will moved but could do nothing to help him as the men struggled with all the power they could muster. Will had at first overpowered Jim, then the battle turned as the poker was wrestled from Will's hand and fell to the floor; Will was on the floor and Jim above him as he fought to hold the grasping hands away. Everything moved too quickly as Jim's hand came up glinting, the blade of the bread knife threatening in his clenched fist. Jane saw fear in Will's eyes as he glimpsed the shiny object; she moved forward intuitively, adrenalin taking control of her movements just as it had the night Hugh had fought with Will in the driveway. In a flash of arms and a blur of movement, the poker was grabbed from the floor and brought down on the back of Jim's neck.

Jim slumped on top of Will. The poker dropped from Will's hand and both men were still. The speed of Jane's adrenalin surge had been a fraction slower than the speed of a man fighting for his life. It was Will who'd delivered the blow. Will sighed deeply then rolled the stricken man from him and onto the floor. The man was still. Will leaned over him and touched his neck.

'There's a pulse, but I don't know how long for; it doesn't seem very strong.' Will's eyes were pained, regretful.

Jane's thoughts were knotted. 'They said it's Hugh that's bad, Will. What if he's the enemy, not them? Who do we believe?'

The voices still argued and were getting louder, causing them both to look towards the door as Will stood and took Jane's hand. Together they quickly left the room.

The next few minutes passed as a few seconds would. Jane would marvel afterwards at how time can move incredibly fast yet dreadfully slow at the same time.

As they stood motionless and confused in the hallway the noise escalated. It was clear that Hugh and the other man were now fighting too; Will dashed towards the sounds now obviously coming from the dining room, but before Jane could follow all three men tumbled out into the hall. In a knot of fists and flailing bodies, Jane struggled to work out who was who and what was happening; the mass of men crashed and fought towards the kitchen. As they fell and tripped through the doorway a shot exploded into the ball of fighting men.

Jane cried out and dashed forward, unsure who, if anyone, had been hurt.

Will half stood and stumbled back towards her, bloodied. Jane tried to grab him, fearful of his injury, but he pushed her roughly behind him. Damaged by fighting, not gunfire, he shielded her.

Hugh stood up, staggering slightly, leaving the body of the third man on the floor behind him. In Hugh's hand was a gun, a pistol; Jane's fingers instinctively fell upon on the matching item she harboured in her pocket. Hugh's gun was raised towards them and in an instant Jane's was raised towards him, a mirror image; but while his practised hand held firm, Jane's shook.

As Will was in front of Jane he hadn't immediately noticed what she held; now he looked down to see the shaking hand at his side as she slowly edged out from behind him.

'I'm so sorry Will, Jane, but more than one life depends on tonight. Many lives.' Hugh said. 'It wasn't meant to work out like this; we should have parted company as friends. Believe me, if there was any other way out I would grab it.' He aimed the gun. 'I'm sorry Will, I'm so sorry, but Hugh Callaghan has to die tonight.'

'Shoot him,' came the struggling voice. The man behind Hugh raised himself enough from the floor to look at Jane as he spoke 'Do it,' he shouted which made her jump.

'Jane, come on, you know me,' Hugh soothed as he stepped forward, one hand outstretched with an open palm and the other still training its weapon on Will. He almost cooed now, 'Come on, put down the gun.'

'That's far enough Hugh,' Will warned and Hugh stopped. All Will could see was the gun getting closer to Jane, even though it was pointed at him. Will slowly edged away from Jane, hoping that the barrel of Hugh's gun would follow him.

The prone and bleeding man behind Hugh spoke again, clearly struggling, half spitting. There was a horrible wet gurgling sound in the man's throat as he fought the damage inside him. 'You don't know him Jane. Believe me. Believe something other than what he tells you.' Jane's hand shook even more and she grasped her wrist with her free hand to steady it.

Hugh stepped forward again, still aiming at Will.

Still fearing his own proximity to Jane and the risk to her if Hugh fired, Will pushed Jane away and lunged towards Hugh in one smooth movement. Jane's gun discharged and she felt the force of the shot thump her hand and reverberate down her arm like an electric shock. Her arm vibrated so much it hurt.

In that split second, no-one had known what was going on; Will's sudden action, a gunshot, a shout.

The two men fell to the ground.

Then silence.

'Oh my God, oh my God,' Jane repeated over and over and over as she crawled across the floor towards the men. At the shot, she'd dropped the weapon from her hand and her knees to the floor. 'Will, Will, are you alright?' She touched his leg, his arm, and crawled further along towards his face which was turned away. 'Will.'

He moved.

'I'm ok. I'm ok.' He sounded as shocked as Jane and pulled himself slowly to his knees as they both looked down at Hugh. Will's fingers moved to Hugh's neck but in less than a heartbeat he turned to Jane and shook his head.

'I killed a man Will. I shot a man.' Jane started sobbing. 'All these fights. All these struggles. Now I'm a murderer Will.'

'No Jane, I don't think so,' Will said as his hands and eyes moved over the body. 'There's not a mark on him.' Hugh lay on his back and Will was right; there wasn't a mark or a spot of blood to be seen.

Jane felt a moment of panic. There didn't need to be blood.

The bottle she'd opened and the drops she'd put in Hugh's tea flashed into her eyes; shaking hands tipping tiny toxic drops into a cup. Hours, it would have taken hours to filter through his system wreaking its havoc before causing his death.

Then she saw herself tipping the tea away and washing the cup.

She hadn't been able to do it, as close as she came, and had thrown the rest of the bottle's contents away too.

Hugh hadn't been poisoned, but he was dead.

'I don't understand.'

Will gently tipped Hugh onto his side and felt beneath him. His hand came up covered in blood and he looked over to the second, and now quiet, man who lay further along the hallway. He'd crawled across the floor and now lay outstretched with a gun in his hand. Will moved to the second man but found more blood on his own hands, instead of a pulse in the man's body.

'He must have reached for that and done it himself.' Will nodded towards the weapon the second man now held. He'd found enough dying strength to shoot Hugh in the back.

As the words touched her, caressing her conscience, Jane slumped back against the wall; two men were dead but not one because of her. Will was soon next to her and they stayed there for a long time as they held each other, Will wiping Jane's tears away with his hand and stroking her hair as she cried. An actor and a receptionist sat in the silent hall smeared with the blood of the two men who lay dead in front of them.

'Mrs Cartlyn's rooms please.'

When they finally stood up Will led Jane upstairs and sat her down on her bed, then he returned to the hall to call the only person they felt they could.

Jane could hear Will's side of the conversation, seemingly composed; she couldn't see his eyes watching the hall floor the whole time. She heard the words and the pauses in between as Mrs Cartlyn clearly probed and instructed.

'Mrs Cartlyn. It's Will Batten. I'm terribly sorry to telephone at this time of the night, morning. Something really terrible has happened. Yes. Yes. Two men and Hugh. No we're both fine, just shaken. She is. There are two men here now Mrs Cartlyn. It's Hugh and some other man. A third left, but I don't know where he went. Yes. Yes, he did. Should we leave right away? Alright, yes. Yes. Please. Should we, uh, do anything here in the meantime? Alright yes, yes I will. Tomorrow? Of course. Thank you Mrs Cartlyn, thank you so much.'

The receiver was clicked onto its cradle and, not long after, Will jogged back up the stairs. He smiled at Jane as he entered the room. 'The guy in the living room, Jim, he's gone; he must have recovered enough to sneak out. I don't know when. He's certainly not downstairs and I've locked the doors. Mrs Cartlyn's sorting out, uh, she's dealing with…well she's doing everything else.'

'What do we do now?' Jane was shivering, even though she still wore her coat after a walk that seemed an age ago. There were bloody fingerprints on her cheek where Will had touched her after checking Hugh and, against her currently ashen complexion, the red marks looked even brighter; poppies on snow.

'Come on, first thing is to get cleaned up.' Will helped her to stand and took off her coat. Jane noticed his skin as he helped her; the crimson splashes had dried to a deep reddish brown. He lifted her dress over her head, then handed her a towel and left the room to run a bath. When he'd done so, he returned and guided Jane to the bathroom. He turned away as she undressed further, taking off her slip and underwear, and stepped into the hot water; she sat there, knees to her chest and her chin resting on them as she stared at nothing. Knowing she was in the water, he returned to her; kneeling on the floor next to the bath, he picked up a face cloth and gently soaped her face and back. Her hair was falling loose from its ties and Will saw smears of blood in it as he carefully freed the rest and washed it for her. Then she rested her head on his shoulder as he slowly and gently washed another man's blood from her face and his hands.

Will helped Jane from the bath and tenderly dried her shaking body. He walked her back to her room, where he helped her into her nightclothes and tucked her into bed. Neither of them had spoken since Will had left to run the bath. As he turned to leave the room Jane held his hand firm.

'I'll be right back, don't worry,' Will soothed as he left. He soon returned with a sugary cup of tea; it was a simple thing, a tool to provide relief from shock, but the task had been a hard one.

Will had taken a deep breath as he reached the bottom of the stairs and turned the corner into the hall, knowing the macabre sight that would await him. He tried not to look at the two men who lay dead in the house, but couldn't tear his eyes from them as he carefully stepped around their bodies. He tried to convince his eyes that it was a stage and the men merely actors, trying to lie still in their morbid roles. He was pleased when the kettle finally boiled and he could creep past again, as though the men might be disturbed, and head back up the stairs to Jane. He had to be strong for Jane.

As he reached the landing, he turned to glance back down to the hall. Putting down the tea, he searched out fresh bed sheets which he took downstairs and carefully placed over the two men.

Jane was sitting up when Will returned, clearly impatient for his presence. She drank the tea he offered and they sat side by side. Will put the empty cup on the nightstand and his arm around Jane, who was still cold but not shaking quite so much.

'What happens now?'

'Mrs Cartlyn said it's absolutely safe to stay here tonight. She was quite business-like, if that's the right thing to say. She asked'*And who exactly is dead Mr Batten?*'She did seem a tiny bit surprised they'd come, but not shocked; and certainly not at all disturbed by the fact that two of them are lying dead in her house.'

'What if the other one, Jim, comes back? What if he's outside somewhere?' Jane's body stiffened and her eyes widened but Will just held her face gently in response, making her look at him.

'Don't fret, I don't think he's anything to worry about; he's just extra muscle, making up numbers. I can vouch for his knuckles, but I doubt he's anything more than a pair of fists doing as he's told. He's long gone Sunshine, don't worry.' Jane relaxed a little just for a moment, before she got out of bed to turn the key in the bedroom door.

'Just in case,' she said as she got back into bed and they both tried to sleep for the little time that remained before daylight.

The sun rose over the house with four occupants, two living and two dead. The two who still breathed rose and dressed. Will made sure he was the first downstairs, keen to check that no tell-tale scarlet had seeped through the white cotton. Jane followed; she too took a deep breath as she turned into the hall but saw white shrouds not still bodies and her composure remained unsteadily intact. Will made sure Jane was comfortable being downstairs alone then trotted back up to get their bags, which he left by the front door.

'We can't just go Will. What about Mrs Cartlyn's house-keeper? What if Mrs Grey comes in today and sees this? She'll have a heart attack. Two men are dead; and they must have families, people who'll miss them, people who rely on them. There'll be police everywhere and an investigation. We'll be arrested.' She stood next to Will at the front door, her back purposely turned on the white sheets. 'As much as I want to get out of this house, we can't just leave. Can we?'

'Mrs Cartlyn said we should leave today and everything here would be dealt with. She was quite insistent Jane. All we need to do now is load up the Ruby and get going. She said she'll check whether it's safe for us to go home now. Now that this has all…' Will wasn't quite sure what to say and Jane raised her eyebrows in question. 'Now that this has all happened. She also said she has somewhere else we can stay while she does that, while she checks it's all over.'

'Where?' Jane's voice rose slightly.

'I don't know. We're to meet her for lunch and she'll give us the details.'

'Where are we meeting, at the Grandchester? Surely we can't go there.'

'The Savoy.'

'Pardon?' Jane's eyes were once more wide, not this time with horror but surprise.

Will shrugged to express his lack of any more knowledge on the subject and repeated 'The Savoy?'

'Why didn't you tell me this last night?'

'Don't you think you had enough to worry about? You were in shock Jane, shaking like a leaf, cold as ice and just as white; I wanted to look after you.'

Jane smiled and touched Will's arm, 'It's a strange place to meet though, don't you think?'

'Well, apparently the best place to hide is not to hide.' Will shrugged again.

'Mrs Cartlyn has more secrets than a magician.'

'She certainly does.' Will opened the front door and motioned for Jane to go first. Neither turned to look back as they locked the door and left the two bodies behind them.

Second Flight

The drive back to London was many journeys all stuck together, a kaleidoscope trip that changed with every turn. There was silence, discussion, commenting on the passing scenery, spirits lifting, moods sinking, futures planned but pasts longed for. Outside, the world stayed calm and roads led the way they always did. Inside the car, Jane and Will moved through many emotions and their own paths led them in ways they never imagined.

After they closed the door for the last time on Richmond Row and turned their backs on the two lifeless men, they travelled in silence for some miles both deeply buried in their own thoughts.

Will's concerns started with Jane's safety, which led him naturally to dwell on what they would do next and then when he'd return to work. This thought took his heart to visit the Halls, reminding him of his own need to send them more money soon. He also knew that his bid to raise cash had been the cause of this nightmare that couldn't be quelled by waking. He felt guilt and anger. He felt guilt at how little he was doing for the Halls, guilt at the danger he'd unwittingly cast across Jane and anger at himself for the very same reasons. Surprisingly, no anger stirred towards Hugh lying dead miles behind them. Hugh had been a decent man, Will was sure, who loved his country and carried his duty to it and his countrymen with pride; he'd been working towards the 'greater good' and Will hoped that his death hadn't been in vain. Will was also sure that he'd never know what had been going on in Hugh's life, what subterfuge he'd been a part of; he accepted and almost welcomed that. But he hoped that Hugh's last moments hadn't been filled with 'what ifs'. And he hoped that Hugh wouldn't have been able to kill him.

As Will drove, Jane stared unseeing at the passing landscape as she worried about the unidentified and concealed dangers that could be waiting for Will; she hoped but doubted that this part of their story was over. She tried hard to push the leaden weight of two dead men from her mind and her eyes. She wondered when she would see her friends again; wanting especially to call Florence and assure her she was alright. She wanted to stand backstage to watch Will and have picnics of pork pie and hard-boiled egg; she wanted to be at home or working at the hotel. Even sheltering in the underground now emitted a nostalgic glow, as warped as that seemed. Jane closed her eyes as she heard her mother's words; no matter how bad things seem, they could always be worse.

Some things were the same in both Jane's and Will's minds; matching thoughts that started with fear for each other. Both wanted their lives back; they yearned to be just a young couple living their lives in London as they chose and no-one else dictated, knowing the dangers they faced and with their fears in the open. They longed for their fears to once more be the same as everyone else's.

As fields and farms were replaced with villages then towns, Jane felt butterflies stretch their wings within her. When the quiet roads bore houses, then tall buildings, shops and hotels, Jane felt nauseous. It was strange to feel such apprehension; usually this started when security and familiarity was replaced with the unknown and there was a longing to turn back to safety and reassurance. Today Jane hadn't left safety and comfort but sharp, deeply penetrating fear; disbelief felt like it punctured her heart and her brain, seeping bloodied horror everywhere. She didn't want to turn back, knowing what lay in the house they'd left behind, but didn't want to go forward either. She wanted to stop and stay completely still in time, where neither the past could haunt nor the future threaten.

As Will parked the car in a relatively quiet side road a few streets from the Strand and the Savoy, all was quiet. The two returning travellers were still for a moment. Will leaned back in his seat and sighed before turning to Jane. 'Ok?' Jane nodded in reply, a hundred fears haunting her eyes. Will got out and walked round to open the passenger door for her. 'We'll leave our bags with Ruby until we know what we're doing.' On the pavement they both paused. Will took Jane's hand then a deep breath, and walked her to The Savoy.

The doorman greeted them with a smile and stood aside for Jane and Will to enter. They stepped from the grey street, where people wore thick coats and avoided puddles, into the shine and sparkle of the hotel. Glass met crystal and carpet met marble. Everyone inside had a gleam somehow; it wasn't their attire (although everyone was dressed appropriately for their role in the hotel, whether their guise was visitor, guest or staff) but in their demeanour and their essence. The outside world, grey and wet, seemed forgotten and Jane recognised just how much she missed her job; it wasn't just the normality of life 'before' that she pined for, but the magic of the hotel - the escapist glamour of a world miles apart from most people's lives, yet only a few metres away, was addictive.

Will gently tugged Jane's hand as she'd stopped just inside the door and hadn't moved forward, absorbing the sights and sounds of the lobby and those who moved within it. 'Come on,' he urged, 'We need to find Mrs Cartlyn.'

As Will told the maitre d' at the Savoy Grill who they were meeting, Jane's eyes scanned the diners and spotted their host just as the very smart and amenable man started to guide them to her table. Mrs Cartlyn was seated at the edge of the room, looking immaculate and refined. She didn't smile as they approached, but nodded at the maitre d' who left the moment he'd pulled out a chair for Jane. It dawned on Jane then that she didn't think she'd ever seen Mrs Cartlyn offer a real smile, a happy to see you smile or an I love you smile, to anyone.

Jane felt Will's hand seek hers out under the table, and was glad of the contact as dark butterflies soared.

'Welcome back.' Mrs Cartlyn eyed the young couple and Jane thought the old lady's face softened as she did so. Both Jane and Will replied in unison with a thank you. 'Not quite the nice little break while things died down that I had envisaged.' She'd been straightening her cutlery as she spoke, then looked up as she finished speaking; neither Jane nor Will knew what to say for a moment and then Will found his voice.

'Mrs Cartlyn, we had no idea Hugh would find us. How did he know where we were?'

'I don't know Mr Batten. I didn't believe for one minute anyone would find you at Richmond Row.' She looked from Will to Jane. 'You must be shaken.'

Jane nodded. 'It was horrible Mrs Cartlyn. Terrifying. The men were there when we came back from a walk, then it was dark all of a sudden. They had guns and then I had a gun and there was a shot and...' Jane couldn't stop until Mrs Cartlyn, in uncharacteristic affection, touched her hand which lay next to a glass.

'It's alright dear,' she patted Jane's cold hand as Will's fingers tightened around the other one. 'Sshhh.' Jane couldn't stop tears running down her face in response to the spoken memory and the old lady's unexpected tenderness.

'Sorry, I'm sorry,' Jane said as she started to withdraw both her hands to find her handbag and a handkerchief. As she pulled her hand away from Mrs Cartlyn's Jane knocked the glass from the table and it hit the floor with a smash. 'Oh no, I'm so sorry.' Within seconds, two waiters were at the table and the shattered glass was gone; a new glass was replaced and all was calm once more.

Will poured Jane some water and she calmed. As two different waiters returned to their table, Mrs Cartlyn said 'I took the liberty of ordering a light lunch for us all.' The three diners were silent while the dishes were served; a variety of dainty sandwiches and small cakes on a stand, salad, fresh water in a beautiful carafe, a bottle of wine. 'Does that suit?' the old lady asked her guests. One of the waiters held the wine bottle in front of her for inspection and she nodded before he poured a small amount into her glass. She sipped, then nodded again without making eye contact with him and he poured wine into the three glasses.

'Yes, of course, it's all lovely thank you Mrs Cartlyn,' Jane replied to their host, and Will echoed her response.

'Right. Down to business.' Mrs Cartlyn said as soon as the three of them were alone again. 'Come on, you eat, I'll talk.' Jane and Will hesitantly started their meal as Mrs Cartlyn spoke. 'Answers before questions.' She took a second taste of wine and winced slightly as she looked at the glass disdainfully, 'It'll do, I suppose, there is a war on.' She put the glass down and her gaze returned to her companions. 'I had no idea that Hugh would follow you to Richmond Row; as for the other fellows, well, that was uncharacteristically careless of him. And while we're on the subject of them, rest assured they have been taken care of. There'll be no repercussions from the incident and you shall hear no more of it. And I expect to hear no more of it.' Jane felt Will's hand move to squeeze her knee.

'Mrs Cartlyn,' Will began, before Mrs Cartlyn held up a hand to stop him.

'Mr Batten, questions later. Although Hugh, sadly, is no longer with us it's still prudent to check that all is safe and the affair has reached its, somewhat unnatural, conclusion. As I mentioned to you over the telephone I have another property, in London, where you can stay. I assure you, with absolute and utter certainty, that no-one will come knocking there. Of course, you can go home if you wish; I have no sway over your choices, but I would advise you,' she hesitated, possibly for emphasis, 'to take up my offer.'

There was a noticeable and awkward silence as Will and Jane gave time for Mrs Cartlyn to continue before they spoke. They both started to speak at once, but Will let Jane talk.

'Mrs Cartlyn, I need to return to work; I can't afford not to work and I can't risk losing my position at the hotel. And I have my room at Mrs Foster's as well.'

'The same goes for me too Mrs Cartlyn; it's very generous and kind of you but I must get back to the theatre. I have to pay my way and I have people depending on me.'

Mrs Cartlyn's lips seeped a small smile. 'The Halls, I know.' Will looked at Jane and both turned to Mrs Cartlyn in startled silence. 'Don't be so surprised. I should have thought the last few weeks would have taught you that. Jane, your job is perfectly safe; maybe you can telephone your landlady to explain that you'll be away a short while longer; Mr Batten, you know the theatre is ever changing. That is the nature of the beast as they say. You'll find work I'm sure. But, for now, for just a few more days, I'd recommend you heed my advice.' Will and Jane sat in doubtful silence as they once again looked at each other. Mrs Cartlyn, exasperation creeping towards her, felt the need for bluntness. 'A job and a room are no use to a dead person.' Her companions' eyes snapped back to her and she felt a little sorry for them, young innocents caught in a sticky web. 'You've seen first-hand that this war isn't just being fought on the continent and among the clouds above us. It's here, all around us, amongst us.' She nodded to the room and Jane and Will followed her gaze as it swept over all their fellow diners.

Everyone in the room looked innocuous enough.

Businessmen, couples, friends;

Smiling, eating, chatting;

Or lying, plotting, spying?

The decision was made.

'Alright.' Will spoke to Mrs Cartlyn first, then turned to Jane. 'I can't let you go home until I know it's safe; you won't go to your mother's so this is the alternative. I can't protect you from Hitler, but I can protect you from whatever I've dragged you into.'

'Will, you go. It's not me who looks like Hugh is it? I can work for both of us; get a second job or extra shifts.' Mrs Cartlyn watched the exchange in silence; tolerant now, anticipating.

'No, it's both of us or neither of us. Final offer, no compromise.'

Jane hesitated, knowing that she could not force any deal with him. Finally she nodded her agreement as Will's face made no other answer possible.

'Alright,' she said and turned to Mrs Cartlyn, 'Thank you, we accept.'

'Good. Now I have the details for you,' Mrs Cartlyn reached for her handbag and pulled out an envelope with very little searching. Jane wondered if she had it to hand all along, knowing that Jane and Will would be going to her house, and had just waited patiently for the inevitable reply. 'The key and the address are in here. I think you'll like it. There's a telephone at the house so I'll be in touch. There's no housekeeper, so there'll be no-one coming in. And I know you can't live on air so there's some money in the envelope too.'

'No Mrs Cartlyn, we can't take any money.' Will beat Jane to it.

'You will Mr Batten.' Mrs Cartlyn said as she stood to leave. Discussion closed. 'And lunch is on my bill'.

Jane and Will finished their lunch quickly so they could leave the environment in which they felt so alien, sure that they stood out like pebbles in a jeweller's shop. It wasn't until they were outside that Will took the envelope from his breast pocket. He looked at Jane before opening it.

'Well, that's that then. Our new home.'

'What does the note say?'

'Just the address and a postscript that says to take a taxi. And there's the key and some cash.' Will held out the note for Jane to read.

Jane sighed 'Well, we'd better do as we're told then.'

'Yes, I suppose so.' Will opened the car and took out their bags before offering Jane the crook of his arm, which she linked her hand through. 'Come on then Sunshine, our next adventure awaits. Let's walk for a while before we get that taxi, I want to savour being home.' Will smiled as they began to walk.

'Do you think it's safe?'

Will smiled. 'Well, if we're unlucky enough to bump into any-one doubtful on the street, I'm up for calling it fate. You just run like hell's doors are opening behind you and get to the Grand-chester.'

'But what if…' Jane started to say.

'What if? What if a bomb hadn't flattened your house? Not all what ifs are bad, Sunshine.' Will turned to look at Jane as they walked and saw her serious expression, so he stopped and put down the cases to hold her close. 'Mrs Cartlyn seems to think it's just familiar haunts, work and home and the like, where we'll come unstuck; if at all. Otherwise she'd be suggesting we leave the city again. I think it's over Jane. I think it's done.'

Despite the cold mid-December air, the sun was trying its best to provide cheer. Despite being a city bending with war the shops looked festive and bright. Despite the daily fear and nightly destruction, people still smiled.

Will and Jane walked for some time, looking in shop win-dows and commenting on things they saw or things that were now missing. After their long journey and the horrors that had occurred before, being back in London was finally a relief. Jane's anxiety as they neared the city had passed, soothed by the familiarity of home. With Will's faded facial injuries from the beating near his flat, visual reminders of their plight were easy to overlook and it was good to feel normal for a little while as they strolled arm in arm along the busy streets, chatting easily. Jane knew that denial of what had happened wouldn't come so easily when Will undressed to reveal the marks that still bore witness to the past.

Eventually, after a long walk and a short taxi ride, the two refugees stood once again outside an unfamiliar front door. The tall Georgian terrace stood firm before them, the ground floor painted white and the upper floors a warm brick. Tall narrow windows looked benignly at them and the black front door waited for the key. Jane's anxious heartbeat had reawakened a small number of butterflies and she held Will's hand tighter without knowing. Will felt the increased pressure of Jane's hand and turned to look at her as he unlocked the door left handed, still anchoring her with his right.

'It'll all be fine here. We're home Sunshine. Hugh's gone. It's over. Alright?'

Jane nodded then whispered 'Alright' and the pair stepped over the threshold together.

'Nice,' said Will as he put down their bags and closed the door behind them.

'Very Mrs Cartlyn,' smiled Jane as she took in the simple but notably expensive surroundings.

'Come on, let's explore.' Will took Jane's hand like an excited schoolboy and dragged her from room to room; kitchen, hall, landing, bedrooms, bathroom, until they ended up in the sitting room again and landed on the settee. 'Ok?'

'Yes.'

Will had lifted her mood as he intended. He smiled then looked serious as he stood up.

'I'm going to phone Maggie and Jack.' Jane nodded as Will left for the hall. Soon she could hear him talking and she quietly walked past to pick up the bags and take them upstairs. Slowly she walked from room to room again, carrying the cases into each room with her. There were four bedrooms; two doubles one twin bedded room and one single, and Jane walked in and out, backwards and forwards. Finally, she put both bags down in one of the double rooms and returned to the hall.

Will's telephone call was ending and he grinned as Jane passed. She went to the kitchen and through that to the back yard, which was small and tidy. She perched on an iron bench a few steps from the back door and shivered as a cold gust of December wind caught her. She closed her eyes as she sat there alone, pleased to be back in London but wondering what the next few days or weeks might bring.

Jane turned at the sound of Will's footsteps walking through the kitchen and watched him look at the sky as he approached. He was carrying a paper bag.

'Rain d'you think?'

'I don't know.'

'At least the skies are quiet.'

'For now,' Jane said sagely. She looked up to the innocent blue grey sky knowing it might later glow red from the burning of the city, and harbour dark machines that looked like evil black birds circling a carcass. She forced the image from her mind, replacing it with friendly faces. 'How are Maggie, Jack and the children?'

'They're doing alright. No news to speak of, which is a good thing I suppose.' Will sat down next to Jane and shuffled his feet about, looking at them as they moved around benignly on the red bricks. Jane knew he must be thinking of Harry and took his empty hand. He passed her the bag from his other hand and she frowned. 'Found it next to the telephone.'

Jane peered inside and was touched to see who it was from, although it could only have been one person. There was no note, just a card inside to give away the identity of the benefactor.

E. Cartlyn was the only text the small white card bore. Small black embossed letters on crisp card. Just like the lady whose name it announced. Small and crisp yet showing it meant business.

Jane smiled at Will, who had clearly also seen the card, as she reached inside to take each item out and place them one by one on the bench beside her; lavender soap wrapped in floral paper, pretty notelets, a dainty ladies' pen, a box of men's cotton handkerchiefs, a metal matches box with an engraved lion on the front and a bar of Fry's chocolate. Jane was moved by the gift from a woman who showed so little emotion or outward warmth. Will put his arm round Jane and squeezed.

'Like I said, there are hidden depths to that woman.' Jane nodded at Will's comment. After a moment he added, 'Should you telephone Florence? You said you wanted to, but I'm surprised it's her of all the girls. I mean, I didn't realise you were so close; I would have imagined you closer to Dorothy - you seem to have more in common.'

Jane knew the time had come for honesty. Honesty about meeting with Florence and then the unexpected meeting with Maria Henderson that had been borne of it. And it was time to tell the truth about the bottle, the contents of which had been secretly poured down the sink at Richmond Row.

When Jane didn't offer a verbal response, but instead just looked sadly at Will, his face changed. There was a look of frightened confusion dawning as he anticipated the falling of bad news from Jane's lips.

'There's something wrong.'

'No, nothing's wrong, not really, not anymore. I just have to tell you about something that happened at Richmond Row, or rather something that didn't happen.'

Will's eyes widened.

'Did Hugh hurt you? Did he do something?'

'No, not at all.' Jane could see where Will's thoughts were charging and was quick to reassure him that Hugh had done nothing that Will didn't already know about. 'No Will, not Hugh; it was me. It's what I could have done to Hugh.'

Will listened as Jane told him how she'd contacted Florence to get a message to Mrs Cartlyn, worried about the meaning of Hugh Callaghan's sudden appearance from the concealing cloak of night. She relived how Maria Henderson had turned up in response to the message, carrying the means to end Hugh's life.

Jane admitted that she'd fought herself over what to do, ashamed that she'd even let the option of murder creep into her head let alone consider it. Will made no sound as she spoke; tears rolled silently down her face as she told him how she'd contaminated Hugh's cup then tipped it away almost immediately, scrubbing the cup ferociously and placing it at the very back of the cupboard before tipping the bottle's contents away too, and then wrapping the small bottle in newspaper and putting it at the very bottom of the dustbin.

She cried as she told Will that she had to protect him but couldn't murder Hugh to do it. She told him how she'd realised during the later bloodshed that she could fire a gun in the heat of a confused moment when Will's immediate danger was pushed in her face, but that calculated pre-meditated murder was an act she couldn't complete. She felt a heavy conflict of guilt as she spoke - she'd contemplated murder but then hadn't been able to carry it out, even for Will. Fire and ice were battling inside her conscience.

When Jane finished talking, Will wrapped his arms round her weeping form and gently rocked her as he whispered 'Ssshhhh' into her hair.

'What do you think of me now, now I'm almost a murderer?'

Will found humour in her comment but she couldn't see his face. He was moved by what she had wanted to do but utterly glad she couldn't. 'Almost is a long way away Sunshine.'

Jane felt purged after revealing the whole story of Richmond Row to Will. Her shoulders seemed lighter without the burden of the secret; for a small bottle it had weighed heavy on her. She hadn't known how heavy it was until Will brushed it from her conscience. What had happened there would never leave them, but they had at least left physically unscathed apart from the few fresh bruises Will still fostered after the scuffle with Hugh. Jane and Will were escapees from an inevitable event, people who never should have been involved in the first place. They knew that Hugh had chosen to walk a perilous road, a delicately balanced route that was easily tipped.

Jane telephoned Florence as soon as they were back indoors to tell her they'd returned to London, but were temporarily staying somewhere else.

'Where are you then?'

'I can't tell you Florence.'

'How long will you be there?'

'I don't know. Not long I hope. Look, I know you have lots of questions and I promise I'll answer them when it's all over.'

'When will 'over' be though Jane?'

'Soon I hope. I promise I'll be in touch soon.'

Florence hesitated before replying. 'Alright, if you say so. Just please get in touch if you need me, or any of us. You know we'll be there in a flash.'

'I know darling, I know you will, thank you. Thank you for rushing to see me when I called.' To avoid enlarging on the events that followed their meeting, Jane changed the subject. 'I wrote to Mrs Cavendish a couple of weeks ago; I haven't heard back yet. Have you had a letter or anything?'

'No, I haven't. I'm sure she's absolutely fine. Clever changing of the subject though Jane.'

Jane was defeated. 'I'm sorry. I just can't tell you every-thing now. Please trust me. I'm fine and Will's fine. We're safe.' There was a pause in the conversation as Florence intentionally waited, hoping Jane would feel the need to continue, and Jane waited hoping that Florence would fill the silence. In the end, it was Jane who did so. 'Say hi to the girls when you see them.' Jane wanted to feel the warmth that came from her friends, each very different but a vital quarter of their whole. 'I miss you all.'

'We miss you too. And Jane?'

'Yes.'

'Merry Christmas.'

Jane was startled at Florence's words and took a moment before replying. 'Merry Christmas Florence' she said.

As Jane put the receiver down, she sighed. With all that had been going on she hadn't thought about Christmas; it was the twenty third of December. Wednesday would be Christmas Day. She hoped that the imminent birth of 1941 would bring peace.

Jane sat quietly in the hall for a little while before Will appeared. He pulled her to her feet.

'There's really not much to eat, understandably. Mrs Cartlyn, bless her, has managed to have a few bits put in the kitchen, heaven knows how, but it's not like the supplies she arranged out in the countryside at Richmond Row. We'll need to batter the ration books some more. Tea and sugar rations have increased a bit leading up to Wednesday, so if we pool what we've got we'll be ok. If we can avoid spending Mrs Cartlyn's cash, I'll be pleased. I don't like the thought of taking it.'

'Me neither,' Jane said. 'Why don't I go out and get some things while you unpack.'

Will laughed. 'And how long do you think it will take me to unpack then?' he asked. Jane didn't answer. 'I know you're trying to keep me out of harm's way, Sunshine, but there's no need. Look, there's that market we passed and a few shops a couple of streets away; we'll go together. We're not close enough to home to be in any danger.' Without waiting for a response from Jane, he took her coat from the rack on the wall and held it out for her. She slid her arms in without argument and buttoned up the coat as Will shrugged his on. Despite his reassurance, she knew that he didn't want her out alone. Cementing this, he added a further excuse. 'Anyway, who's going to find you a cuppa if the air raid warning goes off and you have to shelter alone?'

Soon they were arm in arm among the shoppers; they were like everyone else again, sharing the cold streets and the difficulty of finding what they wanted to buy. Their difference to the crowds, their shared and forcefully buried memories of Hugh Callaghan, their experience of violence and murder, were hidden from all. They even tried to conceal these things from their own consciousness, veiling them with thoughts of normal tasks.

Jane was a little nervous at first, eyeing strange men with suspicion and looking around to see if anyone watched them; no-one did. No-one appeared to.

Between the market stalls and a couple of shops they were able to collect most of the necessary basics, even if Christmas dinner would be fish and not turkey. Without Will noticing as he hovered outside one of the shops, Jane bought some Christmas cards and made a mental note to phone her mother, in lieu of a card, on Christmas Eve. As Jane saw Will through the window before she went outside to join him again, she smiled. He looked casual but debonair as his gaze returned to the street, relaxed but somehow wary. Jane knew as she saw him watching, looking, checking, vetting each man he saw, just how much his reassurance that all was now normal was for her benefit. She felt a thread of ice run though her warm body. The ice didn't last long, overpowered by the melting heat of knowing Will was protecting her and she protecting him as they once again linked their fingers together and walked.

When they returned to their temporary lodgings, Jane unpacked the meagre shopping haul then went upstairs to unpack their cases. As she finished, she heard the front door shut and rushed to the window to look out. She could see Will walking down the street and fumbled with the window, trying to open it to call out to him; she couldn't get the latch to move and turned to run down the stairs instead. She burst through the front door and into the street; but Will was gone.

As she stepped back through the door, she noticed Will's note poked into the corner of the mirror on the coat rack 'Back soon. Don't worry x'

Time moved so slowly Jane wondered if it was going backwards. With no idea where he might have gone, she could do nothing to hasten Will's return. Worried, she wandered through the house as she waited. When almost an hour had passed, Jane gave herself a verbal slap saying 'Pull yourself together you idiot.' As early evening approached, Jane laid and lit the fire in the sitting room, and then she made herself busy in the kitchen preparing corned beef sandwiches. Once done, she headed upstairs, where she wrote the Christmas cards she'd bought for Will and her girlfriends. After each task she checked the time; at each sound she paused, hoping it was Will.

Running out of things to do, Jane washed her hands and face and brushed her hair. Then she walked from room to room again, glancing at every piece of furniture and every picture. Back in the bedroom where she'd unpacked their things she lay down on the bed, checking her watch again.

Jane jumped when she heard a noise downstairs. Her heart beat so fast she could hear its blood pump throbbing in her ears. Disorientated for a moment, she sat up and gently placed her feet to the floor. She quickly but quietly moved behind the open bedroom door, willing her heart into calm in case it gave her hiding place away. She was angry at herself for falling asleep, ashamed at sleeping when she feared for Will's safety and waited for his return. Looking about for a heavy object to arm herself with she saw nothing, her eyes unseeing in the darkness. Her mind was soon distracted from her pointless visual search by the sound of gentle footsteps climbing the stairs. She prayed it was Will, but couldn't be sure.

A shadow fell across the bedroom floor, illuminated from the fresh landing light. Jane closed her eyes, held her breath. Now she could see she didn't want to. The bedroom door was gently pushed from the other side, reducing Jane's hiding place.

'Jane?' the worried voice quietly called. On hearing the exhalation of breath that had been released from behind the door, Will pulled the handle and peered round to see Jane leaning against the wall behind. In an instant Jane had thawed from cold unbreathing tension, stiff and alert, to a melting breath of relief.

'Bloody hell, Jane,' came the sigh, 'you've got to stop doing this to me.' Jane stepped forward. 'Not a week seems to go by when I don't think you've been kidnapped, killed or otherwise lost.' Despite his jest, Jane could see the utter relief in Will's eyes.

'Sorry, I thought you were...I don't know who I thought you were.'

Will's moment of vulnerability was set aside by his role as protector, pushed back harshly by his need to look after Jane.

'It's all over Sunshine, don't worry. No more doubt and despair, we look forward now not back. The only looking over our shoulder we're going to do now is when we're smiling back at happy memories.' Will took Jane's hand and led her downstairs. When they got to the hallway, he stopped. 'Close your eyes.' Will moved next to Jane, covered her eyes with one hand and held her arm gently with the other.

'What on earth...'

'You have to trust me Jane.' Will ushered her forward and she heard him open the sitting room door, leading her in. They stopped a few steps inside and Will removed his hand. Jane gasped as she opened her eyes to see a Christmas tree, too large for the room, standing in the corner. It was sparsely dressed with odd decorations and random small items but, with light bouncing around it as the flames from the freshly stoked fire settled on the few unrelated ornaments, it looked lovely. 'I know it's too big,' Will apologised.

'It's not. It's lovely, Will.' The tree was comically big; not only too tall but also too full, and Will had moved furniture to accommodate it. Considering the proportions of the lovely Georgian home, to install a tree that was actually too big was quite an accomplishment and Jane was amazed at what Will had managed without waking her.

'I'm glad you like it; it wouldn't be Christmas without a tree. But it is too big. There's a real shortage of small trees; everyone's bought them to fit in their shelters apparently. Would you believe it? Only big bloody brutes left, especially this close to Christmas. I was going to cut it down a bit but it seemed a shame; that and I had nothing man enough to cut it with.' Jane's delight at Will's gesture was heightened by the relief of having him back safely and knowing that there had been no sinister reason for his disappearance. Will knew he'd frightened her with his long absence and added, 'I didn't intend to be gone for so long, I'm sorry if I worried you.'

'It was a lovely surprise, thank you.'

The rest of the evening was spent sitting together in the semi darkness, watching the flames dance in the fireplace and enjoying the fresh green smell of the tree as it reminded them of past Christmases and gave them hope for future ones.

'Happy Christmas Eve,' came the gentle voice in Jane's ear as she dozed on Will's shoulder.

'Gosh, is that the time? Really?'

'Yep, we should go to bed. Or we could just sit here; I'd be happy to stay here like this.' He was quick to reassure, not wanting to disturb the warm comfort that brought such peace to them both.

'Me too.' Jane kissed Will's cheek and settled back down to rest her head on his chest and inhale the scent of cotton shirt mixed with faint aftershave and the warmth of a gently rising and falling chest underneath. Not even the siren and the sounds that followed moved them from their settled embrace.

When Jane woke the next morning she found herself on the settee alone, covered by a blanket. She checked her watch to find that it was past nine o'clock. She listened for sounds of Will in the house, panic tapping at her chest. At the sound of Will whistling Little Brown Jug somewhere in the house, the panic was turned away and Jane sat up, swinging her legs to the floor. She turned as she heard Will come into the room.

'Morning,' he smiled.

'Good morning.'

'What's the plan for today then Sunshine? We've not heard from Mrs Cartlyn, so I'm guessing we're fugitives 'til after Christmas. I telephoned Jack a few minutes ago and they've invited us to the farm. We can go, or stay here. We'll do whatever you want, just say the word. I'm guessing you might want to see the girls too and speak to your mum?'

'Oh blimey, hang on a minute, let me wake up first.'

'Sorry.' Will took Jane's hand. 'I just want to make the most of every minute.' He helped Jane to her feet. 'I noticed that you put both of our bags in the front bedroom.'

Jane, finding a forwardness she'd never had before, raised her eyebrows.

'I just want to make the most of every minute.'

'Touché,' Will conceded quite happily.

Turning back to the mention of Jack, Jane was worried.

'You say we've been invited to the farm, which is absolutely lovely, but that's somewhere you're known. The very people we're hiding from were at the farm. They've been there Will, the night they tampered with Sunbeam.'

'I know.' He looked down. 'I know.' He closed his eyes and rubbed his forehead with his fingers. 'My brain is telling me to stay put, but my heart is saying I need to go.' He looked up and shrugged. 'Then there's my gut; that's telling me that it's over, that we'll be alright at the farm. I think Mrs Cartlyn will give us the all clear soon anyway. And if I don't see Jack and Maggie over Christmas, they'll worry. I don't want to do that to them, not now. And heaven help me if Maggie sends Jack to check up on me. He'll find me missing from the flat *and* the theatre; then what do I do?'

Jane hesitated, then found the answer clear. 'I say we go.'

'Do you?'

'Yes. You're right. I think.' The decision was made in optimism, hope and love but Will knew that he'd be extra vigilant at every step.

Christmas 1940

With a sense of optimism that hadn't settled on Jane for weeks the young pair set off for the farm reunited with the sloper, which itself brought a happy familiarity. Will had talked of how pleased he'd be to get Sunbeam back and how he was keen to get going, but Jane knew that his real impatience lay at the feet of the Hall family.

Jane was surprised to feel comfort and confidence on the back of the motorcycle; no doubt aided by the reassuring tightness with which she wrapped her arms around Will. She didn't know that he winced as she tightened her grip on his still tender ribcage. Any nerves that came with her first motorcycle ride since the accident were lost amid the excitement of their impending visit. In the growing darkness of Christmas Eve, Jane's mind drifted cloud-like over the morning. Arrangements for Christmas were finalised and packing done, numerous telephone calls were made and her mum reassured and cheered.

Jane had arranged a get together with Florence, Aggie and Dorothy over lunch, surprised that she'd been able to get hold of her girlfriends and that they'd been free at such short notice. She didn't know that Florence and Aggie had both confirmed their attendance then hastily cancelled prior engagements without question in order to see her. Aggie and Dorothy were a little surprised, but not bothered, by the choice of venue; it was a small restaurant they'd not visited previously. Despite Will's assumption that normality was restored, in the absence of Mrs Cartlyn's confirmation of this fact, Will wouldn't let Jane return to any of her usual haunts. Florence, of course, harboured no surprise at the virgin venue.

The girls all greeted each other like they'd been apart for years rather than weeks, the extra fervour due to their awareness that the separation had been ugly, scary.

The last thing Aggie and Dorothy knew was that Will had been drawn into a deception that was deeper and darker than he had at first known; that Florence had said six words that shocked them all; that the six words were hateful and scandalous but scarily insightful and accurate - apparently giving voice to the only way out.

The last thing Florence had known was that Jane and Will were back in the city waiting for their very own all clear siren; she didn't know what finally came to pass during their forced exile.

As she walked to meet her friends Jane decided that they could not know the whole story, not yet. Maybe when the war was long past she would tell the tale from start to end with no censorship. For now she would give a gentle version, a reassuring and abridged version. Jane had wrestled with this decision since arranging their lunch and still fought with it all the way there. She trusted her friends with her life, but wanted to protect not only their bodies (from a force she couldn't see and wasn't sure existed) but also the love and innocence in their hearts; she shielded them from worry and fear like a mother would guard her child.

As Jane told the simplified and gentler tale, she knew Florence's eyes were upon her. The large eyes veiled a little by the waves of red hair weren't watching with tender care as the other two pairs of eyes did, but with a suspicion borne of knowledge. Florence knew that Jane wasn't serving up the whole story to her friends, but had cut off the juicier, meatier, bloodier parts and kept those safely tucked away.

Jane's story, and the answers she offered to her friends' concerned questions, didn't take long and she was thankful that she and Florence were able to steer the conversation to safer subjects; what the girls had been doing, their festive preparations and plans, jobs, air raids, rationing.

Aggie and Dorothy seemed satisfied with the outcome of Jane's recent adventure, having no reason to doubt the diluted story she told. Florence, as Jane knew, wasn't. She hovered a little longer as the girls exchanged Christmas cards and wishes, hugs and kisses, and then parted, hanging back and catching Jane's arm to stop her walking away. Jane turned, knowing and dreading the conversation to come.

'Well?' Jane sighed and looked into the beautiful but steely eyes of her friend. Jane didn't say anything and Florence continued. 'When we spoke the other day you said you'd answer all my questions when it was over.'

'I know I did, but I'm not sure it is all over.'

'Sorry, that's not good enough. You're home so everything must be heading in the right direction.' The two friends looked at each other, almost staring, before Jane reached out and took Florence's hand.

'Alright. Alright.' The two girls walked away from the restaurant and soon found a bench in a quiet little square. There they sat down, just as they had during Florence's visit to Jane, and Jane told the whole, unedited, bloody and murderous story.

Purged of her secret once again, Jane felt almost absolved. As dark and surreal as Richmond Row had been, it somehow didn't seem as sordid now someone else, unconnected and sunny, knew the truth.

When Florence voiced the words, quite independently and unprompted, that Jane had been telling herself for days, they held more credence.

'Jane, listen to me,' Florence had said as she squeezed Jane's hands gently, 'Hugh was going to die; it doesn't matter when or where, he was going to die. The simple solitary fact is that you and Will were there because Will had been trying to help. Neither of you pulled that trigger and neither of you led those men there, to him.' Florence gently tucked Jane's hair behind her ear, the pair closer than they'd ever been. 'None of it can be changed Jane. I know it will always be with you; it has to be inside you always or you wouldn't be a decent person, but now you have to move on.' Judgement was passed.

Florence's words drifted away as the wind hit Jane's face on another turn along the winding country lanes. She smiled to herself and held Will tighter, causing him to turn his head slightly in response. Florence must be right; many people had witnessed things that they would never forget but which they locked away. They kept the key safe but almost out of reach. Jane was now one of them. In a bid to start afresh and cleanse her soul she pressed even further into Will's back, closed her eyes tight and sighed deeply in a bid to squeeze the vision from her eyes and expel the feelings from her chest.

Darkness shrouded Will and Jane as they pulled into the farm-yard. No sooner had the engine turned off than the kitchen door was opened and there were hugs and welcomes. Bags were un-strapped from the bike and the visitors ushered indoors. The kitchen was more welcoming than ever and it was clear that, even in here, the children had been busy making Christmas decorations. Newspaper chains were festooned throughout and sprigs of greenery generously balanced on every picture frame and window sill.

In the living room, where the travellers were shepherded to sit down after their journey, a pretty Christmas tree stood proudly in the corner. It was lovingly decorated with items clearly col-lected over many years; some bought from shops, others hand-made. Beneath the tree, wrapped in a variety of papers and cloths, was a small stack of gifts. The wireless played gently in the background trying bravely to be heard amid the excited bustling of the Hall children and the chatting of the adults. Jane noticed that the mantelpiece was also laden with greenery and decorations made by childish hands. All the normal items that called the mantelpiece home were hidden from view by the festive decorations; except one - Harry's picture had been moved to the fore, left fully on view.

After the initial excitement of their arrival, Jane was pleased when things calmed a little and she had a moment to herself. She offered to help Maggie in the kitchen but was shooed away kindly as Maggie put the kettle on then disappeared into the large farmhouse pantry. Jane couldn't imagine what emotions rained on Maggie and her family knowing that their loss must be felt even sharper at this time of year when families shared time together or, at the very least, greetings from one another.

Jane left the warm kitchen and the chatter of the living room and felt the air cooling as she climbed the stairs to her room. She opened the door on the now familiar space to see Will's bag next to hers on the bed. She was surprised that his hadn't been taken straight into the boys' room. Jane sat on the edge of the soft bed and pulled her bag towards her. She was pleased that they'd brought bags and not cases; cases reminded her of their flight to Richmond Row.

Shaking the memory from her head, Jane opened the smaller of her two bags; it held the gifts she'd hastily pulled together for their visit, now wrapped neatly in paper. Thankfully, Mrs Cartlyn's bag of treasures hadn't been opened again after the initial viewing on the bench; it didn't matter that neither Jane nor Will would use any of the items themselves. Knowing that they had been given by the secretly soft centred old lady was gift enough.

Although the Halls had expressly asked Will and Jane not to take them any gifts or go to any trouble, the soap, notelets and pen, handkerchiefs, matches box and chocolate were neatly labelled, one for each member of the Hall family. An additional gift was labelled for Will and Jane was pleased that he knew nothing about it. She'd stumbled across a postcard, completely unexpectedly, when she'd started to give up all hope of finding Will a Christmas gift that was both appropriate and affordable. The postcard showed London at night from a very similar spot to that where they'd shared their first picnic and watched the moon send its shimmery messengers to the Thames. The picture was pretty and made Jane happy the moment she saw it. She'd quickly purchased it and found a small frame on the nearby market. A sound on the landing made Jane quickly push the gift to the bottom of the pile.

Will came into the room.

'Are you alright?'

'Yes, just getting the gifts to put under the tree.'

Will smiled.

'They'll tell us off you know.' He sat on the bed next to Jane. 'I hope you don't mind, but they've put us in together.'

'I saw the bags.'

'I kind of asked.'

'Kind of?'

'I asked.'

'What on earth must they think Will?' Jane looked worried.

'They think life's brief Jane, that's what they think. And they'd be right. I can't miss a single chance to fall asleep next to you and wake up with you in my arms.'

A voice called their names from downstairs and the moment of depth, of serious discussion, of romance, was snapped. Sylvie shouted up to them that it was time to put out treats for Father Christmas and his reindeer and Jane and Will responded to the call with childlike enthusiasm.

Once Sylvie and Jacob were excitedly tucked up in bed, the adults and Daniel sat in the living room listening to the wireless. Four extra glasses of sherry, and half a glass for Daniel, had been poured as Father Christmas's tipple was prepared. Four now sat, glasses in hands, as Jack stood to speak.

'Here's to the end of war, here's to those still fighting it, here's to King and country and here's to absent loved ones,' he bravely toasted. Maggie, Daniel, Will and Jane all stood to raise their glasses and take a sip. 'Cheers.' Maggie silently wiped her eyes with her handkerchief and Daniel stood straighter as he put his hand on her shoulder, valiantly holding back his own tears. Jack's voice cracked as he looked at Will and Jane. 'Thank you for coming.' Then he added. 'Here's to your safe return to us Will.' Will nodded as he reached out to take Maggie's hand and another toast was raised.

Jane wasn't quite sure what to do as she watched the pain in their eyes and tried not to register the final toast. Although she felt a deep sorrow at Harry's loss, it was an ache for Will and this lovely family rather than a void she felt herself. As much as she had a vision in her head of Harry and the man he'd been, provided by the collage of different images given to her by those who loved him, it wasn't enough.

Jane was disturbed from her thoughts by Maggie's voice.

'Come on now. It's Christmas; a time to rejoice in what and who we have. Harry's here in our hearts.'

'And probably shaking his head at us,' added Daniel. Everyone nodded, agreed or chuckled. Then the moment of joint recollection and reflection was over and the party dispersed, each keen to deal with the moment in their own way. Jack headed outside, followed by Daniel, and Maggie left quietly for the kitchen.

'Should we help?' Jane asked Will.

'No sweetheart, leave them to their thoughts,' was Will's advice as they sat down, both perched on the edge of the settee. Will watched the flames leaping carefree in the hearth and Jane followed his gaze. They sat quietly for a while before Will relaxed back into the chair. 'You know, Jack and I had quite a chat earlier.' Jane didn't comment and let him carry on. 'He was saying how we all declare that life's precious but we don't *really* know it until we lose someone, especially someone young. It's like saying a flower or a day is beautiful; we don't really see it, we just say it because that's what we say. So many things are said for the sake of being said, just because that's the done thing. We sometimes say what we feel, but we rarely *feel* what we say. We don't stop to truly appreciate things do we?'

'No, I suppose we don't.'

'What I'm trying to say, in my clumsy way, is that I'm going to enlist as soon as I can.' Jane wasn't sure exactly what she'd expected Will to say but it wasn't the sentence she heard. Not yet. She nodded, numb. The connection between this statement and his previous profundity was quite blurry. 'I'm amazed that I haven't been called yet, but I pray it waits just a little longer; so I know that this nightmare is truly over before I leave you. Then, if I've not heard, I'm stepping up.'

'Then another nightmare begins.'

'Maybe, but that's a nightmare the whole country shares. Life is precious Jane, and if we don't stand up and fight for it our lives won't be the same. Call it duty, obligation, whatever you want. Maybe it's fear of the alternative, or thinking we might just be the one person who tips the balance.' He watched Jane for a response and finding none he carried on. 'I won't leave you until Mrs Cartlyn says everything's over, until I know you're safe. I know that she somehow safeguarded your job, but can you think about maybe coming out here instead, staying on the farm?'

Jane hadn't seen this coming either.

'No Will, I can't. I couldn't.'

Will took her face in his hands. 'Just think about it. Please.' His hands dropped and found Jane's. 'Jack knows I'm going, but I haven't told Maggie yet. He said they'd love to have you and I know Maggie will be over the moon if you do come to stay. Please, don't dismiss the idea yet. Just think about it.' Jane nodded and the room was silent apart from the gentle strains of Over the Rainbow reaching their ears from the wireless. 'There's something else too.' Jane wasn't sure she wanted to hear more;

losing Will to the forces and being asked to leave her job and the city were more than enough.

'Will, no more please. I don't want to hear any more.' He kissed her lips to silence her, then drew back to look her in the eyes.

'This is different Jane, I promise.' Jane looked away. 'Please Sunshine, listen to me.' Will bent his head into her line of sight and she gave up and turned back to him. 'I won't do what a lot of the lads have done, hastily marrying their sweethearts before they leave.' Jane felt a blush rising up her chest. 'But I'm warning you now; the moment it's all over and I'm back for good, I'm going to ask you to marry me so get your excuses ready if you don't want to marry a struggling actor.' Jane's face tilted downward again, camouflaging its self-conscious flush with shadow and the glow of the fire, but Will bent his face down to meet hers. 'Is that alright?'

'It's alright.'

Maggie returned to the living room not long after, proudly carrying a tray bearing slices of cake. She'd saved coupons and 'put by' ingredients bit by bit so that she could afford her family the luxury of what she called real cake. Soon, Jack and Daniel appeared and Daniel said a quick goodnight and left for bed. The adults were left alone to talk of the farm, friends and local news then to listen to the latest announcements from London before discussing these too. By the time the mantel clock's delicate hands pointed to the twelve of Christmas Day, the room had fallen silent in anticipation. Will, Jane, Jack and Maggie all wished each other a Merry Christmas, with each one silently praying for the gift of peace and safety above all else.

As Will and Jane retired to their room they both thought of friends and loved ones. Jane tried not to let her face show her feelings when Will removed his shirt and the legacy of his beating could still be seen. She was shocked, despite knowing that he'd still bear the marks of the men who'd flogged him. She wondered how much pain he still bore silently and turned discreetly away; she didn't want to see any more of his bruised skin. They climbed into bed, letting the comfort of the farm and the season overpower any sadness that they felt, and lay there silently. Eventually Jane laid a hand across Will's bare chest, gently touching the worst of his injuries.

'Is it still hurting you?'

Will's hand covered hers.

'No. Not really. I promise it all looks worse than it feels. I'm just going for the sympathy vote.'

Before leaving the living room, Jane had discreetly picked up the small, flat rectangular gift that was under the tree. She rolled away from Will and leaned down to pick this up from its new hiding place just under the bed and sat up to hand it to Will.

'I'd like to give you this now if that's alright. Merry Christmas.' Will looked surprised to receive a gift. 'It's only something small.'

Will sat up and unwrapped the small parcel, beaming with delight when he saw the framed postcard and remembering their pork pie picnic. He leaned across to thank Jane with a kiss.

'Thank you. It's perfect.' To his surprise, Jane took it from him and started to remove the back of the frame to take out the card. 'What are you doing?' Will tried to retrieve his present but Jane pushed his hands away as she withdrew the card and put the frame on the bed.

'No, please, just a minute.' Jane hopped out of bed to reach for her handbag, then pulled a pen from its depths and returned to the bed. Leaning on her knees she wrote on the back of the card as she spoke. 'As you'll be leaving me soon, I want you to take this with you. You can keep it in your wallet, or wherever. We can put it back in the frame when you come home.' Jane handed him the card.

Will took the card from her and turned it over to read the new inscription. Until we meet again. Will paused for a moment, then to lift the melancholy he said 'Here, Merry Christmas' as he handed Jane the discarded empty frame.

Jane feigned annoyance with a raised eyebrow until Will jumped out of bed and moved towards his clothes on the chair. From his jacket pocket he pulled out an envelope. Coming back to kneel on the bed next to Jane, he smiled and handed it to her. Jane nervously opened the envelope and pulled out a small piece of newspaper, neatly cut out. She frowned as Will smiled. 'Turn it over,' he instructed. Jane did as she was told to see a modest advert for a jeweller's shop, with a sketch of a pretty ring part of the advert. Handwritten neatly above it was an IOU. Will winked.

'Well, I'm keeping *that* safe and sound. You do realise that's as good as a contract, a binding agreement?' Jane teased as she flamboyantly tucked the piece of paper down her top.

'I do.' Will declared solemnly before they both started to giggle like schoolchildren, each shushing the other with a finger to their lips.

Christmas was soon over, lost in an excited haze of children, singing and playing games, simple gifts and sharing meals. The morning had raised the household early with Sylvie rapping on each bedroom door as she ran past giggling. Everyone assembled downstairs as the children examined the contents of their stockings. With animals fed and checked by Jack and Daniel, and lunch ably in hand courtesy of Maggie, everyone ate breakfast together before heading off to church bundled up against the cold.

Although an inflated price could easily be asked, Maggie and Jack had decided that one of their chickens would not be sold or even kept for eggs but served for Christmas lunch. Because of this the returning party were welcomed by a wondrous smell that was both foreign and familiar. When lunch was consumed and dishes washed, gifts were exchanged and boisterous games played. The afternoon brought quieter pursuits as everyone settled in the living room. Evening approached quickly, bringing with it a warm and relaxed atmosphere.

Jane felt a mix of emotions as she watched the others in the room between her goes at a variety of gentle children's games. Part of her wasn't looking forward to heading back to London the next day as she'd enjoyed her time at the farm so much, yet she had to find out from their elderly protector whether the adventure was over. Despite musing over the next day's practicalities, the biggest share of her thoughts was taken up with the awareness and dread that sooner or later she'd be on her own without Will and he'd be in danger once again.

Maggie was watching Jane and, as their eyes met, Jane blushed a little knowing that she'd been caught staring at Will and daydreaming. Maggie smiled and stood up, touching Jane's shoulder as she passed. Jane followed shortly after. Will looked up from his discussion with Jack over a world map and winked at Jane as she passed.

Maggie was starting to put clean dishes away in the kitchen when Jane walked in. Maggie, although now on her knees and reaching into the back of a low cupboard, knew from the footsteps that it was Jane who'd joined her. She stood up and closed the cupboard, then turned to Jane.

'Troubled?'

'A little.' Jane didn't want or need to lie. Maggie beckoned her to sit at the table and both women sat down next to each other. The older woman waited for Jane to talk. 'I don't quite know where to start.'

'Anywhere.' Jane laughed a little, more of a nervous puff than anything else. 'Shall I help?' Jane nodded. 'Alright. Well, I know what Will is planning. I know he's going to join up despite him and Jack trying to keep it from me at the moment. Is that what's bothering you love, Will leaving?'

Jane wasn't sure how Maggie was so certain of Will's plan, but nodded. 'Yes; that and so many other things.' She knew that she couldn't mention the events of recent weeks; Will's beatings, the exodus to Richmond Row, hiding at the house in London. 'Will wants me to leave the city too.'

'He won't want you there if he's not with you, with air raids every night now.' Maggie was right but Jane knew that her appraisal was just the tip of the iceberg as to why Will didn't want Jane in the city, especially alone. 'You really are more than welcome here; I don't need to tell you that. We'd love to have you.'

'Thank you Maggie.' Jane put her hand over Maggie's.

'You have to let him go love.' Maggie now took her turn to cover Jane's hand, sandwiching it between hers. 'We have to let our young men do what they know is right, no matter how it tears our hearts out.' Her eyes dipped momentarily, looking for a composure she'd temporarily lost. 'No matter what happens.' The last of four hands, Jane's now lay on top and completed the pile.

'I'm so terribly sorry for your loss Maggie.' Jane had said it before but never in the way she felt it now, in a moment where it meant more and touched her more. 'I really wish I'd met Harry.' Jane felt a squeeze from one of Maggie's hands beneath her own in the pile as they sat there entangled but not freeing themselves.

'Yes, so do I love.' Maggie looked thoughtful for a moment. 'You've not heard his voice or felt his embrace, but you've met him in Daniel, Sylvie and Jacob, in Jack and in me, in Will. You've seen a hundred parts of him in everyone who loved him.' Maggie smiled and seemed more at peace in her smile than before.

A quiet moment of connection followed. The two women sat together sharing but alone with their thoughts; happy and peaceful and hands still piled together.

'Are you alright ladies?' A gentle question from the doorway. Jane and Maggie turned to greet Will. On seeing that the two were genuinely smiling at him, and all was indeed alright, he felt it acceptable to joke. 'We suspected you might be in here knocking back the cooking sherry.' Maggie stood up and started scolding him, smacking at his backside with a tea towel. 'But I see you were just playing One Potato, Two!'

'Get away with you,' she called as she chased Will around the table pretending to give him a good hiding for his cheek. Jane was still laughing as the pair stopped their charade and Will pulled Maggie into his arms for a hug, just as Jane thought Harry might have done had he been there acting the fool instead of Will. He kissed the top of her head.

'Is it alright if I whisk Jane away mother?'

'Of course, go on.' Maggie said as she turned back towards the living room, giving Jane a warm and knowing look as she passed.

Will and Jane sat in the same spot they'd chosen during their first visit to the farm together. London rested in the distance, shrouded in darkness with hardly any illumination to be found. Jane sheltered under Will's arm, neither having put on a coat to venture into the cold night.

'Home in the morning then.' Will said.

'Yes.'

'I'm going to telephone Mrs Cartlyn. I can't wait any longer for her to call.'

'Good idea.' Jane wanted to know as much as Will did, but knew that an all clear from the old lady also signalled his permission to leave Jane.

At her response Will pulled back to look at her. 'You're not going to ask me to wait?' Jane shook her head. 'Why?'

'We can't wait forever. It's tiring looking over our shoulders all the time Will. We're spending so much time looking behind us we're not looking at or enjoying what's in front of us.'

'Profound.' Jane looked at Will, unsure whether he was making fun of her, but she couldn't read his expression in the evening light so she waited for him to carry on. 'It's funny. I'll be glad, obviously, to get rid of this weight that bears down on us, the horror I brought to our door, but part of me will be sad.'

'You're mad,' was Jane's jibe, although she agreed with him wholeheartedly.

'No. Not mad. I've enjoyed spending so much time with you. We wouldn't have been together half as much if all this hadn't happened. We'd have just been grabbing the occasional evening or Sunday afternoon. As it is, we've fitted a year into a few months. I've known you all my life Jane; somehow I've always known you. When we first met in the school hall it wasn't like meeting someone new, it just felt right.' Jane blushed, glad once more of the darkness that concealed her awkward glow.

'What do I do if you don't come back?'

Will pulled Jane closer. 'I will.' He could feel the tension in her shoulders and the dampness on her cheeks as he leaned in to kiss her, so he added. 'Besides, I've got quite used to living in sin.'

When Jane and Will returned to the farmhouse it was still relaxed and calm. The pair joined the others for their final evening there.

When Jane woke the next day she was surprised to see that it was almost ten o'clock. Rubbing the sleep from her eyes and a dream from her mind, she heard the sounds of activity downstairs; Maggie called to one of the children to take a message to Jack on the top field, another called for the whereabouts of their boots, the kettle whistled, a dog barked. Once she registered these sounds of morning routines, Jane jumped from the bed and washed and dressed as fast as she could. Just as she was finishing there was a light knock on the door before it opened and Will's smiling face appeared.

'Out of bed sleepy head.'

'Why didn't you wake me?' Jane wasn't amused, but Will was. He closed the door with his foot as he leapt across the room, tackling Jane to the bed in one swift movement. She struggled from his grasp and stood while he looked up at her, crestfallen. 'I'm cross Will. You should have woken me up, not left me to sleep like a spoilt guest.'

'Sorry.' Will took her hand and tried to pull her back down, but gave up at her resistance. 'Sorry.' He patted the bed in invitation and she begrudgingly sat down, prim and upright on the edge. He sat up next to her. 'Come on, let's not fight. We've got too much to do. As soon as we've spoken to Mrs Cartlyn, we have to get busy.' He moved to sit closer to her and slid each of his fingers between hers. 'There's a lot to organise. I need to give notice at the flat and get my things sorted. I'm going to leave all my kit here, and the Sunbeam; Maggie and Jack are happy for me to use the farm as a base. Makes sense as I'll be coming back here to see you whenever I'm home. We can stay in town for a few days. I'm not sure how long it'll be before I leave.' Will's words ran away from Jane, giving her no time to catch them or trip them up, voice her own or contradict. 'We need to return Mrs Cartlyn's key and her cash. And we'll need to take the Christmas tree down. There'll be your things at Mrs Foster's too; we'll need to collect those. And there's your notice to give at the Grandchester. I bet you'll want to catch up with the girls too. We can still stay at the flat while we're in town, if you're alright with that.' At a pause, Jane saw her chance.

'Yes, we have lots to do. But I'm not coming back to stay with Maggie and Jack, Will.' Eyes met and unspoken arguments danced between them. Both waited for the other, already knowing what they'd say. Will sighed. Jane bit her lip and watched his face. Eventually Will sighed again and stood up, restlessly moving round the room; straightening a picture, closing the wardrobe door.

'I can't make you change your mind can I?'

'No. Sorry.'

'If you're sorry, then why don't you stay?'

'I'm sorry I can't do what you want, not sorry that I'm going to stay in the city.'

'But if you're sorry...' Will didn't finish, knowing his argument was pointless. Instead, he left the room without saying any more while Jane sat on the bed feeling guilty as she watched him go. Although she knew that Will wanted the reassurance of her safety in his impending absence, and although the Halls would embrace her like family, Jane wanted to go home. Strangely, it was Will's absence that increased her need to be in the city; she needed her job, the busy hours, her girlfriends and the familiarity to help her through the coming months.

Jane packed her things ready to leave for home and started down the stairs. The stairs led to a door through which you stepped straight into the kitchen. As she reached the door and pressed her thumb to the latch she heard the Sunbeam start up in the yard. Opening the door and stepping into the warm kitchen, Maggie smiled up at her from her position by the back door. She was wiping the paws of the only one of their four dogs that came into the house.

'Hello love, he's just gone for a ride.'

'Yes, I heard.'

Maggie stood up, patting the little dog's head before she moved away. She pulled out a chair for Jane at the scrubbed table. 'Sit down love. Breakfast? Or just a cuppa?'

'I'll make it Maggie, you sit down.'

'Come on; let me look after my guests. You'll be off soon and it'll be a while before we see you.' As instructed, Jane let Maggie bustle about the kitchen.

'I told Will that I want to stay in the city.'

'Ah, right. I thought you might have, love.'

'He's angry with me.'

Maggie turned to Jane, now seated at the table playing with the corner of the redundant tea cosy. She moved towards Jane to take the tea cosy and held still Jane's fidgeting hands.

'No, love. He's not angry. He's just frightened for you.'

'I'm frightened for him. But if I'm home I'll be nearer to everything I know and I'll feel that I'm nearer to any news and nearer to him.' Jane replayed her words to herself. 'That sounds silly doesn't it?'

'Not at all.'

'I should stay here really, for Will. Then he'll at least have that weight lifted from his mind.'

Maggie shook her head, surprising Jane. 'No you shouldn't. Not if you don't want to. Do what's right for you love. Of course it would be wonderful to have you here and, yes, Will would be relieved to know you weren't in the city. But that's what *he* wants, Jane, and it's not up to him.' Maggie slipped the tea cosy onto the pot, giving it a friendly tap. 'We're here if you change your mind, or if you just want to visit.'

Jane silently questioned her decision not to stay at the farm as she chatted with Maggie about everyday things, nibbled some toast and waited for Will's return. When she heard the Sunbeam pull into the yard, she tried hard not to leap up. Maggie's intuition beat Jane to it and, before Jane had chance, Maggie handed her a large overcoat and tipped her head towards the door. 'Go on. Go and make it right with your boy.' Jane smiled as she took the coat from Maggie, giving her a quick kiss on the cheek before she opened the door to a gust of cold air.

As she turned the corner to the yard, Jane saw that Will was showing Daniel something on the bike. The two looked up as Jane approached and Daniel, ever mature and discreet, said a cheerful good morning to her then headed indoors.

Jane hugged the large coat tighter around her as she smiled tentatively at Will.

'Good ride?'

'Yep, she's running well. It's good to have her back. Sorry I left you. I just wanted to...' He hesitated, looking for the words to explain something he didn't understand. 'I don't know what I wanted.'

'It's fine, I understand.'

'No it's not fine, not really. It was childish to go off and leave you. I'm sorry.'

'Don't be.'

'Well I am, so there.' He winked, then sighed any humour away. 'I don't have any control Jane. Everything's running away with itself. Not so long ago, everything was right. I loved what I did, I had a great time in the city, Harry and the family were all here to visit. The only thing missing back then was you. Now I have you but nearly everything else is gone.' All of a sudden Will looked exasperated and tired. 'I want to stay; God Himself knows how much I want that. But I can't pretend that I shouldn't be doing my bit. I won't hide from it. I've got to go and I want to go now, not wait for conscription.' Jane understood and nodded. 'Things are just dripping though my hands like water, Jane. I can't get back to work, I can't do what I love, I couldn't sort out the Hugh Callaghan mess I made, I can't ease Maggie and Jack's grief. I miss the theatre, I miss home, I miss Harry. I'm going to miss you.' Will touched Jane's hand and, feeling iciness, took both into his to rub them. 'I have to join up, I want to; but once I've done that I'm theirs. I will have no power to do anything but what I'm there for. I asked you to stay at the farm because I just wanted to know that one person was the same, one person was safe. The one person that has to be safe is you. I don't want to control you Jane, I want to protect you.' Jane stepped further into Will's arms. A moment after she did so Will held her back to appraise her, noticing for the first time the coat that she wore. Jane, confused, suddenly understood. It was Harry's coat.

'I'll take it off.' Jane started to slip her arms from the warm sleeves but Will stopped her.

'No, leave it on; you'll get cold. Maybe it can't always be me wrapping you up, maybe Harry's sending me a message.' Will laughed; it was a real, full belly laugh. 'You little blighter Harry,' Will continued to chuckle as his eyes scanned the sky and the stars that were still scattered there. 'Wherever you are mate, you're getting in between me and my girl; we're having a serious chat here.' Will took Jane's hands again and looked at her, still smiling. 'Maybe that's the point. We're being too serious. We can't be serious when you look like one half of Flanagan and Allen.' Jane looked down at herself in the oversized coat and chuckled. 'Come on, Flanagan,' Will said, pulling Jane towards the barn, 'let's see if the kids still use the lair.'

Continuing the joke that so amused him, Will sang Underneath the Arches a la Bud Flanagan as he led an intrigued Jane into the stone barn then helped her up a rickety ladder to the largely empty hay loft. There, some old hessian sacks and wooden crates had been roughly assembled amongst the farmyard detritus to form a hideaway. A few sheets of paper and half a dozen pencils were on the floor of the den, along with a deck of cards and a lone jumper. Will took Jane's hand as she stepped amongst the tools of childhood. Will settled on a crate and invited Jane to do the same.

'We used to be up here a lot. It was quite an adventure, being on the farm.'

'I can imagine.'

'We thought we had so many secret places, but Maggie and Jack knew them all; they just pretended not to. Harry and I would hide up here and spy on Jack. Of course, he knew we were here all along but he never let on; he played his part every time. He'd pretend to hear something and look round so we'd hide.

We'd duck down and try to muffle our laughter. Then Jack'd be on his way and we always thought we'd got one over on him.'

Jane looked down at Harry's coat, optimism light in her mind. 'Will, I still carry hope that Harry will return. He's missing, but he could be injured somewhere, hiding, or a prisoner of war. When it's all over, he might come walking down that lane again.'

'I know there's that tiny chance, and some people might cling to that. We've not given up on Harry without any thought, but I think we're all grieving now because we don't believe we could survive it twice. But, saying that, deep down I really do believe he's gone Jane.' Will's voice splintered as he spoke and he struggled to find composure.

Capturing and holding his eyes Jane deepened the subject, hoping to provide some comfort. 'I know you were laughing when you were telling Harry off a minute ago, but do you really think he's looking down at you?'

Will shrugged. 'I'm not sure. I believe in God and I believe in something after death. Do you?'

Jane nodded. 'Yes. I like to think, wherever he is, that Harry knows how much you all miss him and that everyone's alright.'

'He knows.' Will sounded certain, but the conversation was getting too serious for him. 'Maybe reincarnation's the thing. Maybe he'll come back as a woman. I sincerely hope he's not an actress; it would be mighty awkward if I had to kiss him.' Will pretended to gag as Jane shoved him, before pulling the coat tightly around her again against the cold. Will saw her shiver. 'If I go first, I'm coming back as that coat.' He raised an eyebrow suggestively at the way Jane hugged the coat so closely around her body.

'Well, I'll still be a woman. But I've always wanted to be a Jemima not a Jane. And if I go first,' Jane batted the comment straight back to Will, 'if I go first I'm coming back to check up on you.'

The playfulness stopped at Jane's words and Will looked serious.

'If you go first, Sunshine, I'll be waiting for you. I promise.'

Despite the light tone, the two looked at each other feeling something deeper in the playfulness.

'Another promise Will?'

'One I will keep.'

'Will, I asked you yesterday what I'm going to do if you don't come back. You just said that you will, you will come back.'

'I know.' Will watched her, dreading more.

'You just tell me you'll be alright and make a joke, or change the subject. I know that we can't tell what's going to happen and I know you see the possibilities. There are thousands of women waiting, every day waiting and dreading, but I don't know how to. How will I do it? The possibilities scare me to death, Will; more than any man with a thug's fist or a gun. And I don't know what to do.'

'I don't know how to answer you Jane, really I don't. You know what I'm like; I want to reassure you and make you laugh.' He took a deep breath and ran a hand through his hair. 'I lay awake for a long time last night.'

'I'm sorry. You should have woken me.'

'No, don't be silly. It was all good.' Will fastened the top button of the big coat under Jane's chin and then pulled her closer to him. 'I decided that I don't know what I believe, but I know what I don't. I don't believe that after finding you, death would be the end. I don't pretend to know how it works, but there has to be more. I know we're forced to think of this now because of how the world is. In different times we wouldn't be questioning this for us until we're old and grey. We'll know the answers one day, Sunshine, but not now. I know you're scared of me dying and I can't promise that I won't.' His voice hinted at humour for a moment, despite the subject, then the sparkle of jest in his tone was gone. 'But I promise you with everything I have that

I will try to stay safe.' He could feel from Jane's shoulders and her breathing that she was silently weeping and gently wiped the tears away with his hand. 'I promise I'll do my best.'

'That's two more promises Will. I count three in the last five minutes.'

'Yes, and I promise these I'll keep.'

'Four.'

The seesaw of silly and serious stopped tipping to and fro, settling somewhere in between. Reality yawned itself awake to remind them it was time to return to the city. Jane and Will once more said farewell to their friends and prepared to leave. Maggie, Jack and the children hugged Will tightly not knowing how many more times they'd see him before he joined all the other men answering the call to arms. The extra firm hold didn't go unnoticed by Jane, who knew that it wouldn't be too long before she had to do the same. She kicked the thought away and tried to do the same to the ripping feeling in her chest.

As they rode through the lanes leaving the farm behind, with its waving hands and tearful eyes, Jane held firmly to Will. She knew that she too held him more closely than she needed. As they reached recognisable streets, Jane tried hard to pretend that they were coming home to their old routines; Will to the theatre and some new production, she to the Grandchester, he to his flat, she to Mrs Foster's.

Will had suggested that he and Jane stop off on the way home to make the dreaded and longed for telephone call to Mrs Cartlyn. He was loathe to wait until they were in London to make the call, but didn't want there to be any way that the Halls might get even the slightest scent of anything unusual by calling from the farm. The answer was to stop en route, so they pulled in to a little country pub at about their halfway point. Will bought them both drinks and then made the call while Jane waited, quiet and alone, in a corner of the bar. He returned quickly and slid along the old wooden settle to sit next to Jane.

'It's over Sunshine. It's all done.' He didn't smile, but raised his glass as Jane copied the act.

'That's that then.'

'Yep, that's that.'

They both knew what would come next.

As they continued their onward journey, a surreal haze settled on them. After weeks of adrenalin fuelled fear, of aggression, uncertainty, and murder, it was over. The turmoil and speed was halted in a flash. It was done.

The day was an odd one. A strange deflation settled on the travellers as they reached London. The city, still festive, had enjoyed a brief respite from the daily bombings but no-one dared to hope that it would last. Riding through streets they didn't need to travel to get to Will's flat, the pair braced themselves; they wanted to see but didn't want to see what damage had been done as they rode past places they hadn't been near for a long time. New holes gaped where homes should have been, but the Grandchester, Mrs Foster's building, the Majesty and the building which housed Will's flat still stood, defiant and proud.

The pair based themselves at Will's, unable to force a parting into separate lodgings. Until Will left they'd stay together, whether that was for days or weeks. Will suggested that no-one except the girls and the Halls should know that they were flouting convention and living together without a wedding ring; Jane no longer cared what anyone thought. After the unquestioning acceptance of the Halls, Jane's reticence was washed away; there were more important things to worry about than what society thought. As they continued with their plans, Jane and Will were strangely subdued by the anti-climax. Rather than the elation they'd both expected, the normality and foreboding brought a sad quiet to them.

Mrs Foster had packed up the remaining few belongings that Jane had in her room but kindly offered her room back when Jane and Will collected them. She explained that the number of people wanting lodgings in the city had drastically reduced so the room was still hers if she wanted it. Jane thanked her for everything she'd done and the welcome she still offered, but gracefully declined.

The pair then went back to the house that had been their brief sanctuary when they first returned to London. Both felt a pang of sadness as they removed the trimmings from the tree and it, in turn, hastily dropped its needles to the floor. Will disposed of the ailing tree while Jane carefully packed the redundant decorations into a cardboard box, to be treasured and carried with her, and then ensured that the house would be left as they'd first found it.

On hearing of Jane's return and anticipating her need for somewhere to stay Florence hastily spoke with her bohemian aunt who happily offered her third spare room to Jane, blithely declaring the more the merrier as she downed the last of a brandy before wafting from the house. Florence and Aggie were delighted at the thought of having Jane under the same roof as them again. Although Jane knew she would enjoy spending time with two of her dearest friends, she couldn't look forward to it, as moving in would mean that Will had left.

Will visited the nearest recruiting office alone, signing his allegiance and his life over to the crown. He was told to report the following week, at the very beginning of January 1941, for six weeks of basic training in Kent. After completing that, he would be deemed ready and able for service and his unit would then await, or immediately receive, their posting.

On 28th December Jane returned to work at the Grandchester. Whatever had transpired between Mrs Cartlyn, her erstwhile fairy godmother, and the hotel manager had ensured the safety of Jane's position.

Her colleagues were all pleased to welcome her back, asking after her poorly mother who had been rendered ill by Mrs Cartlyn in a deftly distributed lie. Jane was pleased to report a full recovery.

Familiarising herself with the comings and goings of the guests, Jane scanned through the hotel register. She was saddened afresh to see the absence of Hugh Callaghan as a resident and took a deep breath to calm a sudden flash of nerves. Tracing her finger down the pages she stopped when she noticed another change, this time unexpected. The Hendersons had also left. They'd checked out of the hotel two weeks previously. Jane thumbed through the future bookings, waiting for their names to appear again, but she found nothing. She didn't know why they'd left and had made no advance plans for return; her mind tossed round the possibility that they'd decided to return permanently to their safe country home, or that Mr Henderson's work had invited a move, or possibly that Mrs Henderson, Maria, had forced the change. Jane was sure Mrs Cartlyn would know their reasons, but she wouldn't ask. There were many things Jane wondered about, a myriad of questions that could be posed, but there were an even greater number that she didn't want the answers to.

After finishing work on her first day back Jane visited Mrs Cartlyn, discreetly slipping up the employee staircase with no-one knowing that she hadn't left for home.

Jane knocked lightly on the door, feeling a nervous déjà vu. The old woman called for her to let herself in and Jane once again found herself in the company of the small but formidable woman who'd saved her and Will from something she still didn't fully understand. It seemed an age and a second since their previous meeting in the plush Grandchester suite.

'Hello Jane. Welcome back.'

'Thank you Mrs Cartlyn.' Jane gently closed the door. 'It's lovely to be home at last.' It was a benign semi-truth and Jane turned to see Mrs Cartlyn watching her silently.

'Yes, I'm sure it is.' She paused and watched.

Jane had given a lot of thought to Mrs Cartlyn and her relationship with Mrs Cavendish, discussing this many times with Will. What had transpired in their past caused both question and tremor. Jane hoped that Mrs Cavendish's appeal to Mrs Cartlyn for help was made because of the latter's position; she was a wealthy woman of influence who would quite naturally see Jane regularly at Jane's place of work. Hand in hand with this, she was clearly a trusted friend of Mrs Cavendish, someone who would enquire easily and frequently after Jane and the other girls as required. Jane prayed that the connection between the two women was an innocent one, and nothing to do with the hidden life that Mrs Cartlyn had led. Jane loved Mrs Cavendish and knew that she was a kind and good person. Knowing the strength of her own feeling was the reason Jane chose not to push for any revelation or disclosure from Mrs Cartlyn, or to ever raise the subject of their past with either woman. Enough was enough.

Mrs Cartlyn, in spite of herself, seemed marginally pleased to see Jane. However, business-like and brusque, she accepted the house keys and dismissed Jane's reassurance that the house was clean and tidy as unnecessary information. Despite their recent history and Mrs Cartlyn's warm and generous care of her and Will, Jane knew that she and the remarkable woman would always have an outwardly uninvolved and detached relationship, even if deep down there was mutual affection. Jane wondered if Mrs Cartlyn felt the same warm fondness that she did, although she knew that she had much more reason to feel affection for the old lady than the other way around.

'Mrs Cartlyn?'

'Yes.'

'After today I promise I won't ask another question that has anything to do with the things you've told me; but can I ask you how we move on? I mean, seeing things and knowing things, how can we carry on without being eaten away by...' she struggled with the words 'by events?'

Mrs Cartlyn sighed deeply and turned an impressive cluster of diamonds round and round on her finger.

'For some, nothing is needed. For others, time and answers. You fall into the *others* category. I'd have been disappointed if you hadn't, as then I'd have been wrong about you. You care, and so you should.'

'Time I get Mrs Cartlyn, but answers I don't have.'

'Then I'll give you some.' Jane hadn't been invited to, but she sat down on the edge of the chair opposite her host. One thing Jane hadn't expected was any kind of revelation or insight into what had happened, just hoping for some cover-all advice as to how to move on. Now that answers might actually be offered, she wasn't sure how much she did want to know. Mrs Cartlyn seemed to notice Jane's apprehension. 'Don't worry Jane, I'm not about to divulge anything that will be a threat to national security.' Jane relaxed a little, still feeling the pull of an invisible force that suggested she leave now before she found out anything she might later wish she hadn't.

'Please don't tell me anything about Mrs Cavendish.'

'I don't intend to. But I think knowing a little more about what your young man and Hugh Callaghan have been through will help.' Jane nodded. 'I think we all know what the gossips in this hotel say about Hugh.' Jane hoped she wasn't blushing, knowing that she'd been party to such conversations among the staff. 'I'm sure some of their words have bordered on accuracy. He was a ladies' man, debonair yet roguish. He was also a man's man; sharing a drink, a cigarette and a risqué anecdote. But his exploits in the bars and clubs, and I don't doubt in the bedrooms, were for a purpose.'Mrs Cartlyn looked at Jane and revealed an affectionate glint. 'I'm sure that there were aspects of his occupation that he sincerely enjoyed.' Jane blushed a little, wondering what the man had done in the line of duty. 'My late husband certainly saw their profession more as a calling than merely a job. I know Hugh Callaghan was the same. Both would do anything required in the pursuit of their goal, for the protection of their country.'

Jane spoke so quietly that Mrs Cartlyn had to lean forward to hear her.

'So it's as everyone thought. Hugh was spying, selling secrets?' She didn't dare mention Mr Cartlyn, although she felt the answer would be all inclusive.

Mrs Cartlyn smiled.

'It's so simple to anyone not involved. Hugh's profession has been around for hundreds of years in one form or another. Wherever there is fighting or discord, or war, there are people who are employed to find out more, to listen, to delve and to dig. I don't like the word spy; I prefer scout or emissary. We reconnoitre.' We? We? Jane felt herself turn hot, then cold. 'Yes, I said *we*.' Mrs Cartlyn seemed party to Jane's thoughts. 'You look flustered girl, would you like some water?'

'No, I'm fine thank you.'

Mrs Cartlyn pursed her lips for a moment then continued.

'My husband and I met twenty-five years ago, when another war was threatening all our lives. We did what we could to help; we fought our own battles that most people didn't see. We were the hidden army. Hugh was doing the same. Sadly, through a chain of events I won't bore you with, he was noticed by some individuals and that forced him to change tactics.' She sighed. 'Sadly these tactics were misconstrued by some.'

'I don't understand Mrs Cartlyn.'

'Some... *groups* thought he'd turned traitor. I didn't realise that Maria Henderson subscribed to this view until I found out she'd intercepted the message you sent via Florence.'

'But Mrs Cartlyn, why didn't you tell me this earlier? You didn't get the message at all? Did you not know that Maria came to see me, give me poison?' Jane started to feel sick.

'Telling you would have served no purpose Jane; when I next saw you, all was done.' Mrs Cartlyn leaned forward and poured a glass of water from a glistening crystal decanter, then handed it to Jane. Jane tipped the glass to her lips, and then coughed as the burning liquid scolded her tongue. 'A stiff drink Jane, slow down.'

'I thought it was water,' she spluttered.

'Anyway, remonstrations aside, I didn't tell you but now I am. Maria Henderson genuinely believed Hugh was a traitor and a danger and took the steps she thought right.'

'He wasn't a traitor?'

'No. He led the Germans to believe he had turned. He did too good a job; he had to make everyone believe it was genuine for it to work. Only a few knew the actual story. He was true to King and country to the end.'

'But *you* knew?'

'Not for sure, not until recently. I had to dig very deep and call on old...' she paused, then threw caution to the wind, 'well, old lovers to be frank. I had to call on men I'd not spoken with in years to find out the truth. Some now occupy certain positions of importance in the war office.'

Jane stumbled over words and thoughts and questions, images of an old woman's past life of secrecy and scandal rushing past her eyes. She shook all thought of Mrs Cartlyn's past from her mind.

'So Hugh was a good man pursued by those who thought he'd betrayed his country? And he was asking Will to be him, to take his risk so Hugh could be somewhere else?'

Mrs Cartlyn nodded.

'In very simple terms, yes. He was watched by those on both sides who weren't sure of his motives and he was sought out by others on both sides who thought they knew his motives. He needed space and time, and Will provided that.'

'And the thing he came to ask for at Richmond Row?'

'The last thing he asked Will to do was for him to be seen to attend a big meeting at Whitehall. It was intentionally leaked that a top secret meeting was going to take place over several days. There were many reasons for the false meeting and Hugh also saw it as his opportunity to get out of the country. He would be going to Berlin, heading into the thick of it, and unlikely to come back. He needed the eyes that normally watched him to be watching Will, and yes, he told Will they might not stop at watching.'

'Will knew he might have been killed.'

'Will knew,' nodded Mrs Cartlyn.

Jane sat back in her chair and took another sip of the liquid that was normally so foreign to her. Her voice was still quiet and emotional.

'Will believed in him.'

'Yes, he did. I did too. We were right. And Maria Henderson was misinformed.'

Jane's mind pictured the exquisite form of Maria Henderson, also fighting for her country but aiming at a friend not a foe.

'Did Hugh have any family Mrs Cartlyn?' Mrs Cartlyn seemed surprised by the question.

'No Jane, I don't believe he did. An only child from a wealthy family, all long gone; he lived and died for his country.' Mrs Cartlyn watched Jane, then summarised. 'The answers are all there Jane. It's complicated yet simple. Now you must let it rest somewhere.'

Sunday 29 December 1940

Jane, although pleased to be working again and relieved that there was no longer a need to look over her shoulder or behind a door, was looking forward to the next day; despite only returning to work on the Saturday, Sunday had worked out as her rostered day off. It would be Will and Jane's last full day together before Will was due to leave a few days later.

Will's flatmate was away over the Christmas period, so Jane knew it was Will that she heard in the kitchen when she woke up on Sunday morning. It must be Will. For the tiniest moment, a sickness of fear rose through her body as she heard the sound of movement and feared it might not be Will but someone else, possibly the missing Jim. Jane sat up slowly. She held her breath, swallowing back the nausea that threatened. The flat fell silent. No movement and no sound. Then the whistling of You Are My Sunshine. Jane relaxed and breathed again. Only Will. Even though Jane knew that their brush with Hugh's secret life was over, it had left a faint shadow that she sometimes stepped into. She'd asked Will on more than one occasion if he felt the same, but he'd just joked and smiled and reassured, always trying to make her feel better.

She lay back in bed listening and enjoying the sound of nothing but the two of them alone. Before she could follow Will to the kitchen, he appeared in the doorway carrying a tray.

'That's not fair, I wanted to wake you with breakfast in bed,' he grumbled, as Jane sat up again. Laying the tray on the covers, and revealing its bounty of tea and toast, he sat down at the foot of the bed. 'What would you like to do? The whole day is ours.'

Jane had thought about today so much already. 'Would you like to visit Maggie and Jack? Before you leave?'

Will shook his head. 'No. I said goodbye the other day and I spoke with them yesterday while you were at work. They know today's our day.' Jane opened her mouth to speak but was silenced. 'No arguing.'

'In that case, I don't know. Shall we go for a ride? When will you get Sunbeam to the farm?'

'I already arranged with Jack that he'll come next week and get her and my things.'

'Oh, right.' Jane's stomach lurched as the arrangements became final.

'Come on Sunshine,' Will beamed. 'Look,' he leapt up and ripped back the curtains 'the sun's shining, all is well.' He came back to the bed and handed Jane her cup of tea. 'Come on, it's spoily day. I'm going to run you a bath.' Then he added in a conspiratorial stage whisper 'and I have girls' stuff to put in it; all manner of bubbles and salts in pink bottles' and then he was gone. Jane was trying to be happy as she leaned back against the pillows; the only thing she could do was to go along with Will's buoyant mood and hope that the carefree feeling would be catching.

Jane bathed and dressed as quickly as was possible without seeming ungrateful for Will's pampering and they set off on the Sunbeam in the winter sunshine. Neither was sure where they were going, and neither cared, as they rode further from the city and the scenery before them changed.

They finally stopped in Marlow, eating lunch in a friendly pub and then strolling through the town. They crossed the suspension bridge and wandered into the church which sat next to the river just a few steps from the bridge. The church was quiet, between the morning and evening services, and Will and Jane sat down side by side in one of the oak pews.

They sat quietly with their thoughts for a while before Will whispered, without turning his gaze from the altar, 'This would be a great church for a wedding.'

Jane didn't turn her head either, but responded with, 'yes, it would.'

'A nice town to raise a family in too.'

'Yes, it is.'

Then footsteps were heard and they sat in silence again as a lady walked past them to the altar; she crossed herself, whispered a few words, paused for a moment then turned to walk back down the aisle nodding to Jane and Will as she passed. They nodded and smiled back. When she'd left, Will whispered again.

'How quickly do you think we can do it?'

'Do what?'

'Get married.'

Jane was taken completely by surprise at Will's words, but chose to assume his question was hypothetical after his previous vow to wait.

'Oh, I don't know; a couple of weeks maybe? I really don't know. Special licences would be quicker I suppose.'

Will finally turned to look at Jane and she knew that his question wasn't what she had assumed.

'I'm sorry Jane; I've misled you. Unintentionally.' Jane frowned. 'I gave a great big speech about waiting, not rushing. But I can't.' Jane's heart started to beat dangerously fast as Will stood up. He gently took her hand and pulled her to her feet, leading her from the pew and down the aisle towards the altar. A few steps from the altar they stopped.

For a moment they both stood there in the light from the window behind the altar. As the December sun shone into the stained glass it sent a myriad of muted reflections through the air inside the quiet church and threw them onto the flagstones at their feet. Jane wanted to speak but couldn't; she wanted to breathe normally but couldn't; she wanted to slow her heart but couldn't.

Will bent down on one knee as Jane's emotions wobbled between nausea, desire and delirium. Taking both her hands tenderly in his and looking up at Jane in the beautiful kaleidoscope of dappled light, he proposed.

When they finally left the church, Will apologised.

'I'm sorry I don't have a ring yet.'

'I don't mind. I don't need a ring.'

'I didn't plan to propose. Not now, I mean. You must think I'm such a hypocrite. I really did mean all I said about waiting, or I believed I did. But sitting in the church, at that moment…I don't know what happened, it just seemed that there would never be a better moment.'

'There won't be.'

They strolled on hand in hand through the town and back to the Sunbeam, waiting shiny and patient for their return.

'We ought to head back I guess.'

Jane nodded, disappointed. 'I suppose so.'

Standing by their faithful transport, Will looked at Jane with a glint in his eyes and a little boy smile on his face.

'What?' Jane half laughed. 'What is it? Why are you laughing?'

'Seeing as I've completely contradicted myself by proposing, how about we see if we can get married before I leave?' His teasing eyes were hopeful.

Jane smiled the smile of an accomplice. 'Yes. Yes please.'

As usual, the ride home seemed quicker than the ride out. It seemed even more so this time as Jane's mind danced lightly amid thoughts and plans. Could they get married that quickly? Was there any way of dashing down to see her mum, or could she catch the next train to London? How would the girls react? Jane wasn't sure whether the cold dampness on her cheek was a tear forced by the cold wind or a tear driven by joy.

Soon Will and Jane were greeted by old sights once more. They pulled up a street away from the flat and climbed from the motorbike.

'Home again,' Jane reported unhappily.

'That we are.' Will rocked the machine onto its stand and turned to look at Jane. 'What next? Fancy doing anything in particular?'

'Not really.'

'Well then, how about we freshen up at the flat and have a drink or something then go for a long newly-betrothed-couple wander? It's been quiet overhead the last few days so why don't we head up towards the palace and then through the square mile. I might even take you in somewhere for a celebratory pint.' He winked.

'Sounds perfect.'

They walked slowly to the flat, trying to make the most of every minute of the day and hoping that the slower they walked the slower time would pass. Refreshed and keen to continue the evening for as long as possible, they left after adding hats and scarves to fight against the cold.

The warm romance of the city couldn't be dampened by the sight of bomb damage or preparation. Boarded windows and sandbags were so common they'd almost become invisible, as had the white criss-cross of window tape and the occasional movement of a fire watcher on the top of a tall building.

Will and Jane wandered further into the city where financial institutions and offices stood quiet and dark, waiting for the active bustle of Monday morning business just hours away.

'Come on, it's almost six, let's head somewhere more lively and find some supper.'

'I'm happy just to keep walking Will. I'm not really hungry anyway.'

'Alright, but I want us to be near a shelter. Let's turn towards home and see where our feet take us on the way.'

As they turned to start the long walk in the general direction of home, the familiar noise of fighter planes burned in the clouds. Will's hand tightened around Jane's and his footsteps sped, eager to get her to safety. Jane found that her steps didn't follow suit, so keen was she to make the evening's solitude last. Will was now almost pulling her along, aiming for the protection of the nearest station while Jane was unable to see anything in the evening ahead of them but the jamming together of hundreds of people instead of the closeness of just two.

'Come on sweetheart, step to it. We're streets away yet and those planes sound like they're gaining on us.'

Jane couldn't answer. Her reluctance to join the masses of sheltering people and lose her time alone with Will was scrubbed away. Her ears told her that tonight was different. Somehow the noises above them had changed. She couldn't pinpoint how, but the humming seemed greater and more urgent. The air raid siren called out to everyone, warning and pushing, calling and preparing.

As they got closer to sanctuary the urgency of the situation became clearer and louder; civilians appeared dragging loved ones and rushing towards safety, firemen converged pulling stirrup pumps and running away from safety. Calls and shouts carried through the streets as people hurried towards shelter. It took moments for the flood of incendiary bombs to begin dropping. Amidst the onslaught of explosions and terror as death fell from dark skies, people cried and ran and sirens screamed and water pumped.

In the distance the yawning opening of an underground station called to Will and Jane as the whole city seemed to quake beneath the vicious onslaught of explosion and fire. Flames could be seen reaching towards the sky, lighting up the buildings beneath the clouds and providing hot points of reference for the next wave of aircraft to use.

As a new flock of planes drew near, the terrible droning got louder and the machines that were the cause could just about be picked out against the fire flooded sky. Will knew the planes would be overhead before he and Jane could make it to the station and, seeing it as the only option, dragged Jane under the concrete archway to a pub's side entrance. He pinned her tightly against the wall of the arch and reached his arms up to cross them over her head, desperate to anchor them there against the brick and provide what protection he could against any masonry that might fall as London burned around them.

Sixty Years Later

As the train entered the tunnel, Jem winced. She didn't like the sensation of her eardrums filling with warm water and all sound becoming a watery echo in her head. She swallowed a couple of times then pinched her nose between her fingers and blew. The relief was momentary as her ears filled again; for the length of the tunnel, she would repeatedly hold her nose and blow.

Jem's eardrums seemed to suck in and she closed her eyes as she held her nose yet again. The noise within the train changed as the sound of the train itself changed. It seemed to slow and lose its smooth speeding run along the tracks; it felt strangely slower and the motion less smooth. It took longer to explain than to experience and no sooner had Jem thought about it than the tunnel was left behind and the journey continued in the daylight again. Jem knew they'd left the tunnel as the echoing sounds which bounced from the tunnel walls were lost to space and air; sunlight now bounced from Jem's closed eyelids, rather than the dull luminescence of the carriage lighting alone. She gave one last blow and let go of her nose as she opened her eyes.

Fran laughed and nudged her with her elbow.

'Stop it Jem; you'll blow your brains out through your ears if you're not careful.'

'It's horrible though, isn't it? I hate that feeling. It's the pressure inside the tunnel isn't it? It's odd how that happens.' Jem liked to have an explanation for everything. She liked knowledge and lists and plans and preparation.

Fran, on the other hand, was more spontaneous and laid back and 'take it as it comes'.

Jem rummaged in her roomy bag and pulled out a map of the underground.

'Right, the theatre tickets are here.' She patted the inside pocket of her jacket to indicate their whereabouts, then opened out the map. 'It's the southbound Bakerloo that we need - 5 stops to Piccadilly.'

Fran leaned her head on Jem's shoulder and sighed dramatically.

'What would I do without you Jemima?' Jem shrugged her away, laughing.

'That's it, mock, but I like to know we have the tickets and everything. Just imagine getting there and finding that we've left the tickets behind.'

'A bit late to check now. They can hardly turn the train around.' She patted Jem's hand. 'Don't worry so much. And I don't know why on earth you have this.' She snatched the map. 'It's not like we've never been before.'

The sisters grinned at each other and sat in happy silence as the train hurried onwards and fields and towns passed anonymously by.

Jem found herself listening. Once she'd tuned in she couldn't then tune out from the women in the seats just behind. One of the party of three was obviously sitting across the aisle, so the more vociferous of the two women behind was very kindly talking louder so her friend could hear. Jem, and quite likely everyone else in the carriage, was treated to a guided tour of the woman's ailments and what pills and medication (including full drug names) that she took to combat these. Her companion concurred and sympathised in all the appropriate places, but Jem wondered if she was a little embarrassed by her travel mate. As well as her ailments, the woman told of her neighbour's friend's cousin's wife who had passed suddenly away, of her own prodigiously talented grandchildren, her plans for the weekend in London and what she'd heard about the hotel that they'd booked. She spoke about their rooms and gave a history of the hotel, being built on the site of a rather grand hotel that had been bombed during the war.

As Jem heard the ongoing tales she glanced about trying to block out the women behind, and noticed the solitary traveller just across the aisle. She'd boarded the train at the last stop, quite close to the venue of a music festival, and wore a flowing purple, white and yellow tie-dyed cotton dress that kissed the floor, a faded denim jacket and muddy green wellington boots. When she boarded she had a full set of very long crimson nails (a little incongruous with the earthy and free spirited outfit) and she was now sitting by the window biting at these false additions, only looking away from the view to glance down at her hands and pick at the remnants of the red appendages. By the time she got off, all traces of red would be gone and in their place bare nibbled stubs and ripped cuticles. Her bohemian but slightly eccentric style struck a distant chord with Jem, imagining her in years to come (but somehow visualising it in the past) as some ageing nonconformist with a floaty home and an equally floaty circle of friends.

In front of the lone woman was another chatty person. A very tall man, obvious by the way his legs were folded into the gap between his seat and the one in front. He spoke occasionally to a companion Jem couldn't see and had the merest hint of an accent even though his English was perfect. He wore a very large watch and, on the other wrist, a wide curvy silver bangle. He had the biggest hands Jem had ever seen. To pass his journey he watched a film on his laptop, ears plugged into the sound by white plugs and a long wire. He occasionally laughed out loud and pointed something out to his travelling companion, but that was preferable to the incessant chatter from behind. His softy accented voice and large stature seemed familiar. She could picture him standing in front of a fireplace, flames filling the grate behind, but didn't have a clue why.

Jem decided that she really should try not to be so romantic with her thoughts; even the immaculate old lady sitting at the very front of the carriage had begged recognition when Jem had boarded the train. The lady had been looking out of the window and slowly turning round a rather large diamond that adorned her finger. She turned as Jem walked past; Jem smiled but the old lady just gave her a sort of quarter smile, her lips barely moving, like it was foreign to her.

The quietest passengers in the immediate vicinity were the two men in front of Jem and her sister. Jem had seen them get on when she and Fran did; they both wore ripped jeans, one sported a vest top revealing tattoos and hairy arms, the other a grey sweatshirt. The man with the t-shirt had an intricate spiky hairdo which was shaved at the temples and his friend had no hair at all, just the finest hint of blond stubble covering his round head. All you could hear from them was quiet chat and the occasional psst sound of escaping carbonation as they discreetly opened their next can of lager. Not everyone was like their stereotype.

Jem smiled to herself as she absorbed the people around her, thinking how she was currently and briefly connected with all these individuals on this journey. No-one knew who else would be on this train as they boarded or what their stories might be. Jem often found herself extending normal situations in her thoughts; she would daydream, or maybe even fantasise, and come up with 'what ifs'. She found herself thinking of a scenario, not in words but in images which told their own story. There was no narrative, just visual ideas. Her cerebral pictures weren't based on fear or panic, but on her thoughts about human nature and interaction - 'If we were detached from the rest of the train and found our carriage jammed in a tunnel miles from anywhere, how would we all react and interact? Who would not be at all like we perceive them? Would the tall man with big hands be the protector or the clown? Most likely the two lager drinkers would be the hidden gems and the saviours of the day. Would festival girl be the laid-back earth mother type, or did her nail biting hint at a more nervous disposition? Maybe the woman behind would throw off her mantle of annoying chatterbox and become the warm matriarch of us all?' Jem was a dreamer who loved to drift; to see a glorious old building and wonder at its past, or an ancient tree and question who the many people had been who'd sat in its shade; she loved history and art and music and theatre, with an almost nostalgic fondness of the 30s and 40s, an era long before her time.

'Jem.' Fran nudged her and leaned past her to look out of the window. 'Stop daydreaming. We're nearly there. Next stop Paddington.'

Jem smiled at her sister and felt the flutter of anticipation that she always felt when coming to London. This visit, for a West End show, was excused as the sisters' Christmas gift to themselves even though it was December the 29th. Although born and raised in the beauty of the South West of England, London managed to pull her into its embrace and every excuse to visit (be it for the theatre, museums and galleries, sightseeing or shopping) felt somehow familiar and comfortable but delicately laced with expectancy and excitement.

The End of an Era

As soon as Jane heard the sky screaming, she'd known. Everyone knew. It was coming. It was coming again. No chance of making it underground this time, or into a cupboard under the stairs. 'Oh God,' Jane whispered and she brought the palms of her hands together as she closed her eyes and prayed. Noticing her trembling, a hand slid down to find hers. In that tiniest splinter of a second Jane turned to look up at Will who looked down at her, his face lit from the shadows by the burning red of a city on fire; he held her gaze with an invisible cord to express a thousand things to her in that moment, just in case it was their last. His eyes said don't worry, just keep looking at me. Just keep looking at me.

The shrieking stopped for a second as the world ceased turning. Then all was black and all was silent.

Or Maybe the Beginning...

So when you die the last thing you lose is the power to hear...

Jane. Jane. The man's voice was calling her frantically from an indeterminate distance. It sounded as though she listened through water. Everything hurt. Pain was everywhere but nowhere. His voice betrayed emotional pain as he fought to wake her, to pull her back to him. He was next to her, holding her, above her, all around her. Yet he was far away.

Jem. Jemima, can you hear me? Jem, please be alright. Jem. A woman's voice now. One she knew like her own. It drew her through the watery consciousness, getting closer with each word. It called a name she knew was hers. A hand reached to touch her face.

But then the man's voice called to her again.

Oh please God, please. Come back to me Jane, please, open your eyes. Wake up Sunshine, the desperate voice beseeched. Don't leave me, please. She knew he called to her, a voice crying a name that was right, that was hers, but his words sounded more distant with each second and as much as she tried to reach out to him she couldn't summon the strength. She couldn't open her eyes or force any movement from her body. Her will was no match for the stone from which her muscles seemed to be hewn. With all her might she tried to touch the man who called to her, to open her eyes and see him. Her body wouldn't do as she begged it; there was no power within her and she couldn't fight anymore.

He whispered a promise to wait for her. Another promise. Why did she notice that? And then his voice was gone, and all she heard were his cries as he cradled her and rocked her gently to and fro. And all she felt were his hot tears falling onto her cooling skin as he lost her.

Awakening

'Oh thank God.' Fran cried. Jem's eyes slowly blinked open and began to focus on her sister's tear streaked face through the slowly clearing fogginess behind her eyes. 'Can you hear me, are you alright? Where does it hurt?' As Jem slowly started to absorb the scene above her she saw more concerned faces and heard noise, commotion, the wail of a siren. Not a bomb's wail but confirmation that help was coming or help was there. But why would it be a bomb, why would someone, a man, call her Jane? Why did the name feel absolutely right when she was Jemima? Why did the name Jane seem to call her home?

'It's alright; the ambulance is on its way. You'll be fine. You'll be ok.' Fran offered a tiny reassuring smile.

Jem now realised that she was lying in the road, but she felt no pain just the cold tarmac beneath her. As she carefully checked her awareness of each part of her body and struggled to recall how she'd come to be in this embarrassing place, she saw the crowd moving aside.

Two paramedics soon knelt beside her, one turning to Fran to ask what had happened. She noticed that two policemen were also there now, one talking with a very distressed man by a car who kept looking worryingly at Jem.

Fran's reply as to what had happened, how her sister had been distracted, switched on a light and Jem knew.

A man had called to her. He called the name that felt right but was not her own.

She'd been about to cross the road with Fran but had seen someone in the crowd, the person who'd called the name. It was someone she recognised; a man she knew well, but had no idea how. She'd seen in him a man her whole being knew, or maybe an older version of a man she knew.

Recollection came then of the man calling to her before the car caught her, or was it after? Hadn't he begged her not to leave him? She felt the strongest pulling; she wanted to go to him more than anything else. But she hadn't been able to. Her body hadn't been able to move, so leaden was it that she may as well have been dead. Then she'd fallen asleep. Hadn't she? She'd fallen asleep, not died, and woken up to Fran's frantic begging.

It wasn't a trick played by Jem's mind when she'd blacked out. It was real; the sense of needing this man, this stranger who was so well known to her.

The begging voice circled her. When had she known this man, been begged by him to stay? Now today she'd seen him again, looking different and the same; he'd only been there for an instant, but that was long enough for Jem to take her eyes off the road and step forward. She wanted to close her eyes and go back to the place that the strange but perfectly correct name had taken her, but there were other questions to answer instead.

The car hadn't been going very fast and had clipped her more than knocked her over; but it was enough to spin Jem from her feet and send her into the road. It wasn't the driver's fault, Jem insisted groggily. She wanted to exonerate the poor driver quickly so she could search for the man who called to her; whose voice called to her ears and whose presence called to her soul. She tried to sit up, embarrassed, as the paramedics asked her not to and checked all her vital signs. They carefully put on a neck collar and asked her to lie still, even though she protested that she felt fine as they gently slid a stretcher beneath her. Fran asked her to do as she was told, gently encouraging her compliance. She'd be taken to the hospital and checked over.

As Jem felt herself rise off the floor to be lifted into the ambulance she tried to look around and silently cursed the neck collar which stopped her head from turning. Her eyes darted, looking for

the man in the crowd as best she could, but she couldn't find him.
Hands in surgical gloves held her firm, gently imploring her to
calm down and to lie still. But Jem didn't want to. She had a face
to search for. She didn't know why but she wanted to see that face
and to hold on to the man who called her. And not to let go.

Her brief but lucid moment of knowing she'd been someone else
was over.

Darkness into Light, Present into Past

In the recess of a shop doorway stood the man Jem tried to see. All trace of colour had bled from his face when he'd seen Jem in the crowd; his whole body seemed to drain of blood and be replaced with ice cold water when she'd been knocked down. Unable to reach her across the street before she was surrounded by people, he'd been left with no choice but to fight for broken images through the crowd as he struggled to get closer. When she tried to sit up, looking embarrassed but unhurt, he'd breathed again and the chill in his body warmed. She'd been grasping at eyes, faces in the crowd, and he wondered if she was looking for him.

He raised his hand absentmindedly to touch the worn and folded postcard that lived in his breast pocket. He didn't need to look at it to know what faded words were still visible on the back of the familiar picture of London at night. The card had been his constant companion through loss, life and war; reunions, births and joy.

'Poor girl seems ok thankfully. Pretty young thing,' his elderly companion commented, before elbowing him lightly and adding, 'If I were sixty years younger I might have asked her out.'

He smiled at his own quip and was already walking on ahead when Will replied wistfully, 'Harry, when I was sixty years younger I did.'

Will watched as Jem was lifted into the ambulance and the doors closed on a sixty year old promise.

Full Circle

When the two lifelong friends parted company Will returned to his small flat and sat down in an armchair to visit his favourite place. His mind was many years younger than his body and he had no trouble in recalling and reliving events from the past.

His memories always started at the night that had since become known as the Second Great Fire of London; hours of the city burning around him. The calmness and stoicism of the whole country couldn't lift him from his pain on the night he'd tried to protect Jane's shaking body with his own, fighting in vain to be stronger than forces that brought buildings to their knees. His body was no match for the destructive power that could bring down an office block, reduce masonry to sand and flatten a house of bricks to a house of cards.

So many homes were lost, along with churches, shops and offices; and hotels. The Grandchester received a direct hit, with the loss of the magnificent building and all within it. The mystery past of the grand dame of the hotel was probably confined evermore to the shelves of some forgotten archive. Will still found it hard to grasp that he was now older than Mrs Cartlyn had been when he'd known her all those decades before and she'd given Will and Jane the precious gift of time.

Someone somewhere in the war office had known of Will's subterfuge on Hugh's behalf and there'd been a mysterious deferral of Will's drafting; longer than was needed for him to recover physically from the injuries he'd sustained on the night that Jane died in his arms. When called by officials to discuss his role as Hugh, Will agreed to act once more in the late man's stead. He no longer had anything to lose. The job was done and Hugh at last was laid properly to rest.

During Will's subsequent active service in Italy and France he'd sporadically received letters from Maggie, often with an extra letter inside from one of the children. In the top drawer of a writing desk these letters were still carefully piled, the uppermost of which was the letter Maggie had sent to Will close to the end of the fighting and which retitled Harry as a prisoner of war. Harry had finally returned home to the farm in early 1946 to start a physical recovery that took months and a mental one that took a lifetime. The farm remained a place of refuge and retreat for Will between his theatre roles and later teaching career.

Life was lived and times changed; homes and lives were rebuilt and years grew into decades. Harry's children, and now grandchildren, were like Will's own.

Will heaved himself up from his armchair and huffed with chagrin when his knees clicked like his grandmother's used to. He walked to the mantelpiece and took the empty frame from its resting place there. Withdrawing the folded and frayed postcard from his breast pocket he carefully flattened it back into the frame it had left sixty Christmases ago. He put the frame back in its place on the mantelpiece.

'Well, Sunshine, now we know,' Will smiled, touching the frame tenderly. 'Until we meet again.'

The End

Family of Strangers

What would you do if someone you loved disappeared?

What would you do if you were told they'd never existed?

This nightmare comes true for Eva when her closest friend, Annie, vanishes.

Even Annie's parents deny her existence.

The uncertainty of the early months of 1939 has been eclipsed. Eva's comfortable life becomes despairing and desperate, until a friendly hand reaches out to her. The elderly and eccentric Lola shows no surprise at Eva's tale. Neither does Gabe; young, handsome and distant. They have answers that lead to more questions, and information that leads to confusion. The pair guide Eva through a new and frightening world towards her beloved Annie. Eva is sure that her search has absorbed every part of her, until she realises how close she's becoming to the mysterious but tender Gabe.

As Eva learns more about the hidden world now exposed to her, the depth of which seems infinite, she finds that people can be lost and all memory of them forsaken. Gabe and Lola are lost, just like Annie; but unlike Annie, no-one is looking for them to guide them home. Eva, now attached to Lola and deeply tied to Gabe, struggles to believe that nothing can be done to help them.

Eva's search is littered with many things - doubt, discovery, love, belonging and a myriad of scary jigsaw pieces; lost friends, the giving of gifts, a library of books, a troubled conscience and a brilliant pianist. Can Eva piece it all together to see the picture or has she missed something? Does Eva find Annie? Will Gabe reveal his story and are his and Lola's other lost friends a help or a hindrance?

And is there something crucially important that not one of them is telling Eva?

Excerpt from Family Of Strangers:

When I reached the house I already knew.

But that didn't stop me wrenching the front door open as soon as my shaking hands had fumbled the key into the lock and rushing breathlessly into the empty hallway like a woman possessed, tearing through the barren sitting room into the kitchen where there wasn't a sound or a soul. No odd cups on the table, no whistling kettle, no shopping basket, no cups of tea, no patchwork bag, no apron on the back of the door. There were none of the glorious chaotic things I loved and that welcomed me and made me feel I'd come home. All were gone except a few pieces of furniture left swathed in white, dust sheets covering them like a snowy mountain range.